return to sender

A PINE FALLS NOVEL

JENNIFER PEEL

dedication

To the little girls who live inside each of us
who think they aren't enough.
Please know that you are.

prologue

"Ariana, what if I told you I loved you," Jonah whispered in my ear, bringing me out of my sleepy haze.

I held impossibly still in his arms, hoping he thought I was still asleep. I told him from the beginning not to fall in love with me, and I promised I would never fall in love with him. I supposed we were both liars now.

"I know you're awake." He kissed my head.

I held back my tears and nestled into his chest, knowing this would be the last time. His chest hairs, peeking out from his button-up, tickled my nose. I would miss this. I would miss him more.

"Ariana?"

"Jonah, go back to sleep, you have to be back at the hospital in two hours."

He frequently crashed at my place to catch a few z's during his grueling year of clinical rotations at Pine Falls General in his last year of med school. My apartment was closer, and he was . . . well, he was infectious like a disease, but one you never wanted to be cured of. We were supposed to have remained friends only. That morphed into kissing friends. Then he started showing up at my door late at night or even in the middle of the night saying he needed to see my face or asking if he could just hold me. He'd slept on my couch so much the past several months I should have started charging him rent. I should have never let him in, but there was no saying no to his jade-green eyes and those dimples. Don't get me going on his boyish charm.

"I love you." He nuzzled my ear.

I tried to wiggle out of his arms. "Don't say that. Please," I begged.

He wrapped his arms around me tighter. "I'm not Kaden or your father, and you aren't your mother." The edge in his tone said he couldn't believe I hadn't subscribed to his way of thinking by now. Believe me, he had been difficult to resist, but resist I must.

I gripped his shirt and twisted it in my hands. My tears dripped on the soft fabric.

He stroked my long strawberry blonde hair. "I know you miss her."

I wasn't crying because I missed my mom. I was crying because I already missed *him*.

My relationship with my mother was complicated. She'd put me through so much. I wanted to believe she had done her best, though her best was far below average. But she did end up being right about men: they were nothing but heartache waiting to happen. Maybe Jonah wasn't my father, who I'd never known except for the mysterious letter I received once a year that always went unopened and returned to sender. But for all I knew, Jonah could be a Kaden—seemingly wonderful and true to his word, until I'd found out it was all a lie. Thank goodness my engagement ring had needed to be sized. Had it not, I might have never figured out Kaden was engaged to another woman at the same time he was engaged to me.

With more force this time, I wrestled out of Jonah's arms and sat up on the couch, running my hands through my hair, wishing more than anything that he would have kept to the rules we agreed upon when we became friends. More than that, I wished he could have his wish—me.

"You don't want me," I said. "I don't fit into your doctor world. I didn't even go to college. You'd be better off with Dani or Kinsley." They were my best friends, and technically my aunts, even though they were younger than me.

I blamed Dani for bringing Jonah into my life in the first place. She'd met him along with her own unrequited love, Brock, at school in Boulder. Brock and Jonah were premed while Dani was studying sociology. She was out to save every foster kid she could. She felt she owed the world at least that after Grandma Kay and Grandpa Sam fostered and then adopted her and Kinsley. She credited them for saving their lives. I got pulled into their mix when Brock and Jonah started doing rotations at Pine Falls General last year.

Jonah sat up and leaned against the arm rest, scrubbing a hand over the dark stubble on his face that offset his sandy brown hair. "As much as I admire and respect Dani and Kinsley, they aren't you. Don't dishonor me or you by using your lack of a degree as an excuse. You know that I love what you do." He ran his finger down my bare arm. "Ariana, I've accepted an internal medicine residency offer in Ann Arbor." He paused. "I want you to come with me."

I propelled myself off the couch, my heart about ready to beat out of my chest, and headed toward the kitchen to make coffee. It was too early in the morning for this kind of talk. I couldn't stand the thought of him leaving, but I knew it was for the best. "I can't move to Michigan with you."

He stood and followed me the short distance to the kitchen. He folded his arms and sighed. "You mean you won't."

That was exactly what I meant, but I blamed it on my grandma. "If I leave, Grandma would have to sell her glass art studio." I currently ran the studio and taught most of the classes we offered there. I grabbed the coffee pot to fill with water.

Jonah took it right out of my hands, set it on the cluttered counter, and gently turned me toward him. He tipped up my chin with his finger, making sure our eyes met.

I stared into his bloodshot eyes, wishing things could be different, but life had taught me they never were. We would eventually end, just like over half of the population. I couldn't bear us hating each other, or worse, him proving my mother right. It was best to end it while all my memories of him were fond ones. Like I had always planned on doing for both our sakes. But I hadn't planned on him. I got lost in him and waited too long to walk away.

He rested his hand on my cheek. "You're making excuses."

"I love my job and my life here." That was true.

"I know that, and we would try and come back here eventually, but you can open a studio in Michigan or wherever we end up after my residency."

I turned away from him and grabbed the pot. "Life isn't that simple. And I don't have that kind of money."

"I do." He leaned against the old Formica countertop.

He wasn't helping his plight. It was only a reminder that he came from a "normal" family. His parents had been married forever and were both successful dentists in St. Louis. His mom certainly hadn't blown up her wedding dresses like mine had, or toured the country with her daughter in tow seeing how many worthless men she could marry in the span of fifteen years. To top it off, his parents didn't think too highly of me. They'd made that very clear when they visited last month, even though they believed Jonah and I were only friends. They thought it was a crime that I bucked social norms and skipped out on higher education.

I turned on the water. "I'm not taking your money."

"What if it was ours?"

My head popped up. "What are you saying?" Wait. I didn't want him to say it. I dropped the pot in the sink and rushed to place my finger on his soft lips. The ones I had reveled in feeling against my own many times. "Please don't ask." My voice cracked.

He removed my finger with a hefty exhale. He clasped my hand and let our hands fall together to our sides. "If I don't, I'll always regret it."

"Even if you know the answer will be 'no'?"

"It doesn't have to be," he pled. "We're good together and you know it."

A hundred memories of us played at high speed in my head. They were all wonderful, from taking late-night hikes to eating ice cream in our pajamas at the nearby café. I remembered the first time he'd called and asked me to ice cream, I told him I was in my pajamas and the bra had already come off. He'd said, "Perfect, I'll meet you there in my pajamas, and I won't wear my bra either."

It hadn't been only fun and games though. He was there for the difficult times too. He'd held my hand when my mom slipped into a coma, and never left my side until well after she took her last breath. He stayed even though my mom never hid how displeased she was about our *friendship,* and her final words in his presence were begging me to promise her two things. First, that I would never open the annual envelope I received from my father. And second, that I would never get married, especially to a doctor.

"We are good together *now*," I countered, even though I couldn't make eye contact with him. I didn't want him to see the shadow of doubt that filled my own. He was making me question the cold hard truth I had on my side. I'd seen for myself and had firsthand experience how devastated a man could and would leave you, given the chance. The first man who should have loved me left me before I was even born.

"That's your mom talking."

With my free hand, I held onto the counter for support. "Every man in my life, I've had to return. I refuse to let you be one of them."

He pulled me to him and leaned his forehead against mine. His breath cascaded down my face like a warm waterfall. "What do you think you're doing now?"

"Saving us."

"No, Ariana." He kissed my nose. "You're throwing us away."

"I told you not to fall in love with me," I cried.

His tears mingled with mine. "By then it was too late."

chapter one

Nine Years Later

"Goldie Hawn, now that it's November and officially cold, what outfit should I wear today? Mustard sweater with a hole in the pit, or gray sweatshirt with a gravy stain?" I asked my goldfish while I stretched my arm, trying to reach for the warmer clothes on the top shelf of my closet.

Goldie stopped mid turn in her bowl and flashed me a look that said no grown woman of thirty-five should be asking that question. It was probably a fair assumption, but I ignored her and kept blindly reaching for the clothes. With one more good stretch, I yanked on what I thought was the sweatshirt. Unfortunately, that tipped an old shoebox over and a shower of odds and ends rained down on me.

"Crap!" I tried to cover my head as best I could.

I swore I heard Goldie laugh.

"Keep it up and you'll be taking a joy ride down the toilet," I threw out an empty threat. Goldie knew she was safe. Who else would I discuss my myriad of issues with? She was the cheapest therapist around. Which was probably why I was still dressing like a hobo. You get what you pay for.

Ugh. I bent down to clean up the mess before getting dressed for the day. I grabbed the tattered old shoebox and began gathering my old trinkets—tubes of Lip Smackers lip gloss that were probably dried up and notes folded to look like triangles from high school friends. There were even some old photos. One photo in particular. A photo I wasn't sure why I kept.

I leaned against the wall and stared at the faded polaroid I had salvaged when I was a little girl from a pile of junk my mom was going to throw away. If she had known I saved the photo or even that I knew it existed, she would have been furious. But I had wanted to know what he looked like.

I brushed my finger over the picture of Roger Stanton, the man whose blue eyes and last name I shared. He was standing next to my mom in front of the Camp Alpine sign where they had met as camp counselors several years prior. In the white space under the photo in faded pen it read, *Roger and me,* with a tiny heart next to the script.

I wasn't sure what killed me more, the inscription or my mom's permed blonde hair and shoulder pads. Who needed shoulder pads in a t-shirt? It wasn't as bad as Roger's feathered-back auburn hair and his ridiculously short athletic shorts. I knew it had been the style in the early eighties, but it seemed wrong in any era for men to wear such tight, high shorts. I could see Roger's charm though. He had an athletic build and a handsome, angular face.

When I was growing up, I would secretly hold the picture against my chest whenever I got scared and wish with all I had that Roger would come and rescue me from the madness Mom was subjecting me to. Even now, as I touched the old photo of Roger holding my mom's hand while she smiled up at him as if she could see forever in him, I wondered what had happened. Why had Roger disappeared?

Mom rarely talked about him and when she did it was only after she'd had a few too many drinks. Most of the time it was to warn me to never open the letter from Roger that arrived every Christmas Eve without fail, even if it was on the weekend. A special courier always delivered it.

I'd kept my word and always returned it to sender, though I was more than curious what was in the letter-sized envelope from Dr. R. Stanton. The envelope never had more than his name on it, which spoke volumes to me. He didn't want me to know where he lived. I think that more than anything kept me from opening it. To spite him, somehow.

However, I did once try to search for him when I was twenty-seven. When I googled his name, 7.8 million search results popped up. I went through at least a hundred pages searching for the man who looked like the picture I held. I even tried narrowing it down to Chicago, the only place I'd known he had lived, but all it ever came up with was a bunch of old men who couldn't possibly be him. I gave up after that. He wasn't worth the effort. After all, I could blame him for a lot of the reasons I was seeking therapy from my goldfish.

It was odd, though, how he knew where to find me no matter where we lived. I say odd, but it was unsettling. And sad. If he cared enough to know where I was, why didn't he come himself? My mom wouldn't tell me, so I dreamt up my own reasons. For a long time, I imagined he was a CIA agent and he stayed away to protect me. But when I was around twelve, I figured out that was ridiculous since he was only twenty-one when he met my mom. Too young to be in the CIA, unless he lied about his age.

It made more sense that he was in the witness protection program. *Right.*

And more outlandish was the fantasy I had that he was the prince of a European country and wanted to see what it was like to be a commoner, so he disguised himself as a camp counselor. He didn't count on falling in love with my mom because he was already betrothed. It broke his heart to leave my mom and me, but his family would have disowned him if he didn't.

I came up with this farfetched dream after my mom let it slip that my dad had told her if he ever had a daughter, he wanted her to be named Ariana. That was a pretty royal sounding name to me at the time. I was never sure why Mom honored his wish or gave me his last name. I'd asked, but all she would ever say was it was meant to be my name.

But as I aged, I realized I wasn't going to be a princess, and that Dr. Stanton was really a selfish jerk who impregnated a young woman and didn't want to take responsibility for it. The way Grandma told it, my mom came home from Camp Alpine that year saying she had met the man of her dreams, a premed student from Chicago, and they were planning on getting married when he graduated with his undergrad. She forgot to mention she was pregnant. Or maybe she didn't know right away.

A month later, though, according to Grandma, my mom went crazy after a long-distance phone call to Chicago. Grandma never knew what happened on that call, but she said her Joanie was never the same. It wasn't long after that, Mom left with some guy named Jeff, who I'm sure was a loser because all her men were. Grandma thinks she turned to her wild, free-loving ways to try and fill the void Roger Stanton left.

Little did Roger know he'd created a hole in me too. Not only by ignoring me for my entire life, but by the impact his actions had on my mom.

My life could be broken into two time periods, BC and AD. I wasn't talking about *Before Christ* and *Anno Domini*; I was referring to much more recent and personal eras, *Before Carl* and *After Dynamite.*

My first fifteen years of life were *Before Carl.* During that time, my mom was married four times and had two live-in boyfriends as she tried to fill the crater-sized hole in her heart created by her first love, maybe her only love.

My mom's first husband, Doug, I couldn't remember, but she referred to him as a *deadbeat.* In my opinion, they all fell under that category. Then came Isaac, he was the first stepfather I remembered. He was one of those people who believed children should be seen but not heard. Unfortunately, at the time, I liked to be heard. I was punished plenty for it. Everything from spankings to going without dinner. We lived in Tahoe with him, and the only decent thing he ever did was teach me how to ride a bike.

After Isaac came Tom. Tom was a truck driver and he moved us to North Dakota. Mom "needed to stay warm" in the winter, and with Tom being gone most days of the week, she sought out companionship with Weston. He was the first live-in boyfriend. They were both gone by spring.

After Weston left, we moved back to Pine Falls for a brief stint to live with Grandma and Grandpa. I wanted to stay and begged my grandparents to let me, but Mom wouldn't hear of it. I think it about killed Grandma and Grandpa when Mom married Hank and he took us to South Carolina. It wasn't bad living near the beach, and Hank was probably the nicest of all the men I was subjected to. Which meant he pretty much ignored me.

Unfortunately, Mom was looking for love in all the wrong places. She should have loved herself first. There was no way to calculate the heartache, hers and mine, that could have been avoided if only she had.

After Hank—or during Hank, I should say—came Ed, live-in boyfriend number two. Ed moved us to Texas out in the middle of nowhere. We lived in a trailer with a dust bowl for a front yard. Ed drank too much, so there was a lot of yelling. Mom sought the comfort of Ed's brother, Carl, who she had crowned as her knight in shining armor. She declared she had finally found true love in Carl, the self-proclaimed West

Texas King of Karaoke, so he became husband number five. The balding sleaze ball sold lies to Mom like he was Amazon.com on a bender. She bought them like she had a credit card with an unlimited line of credit. Even at fifteen I knew what a liar he was. I mean, come on, no way was he getting hired every night to do a different karaoke party. We lived in a town with one stoplight, and the median income was at poverty level.

I'll tell you what Carl was doing—well, maybe I won't. I'll tell you this, it wasn't with only my mom. It didn't take long for the rumors about Carl's cheating ways to get back to Mom. The town's population of two thousand was a real killjoy for ol' Carl. Sadly, it wasn't enough for Mom to leave him. The final straw had to come at my expense. Carl's hungry eyes started to rove over me, so I locked and pushed my dresser in front of my bedroom door every night I was home. But then one night he came home drunk, and in front of Mom asked if I wanted him to tuck me in and teach me how to be a woman. I still squirmed thinking about it.

The AD period of my life began with one slap across Carl's face and his clothes being thrown out the apartment window. That night did something to Mom. The impact her choices were having on me finally dawned on her, though it should have been obvious well before that. I was hardly coming home at the time. One of the only friends I had made in that desolate town, Ginny, had the nicest parents who were not fooled by Carl. I had an open invitation to eat with them or spend the night anytime I wanted. I took them up on it, not only because I hated Carl, but because Ginny had an older brother, Riley.

Riley was my first kiss and the first time I ever got an inkling of why Mom was obsessed with the opposite sex. That smooth-talking boy of seventeen used to tell me I was the prettiest girl he'd ever met. Even prettier than the poster he had of Reese Witherspoon in his bedroom. He used to pick me daisies and write me little notes. That case of puppy love didn't last long. It all ended with dynamite.

Mom decided to proclaim herself cured of men in a grand fashion. I'm not sure where she got the idea to blow up all five of her wedding dresses—from the micro white dress all the way to the ball gown she'd worn for her wedding to Carl—or where she got the dynamite. But I'll never forget the night she and I stood on the rocky ridge overlooking a barren wasteland outside of town with her friend Callie, who was higher than a kite. I think Callie was the one who *borrowed* the dynamite. The sun was about to set, and its last rays gave the endless dirt and rocks a little bit of character. Mom held me tight with one hand while she held the detonator with the other. Before God, she swore she was done with men and that they all deserved to be returned to sender.

Then Mom smiled at me with tears streaking down her porcelain face. "Promise me, Ariana, you'll stay away from men, all of them. Promise me you'll return any man that comes your way. They're nothing but a heartache waiting to happen."

I thought about Riley and how sweet he was and his kisses that made me feel warm from the top of my head to the tips of my toes. In my teenage heart, I knew I could and would be smarter than my mom. I was certain I could find a man who didn't ever have to be returned like all the men in my mom's life. In my naivety, I was positive I would always choose nice boys like Riley. But given my mom's unstable state and the fact she was holding a detonator in her hand, I could hardly disagree with her. And in that moment, I wanted her to be happy. I wasn't sure I had ever seen her truly happy. So, I nodded my head with my fingers crossed behind my back. "I promise," I'd said, lying to her for the very first time. It wasn't the last.

Satisfied with my response, Mom squeezed my hand, and with the most maniacal laugh I'd ever heard, she pushed the detonator. I'm not sure how much dynamite she used, but she lit up the night like the Fourth of July. Remnants of the dresses mixed with dirt and gravel rained down on us. Mom twirled around in it like it was washing away every mistake she had ever made. From that night on, she was true to her word. She never again had anything to do with a man except her father. We moved back home to Pine Falls and there she began her life of celibacy.

Meanwhile, I was starting to explore the wonders of the opposite sex. It was unfortunate how wonderful and tingly they could make me feel. Those intoxicating feelings had me lying to Mom about hanging out with friends when I was really meeting boyfriends, whether it was at the movies or school dances. I hated the lying because I'd been lied to so much growing up, but I felt it was unfair for me to miss out on dating just because my mom had a problem. After all, I was *smarter* than her.

I believed that lie until I was twenty-two.

Then I met Kaden, the man I thought I would spend the rest of my life with. He had been on an awkward blind date taking one of the mini mosaic classes I taught at the glass art studio. Kaden flirted with me while I was showing him and his date how to properly grout. I tried not to encourage the flirting, even though his date did seem disinterested in him and spoke more to her friend they were double-dating with. It should have been a warning to me, but I was overly confident and naïve. When he came back that night while I was closing and asked for my number, I gave it to him.

Mom was sticking to her mantra that all men were the spawn of Satan. By that time, she had become a popular indie artist in the area. She had leased the space next to the glass art studio where she opened her own gallery. Our lives were so entangled back then, there was no way to keep her from knowing about my man-loving ways. Besides, I didn't like lying to her, or anyone for that matter. I was going to prove to her that there were still good men and that I could make good choices.

From day one, though, she hated Kaden. Before we parted that night, she said, "Watch your step with that one. He has dark eyes."

I wanted to respond, "I know, aren't they beautiful? Like deep, dark chocolate." Instead I said, "I promise I'll be careful. Besides, it's only one date." Mom had shaken her head at me, walked out, and slammed the door.

That one date led to spending every waking minute we could together between my job at the studio and his as a construction foreman for a housing development in nearby Edenvale. I'd thought we were made for each other. We were both spontaneous and loved adventure. It was nothing for us to decide on a whim Sunday morning to go rock climbing or sign up for scuba diving lessons.

We were head over heels in love. I didn't care that Dani, who had become one of my best friends despite her being my "aunt," began to question Kaden's and my relationship. Even Kinsley, who was only fifteen at the time, expressed her concerns. They said he was too perfect. I knew he was. That's what made him so great. And it was why, when we had only been dating for six months and he asked me to marry him, I said yes. Mom had cried and painted a gruesome picture of a white wedding dress with a knife shoved in the bodice, dripping with blood. She displayed it proudly in her gallery until some jilted woman bought it. Unfortunately, that painting foreshadowed things to come.

After Kaden and I were engaged, the construction company he worked for got a contract for a large development in Denver, four hours away, which meant he was gone during the week and would come home on the weekends when he could. At first, we tried to talk every day, but then he had less and less time. He blamed it on work, but even when he came home, he seemed distracted. He wouldn't set a wedding date with me. He said he just wanted to wake up one weekend and take me to Vegas, but it would be a surprise. That sounded like my style, so I went with it.

This went on for a few months. That was, until I went to the jewelry store to get my ring sized. Kaden had been promising me he would do it, but I was afraid I would lose the rectangle sapphire ring he'd put on my finger. When I looked back, I would be forever grateful for that stupid ring. It saved me from myself.

I wasn't the only woman Kaden was engaged to. It was an awkward moment when I went into the jewelry store and they pulled up his file. He had purchased quite a few rings there. Two, most recently—mine and his other fiancée's. That poor salesclerk about wet her pants when she realized what she had revealed to me. But to this day, I thanked her. I left the ring there and had the jewelry store inform him of the return. What made it worse was Kaden didn't seem to care. I thought he was madly, deeply in love with me, the way I loved him. But he called to say it was better this way. He said the thought of monogamy frightened him. He didn't care that he had crushed my soul or made me question every decision I had ever made and everyone's motives around me.

Mom was downright gleeful about it, which I had to say I resented after all the men and heartbreak she had subjected me to over the years. All I had wanted was a comforting shoulder. My error in judgment had scared me. How could I be so fooled? How had I not learned anything from all the losers my mother had been with? My conclusion was I had no choice but to agree with Mom. Men were nothing but heartache waiting to happen. Unlike her, I didn't swear off men completely, but I would never let one get close enough to hurt me like Kaden had. Like Roger and an entire slew of men had done to my mother and me.

Then a few years later came Jonah. I hadn't meant for us to grow so close.

My eyes welled up with tears while I brushed my fingers over Roger Stanton's face. "I didn't want to return him to sender. That's all you've ever been to me. Why is that?" I asked the picture another poignant question, "Did I make a mistake where Jonah was concerned?"

Roger stared back at me silently.

"Jonah ended up married and happy, as far as I know," I told Roger. "He even has a little girl."

I'd watched her grow up the last four or five years through the Christmas cards Jonah sent Dani. The ones she'd tried to hide from me. Obviously, Jonah and I hadn't done a good enough job keeping our feelings secret even though we never acted like a couple in public, not even in front of our friends. No one ever said anything to me about him over the years. But they must have known, as no one questioned why I didn't get invited to his wedding seven years ago. Our circle of friends here had done a terrible job of keeping their plans from me to fly to Nantucket to watch the blissful event.

Jonah had married a beautiful woman named Eliza, and they had a gorgeous baby named Whitney. Their Christmas card every year was a stab in the heart, but I'm the one who stuck the knife in there, so I had no one but myself to blame. The baby girl with bouncing sandy brown locks and her daddy's green eyes could have been mine, but I had made the right choice. Jonah got the family he always wanted. His wife, Eliza, from all accounts, was lovely and ambitious; a Princeton graduate with an amazing mind for business, as Brock called it. That was before he realized I was in the room.

But looking at Jonah's wedding photos and Christmas cards over the years had cemented my choice. His life was so different from my own. See, I would have never wanted to get married in Nantucket in a dress like Eliza's. Don't get me wrong, she looked lovely in the lace trumpet gown, but I would have preferred a short, cotton, off-the-shoulder number. And I would have been barefoot under some pine trees in the mountains. Definitely not at a country club with several hundred guests all dressed to the nines. And those Christmas cards he sent every year looked like they were posing for a company brochure in front of a boring gray canvas back drop. He and his wife both wore suits and their darling daughter was always dressed in something just as stuffy and stiff. If it was *our* family, we would have been out in a sunflower field and casually dressed. And probably barefoot. I wasn't a fan of shoes.

I was happy for Jonah. Really, I was. If anyone deserved to have the unattainable, it was him. I knew he was meant for a life I couldn't give him. He didn't really want an eclectic artist with an ugly past. He had been wrong—I *did* save us from ourselves. I didn't throw us away, I let us go onto something better. The studio was doing better than ever, and it had been nine years since my heart was broken for the last time.

I took one more good look at the picture of my parents. I was sure my twenty-year-old mom thought her life would turn out much different than the one she ended up living. She'd chased after that dream for many years, the white-picket fence complete with an adoring husband. As happy as I was when she gave up on men, I was always sad she never had what she desired. She was never happy. She literally died trying to fill the void Roger Stanton left in her—she'd contracted hepatitis B from one of her lovely husbands and, unfortunately, it turned chronic and eventually into liver cancer. At least now she was at peace.

I wiped a tear off my cheek. "I am happy, Roger," I lied to him. "Unlike Mom, I never needed you for that." Or did I? Would I have been happier if he'd rescued me? Could he have changed my life? Would I be with Jonah now? I couldn't think like that.

I threw the stupid picture in the box and buried it under all the rest of the crap from my past before I shoved it back in the closet.

I held up the stained sweatshirt and the holey mustard sweater. "Which one, Goldie?"

She swished her fin at me in disapproval, clearly communicating, "You need help."

I know.

chapter two

"Why are you both staring at me like that?" Dani and Kinsley had been shooting furtive glances to each other then at me all night. I didn't have time to keep guessing why—I assumed they had some unpleasant news to share and I just wanted them to get it over with. I'd had a customer special order custom Tiffany-style Christmas ornaments, and she wanted them well before Thanksgiving. She should have thought about that before placing the order on November 5th.

I was sneaking in working on them any time I could get. Between our busy holiday class schedule at the studio and the large stained glass piece of a dove with a starburst behind it a pastor had commissioned for his church in Carrington Cove that was being renovated, I'd had to start working late into the night in the loft above the studio I'd moved into a few years ago with Dani and Kinsley. It was a great way to save money. And I enjoyed not being home alone every night.

Dani was tapping her fingers against our table that frequently functioned as my workspace, and Kinsley was twirling her long blonde hair as I wrapped copper tape around a piece of stained glass shaped like the crook of a candy cane. Something was definitely up, but neither of them was being forthcoming, so I changed the subject.

"How are restaurant and non-profit life going?" I asked.

Kinsley had opened a new restaurant called Two Girls and a Guy with some friends she'd met at culinary school. It was an awkward situation, if you asked me. One Dani and I had warned her about. Not only was the restaurant theme based on love triangles, but it was obvious Kinsley and Gisele both had a thing for Carter, their other partner.

Not that Dani had a lot of room to talk. She had her own weird triangle thing going on. She was in love with Brock Holland, who might have feelings for her as well, but I swore his identical twin, Brant, also had feelings for Dani. Brock and Brant Holland lived nearby in Carrington Cove and were from a wealthy and powerful family. Their dad owned a gas and oil company here in Colorado and had been a US senator. Dani, Brock, and Brant had a three-musketeer vibe between them. She even had a "Dani test" that all the women the brothers dated had to pass.

Basically, we were all a mess when it came to love.

"Our holiday donations for Children to Love are up this year," Dani answered first. Children to Love was the non-profit she ran for kids still in the foster system and for those that had aged out. She and her organization made sure each child in a foster home in the three surrounding counties received a Christmas gift every year. They also provided mentors and job training for those aging out of the system. I had hired a great young woman who'd graduated from their program to help in the studio. She answered the phones for us and handled all our scheduling. Dani was doing great things. It was amazing considering where she came from, a child of the system herself.

"That's great," I commented while smoothing out the copper tape. "The donation box at the studio is full already. I'll make sure to drop off the toys during lunch tomorrow."

"I can grab them in the morning and take them in," Dani offered.

"I suppose that would work too." I grinned.

Kinsley, with her nervous energy, jumped up. "I've been working on a new chocolate peanut butter dessert. Do you want to try it?"

Chocolate and peanut butter were my true loves. "Always yes, but first, why don't you tell me what you're both hiding from me."

Dani and Kinsley gave each other uh-oh looks.

"That bad, huh?" I set down the piece I was working on.

Kinsley sat back down while Dani let her gorgeous ebony hair out of her ponytail. Her hair fell nicely at her shoulders. I looked between my two friends, sisters really, wondering who would cave first.

In their silence, I reflected on how thankful I was Grandma and Grandpa brought them into our lives. We may not look a thing like each other, but we were family in the truest sense of the word. Dani with her olive skin and grey eyes looked as if she had some Middle Eastern blood in her, but like me, she only ever knew her mother, who was Caucasian, so it was only a guess. Kinsley and I both had fair skin, but she looked like an all-American girl with her blonde hair and big brown eyes. She was cute and perky, the youngest of us at twenty-eight. Dani was thirty-three, so that made me the oldest "sister" at thirty-five. I was neither cute and perky nor exotically beautiful. I was more of a hot mess, emphasis on mess. I was a throw my hair in a messy bun or put a hat on if I didn't have time, baggy jeans, and loose t-shirts and sweaters kind of girl. And shoes only when necessary, which was more than I liked since I worked with sharp objects and 350-degree solder irons.

"I assume no one we know died, since there are no tears," I threw out into the silent abyss.

"Fine." Dani sat up straight and let out a deep breath. "Brock," she always said his name wistfully, "had lunch with Jonah today."

I swallowed down my heart like I always did when his name was mentioned. "I didn't know Brock was out of town." I did my best to sound unaffected and picked up the candy cane piece again to fiddle with it.

Kinsley reached out and rubbed my arm. "He's not. Jonah's here."

Oh. I shrugged. "That's nice." What did I care if he was visiting? The *married* man was free to do whatever he wanted. We were ancient history. "How long is he in town?" I thought to ask, to make sure I avoided him while he visited.

"Well . . ." Dani bit her perfectly pouty lips, "for a while."

"How long is 'a while'?"

"Maybe forever." She tensed and leaned away from me.

I dropped the stained glass and it clanged against the table. "Define forever."

"He moved back," Kinsley rushed to say before her hands flew to her mouth as if she'd said a bad word.

A loud ringing started in my ears. I think it might have been from all the extra blood being pumped by my erratically beating heart. "Super. Fantastic. Great," I breathed out maniacally. "I mean, he always wanted to move back here. I'm happy for him and his family." I pushed my chair back and stood. I needed that chocolate peanut butter dessert Kinsley was working on. I headed straight for the commercial-size fridge we had for Kinsley's benefit.

Dani and Kinsley tiptoed after me.

I threw open the fridge door and let the cold wash over me, inhaling and exhaling deeply, mad at myself that he could still affect me this way. He was married with a child. I had no business feeling this out of sorts about him. But all I could think about was the last time I saw him. He had gently kissed me and said, "I love you. Say you love me too. Please." I'd wanted to. I almost had, but I knew he wouldn't have left if I had, or he would have begged me again to come with him. He wouldn't have led the life he was meant to live. I'd guaranteed us our happy ending—we'd never have to grow apart or end up hating each other. When I hadn't said it, he had taken my face in his hands, pressed his lips against mine, and hungrily kissed me, bleeding into my lips every feeling he'd ever had for me, and they were all beautiful. Tears had streamed down both our faces. Then he'd pushed away from me and walked out the door. I'd never heard from him again. But I could still remember the way he tasted like Skittles. He'd loved them and ate them by the handful. I hadn't touched a Skittle since he left.

Kinsley rubbed my back. "Maybe we shouldn't tell her the rest."

I whipped my head toward the two. "The rest?"

"Maybe you should sit down," Dani suggested.

"Why?" What could be worse than living in the same zip code as him and his beautiful family?

"He's divorced," Kinsley blurted.

It felt as if someone ripped the band-aid off an infected wound. I held onto both of them for support. "What? How? I saw all the Christmas cards you hid from me. He looked happy. His wife is gorgeous and successful. They have a beautiful little girl." I paused, realizing how I was basically spelling out the feelings I had for him that I had tried to keep hidden from everyone. "I mean, what does that have to do with me? We were friends. That's it."

They wrapped their arms around me, sandwiching me between them.

"Nice try, Ariana, but you're not fooling anyone. You never did." Dani squeezed a bit tighter.

I took a moment to revel in the comfort of their arms before I whispered, "What happened?" Honestly, I thought if anyone would get the pie-in-the-sky dream, it would be him.

Dani led me to the couch while Kinsley grabbed her masterpiece and three spoons. We sat on the old burnt orange couch we'd inherited from Grandma Kay. She'd called it a housewarming gift when we'd all decided to move in together a few years ago. We didn't particularly want it, but Grandma was a waste not, want not kind of lady and she wanted a new couch, so we got saddled with the 70s relic.

Obviously, Jonah moving back here had nothing to do with me. He probably hadn't thought about me in years. Still, I sat there holding Dani's hand, trying not to hyperventilate. Kinsley sat on the coffee table and held up the pan full of rich chocolate with swirls of peanut butter. I grabbed one of the spoons and scooped out a large bite before shoving it in my mouth. I closed my eyes for a moment and basked in dessert heaven. My breathing slowed and my heartrate lowered. I opened my eyes to find my two best friends staring at me, assessing my mental health.

"I'm fine." I pointed with my spoon toward the dessert. "By the way, Kinsley, your new creation gets an A+."

Kinsley set her yummy dessert to the side. She rested her hands on my legs and got nose to nose with me. "You need to own your feelings for a change."

I leaned away and pulled my knees up to my chest. Feelings were dangerous. They meant you could get hurt.

Dani leaned back with me, not letting me off the hook, no matter what my body language was saying. She forced my head to lay on her shoulder. Kinsley moved to the couch and sat on my other side, taking my hand.

"Jonah asked Brock about you—a lot," Dani hesitated to say.

"Really? Why?"

"Why do you think?" Dani stroked my hair.

"Curiosity," I guessed.

Kinsley and Dani laughed.

"He mentioned to Brock that he had proposed to you once upon a time. Is that true?" Dani's voice was strained, indicating she was hurt that I had never told her.

I leaned forward to rest my head on my legs and turned toward Dani. "I begged him not to."

Dani pressed her lips together, shaking her head. "It's a shame."

"Why?"

"Because," Kinsley jumped in, "you were good for each other."

I sat up straight and ran a hand through my hair, undoing the loose bun it was in. "No. He deserved better."

"You're right," Dani said.

Ouch. I grabbed my stomach.

Dani put her arm around me. "You're taking that wrong. I meant he would have been happier with you."

My head snapped toward her. "I saw the pictures and read the Christmas letters he sent every year. I've never seen a happier family." He was part of a successful practice and his wife was some high-power corporate consultant type, teaching companies how to be more productive and create better relationships between employees and management. She traveled all over the world and the letters made it sound like Jonah and their daughter at times traveled with her.

"You saw what you wanted to see," Dani disagreed with me. "Did you ever notice his eyes?"

I hadn't. I couldn't afford to get lost in those green jewels. They weren't mine to own. I shook my head.

Dani nodded as if she understood. "Had you, you would have seen that the light had gone out of them."

I rubbed my face in my hands. "I don't understand."

Kinsley petted my head like I was a lost puppy.

"Ariana," Dani drew my attention back to her, "Jonah was living the life his family thought he should lead."

That wasn't too surprising. His parents were less than impressed by my lifestyle, not to mention the lack of proper upbringing. "He wouldn't marry someone he didn't love. And what about his little girl?"

"Of course Jonah loved Eliza. And Whitney will be living with him," Dani informed me.

"Did he cheat?" Isn't that how it always went? Though if I was honest, I didn't see Jonah cheating, but that's how men got you. They were all wonderful upfront and then boom, you're going to the jewelry store to get your engagement ring sized and you walk out single, feeling like the world's biggest fool.

"Ugh," they grunted in unison.

"What? That's what always happens."

Kinsley threw her hands up in the air. "That's not what always happens. Grandma and Grandpa are still together and neither have had an affair."

"But," I interjected, "Grandma told me that she almost divorced him after my mom was born because he was a selfish jerk."

"But she didn't." Dani turned so she could shake my shoulders. "You know why?" She didn't wait for my reply. "Because she saw something worth saving. And aren't you glad?"

I looked up at the steel beamed ceiling. "Of course I am," I whispered.

"All right then." Dani sat back and sighed. "Jonah's wife left him. She wanted to focus on her career."

Oh. I bit my lip. "That's awful."

Dani shrugged. "Brock said Jonah seems to be taking it well."

"So, why did he move back here?"

Kinsley and Dani leaned forward to look at one another, deliberating about what they should say.

"What aren't you telling me?"

They both sat back and fidgeted for a bit.

Kinsley eventually took my hand. "Well . . . the truth is, the happiest he's ever been in his life was when he lived in Pine Falls."

"No," Dani disagreed, "the happiest he's ever been in his life was when he was with you, Ariana." Dani's eyes and words hit me like a freight train.

"Oh," I squeaked.

chapter three

I decided the best way to deal with Jonah being back in town was to avoid him at all costs. Which meant never hanging out with Dani and Kinsley in a social setting. I was onto them. "Let's meet for dinner at the new eatery," Dani had suggested last week. "Will anyone be joining us?" I'd asked. Her olive cheeks had pinked.

If Jonah really wanted to see me, he knew where I worked. The glass art studio was where it had always been at, the old mill near the river.

I was honestly afraid one day he would show up. Each time the door chimed at the studio during the last two weeks, I'd jumped. That was a lot of jumps, as it was our busiest time of year. People loved getting an early start on their holiday shopping, and we always had a lot of homeschool groups bring their kids in this time of year to make their own ornaments. Not to mention we had become a popular date night destination on Friday nights. I had named our Friday night workshops *Sip and Solder.* Only nonalcoholic beverages were served. You know, on account of us dealing with 350 degrees of melt-your-skin-off heat.

I knew Dani and Kinsley had seen him; they were done hiding their contact with him. They gushed about how cute his little girl, Whitney, was and how charming Jonah still was. "He moved into the new Creekside development south of town. Isn't that nice?" Kinsley asked. Or Dani would mention, "The years have been really good to him." That I already knew from the Christmas cards. It didn't matter what kind of information they gave me about him, I never asked them to elaborate.

Since they couldn't bait me verbally, Dani started leaving mental health pamphlets around the house. They ranged from coping with traumatic events and abandonment all the way to how to manage anxiety. Uh, I hadn't been anxious until two weeks ago. She even left a business card on my pillow for a local therapist she admired. On the back of it, Dani wrote, *Living in fear is the worst terror there is. Stop tormenting yourself. You're not your mother. And if you ask me, your mother emotionally abused you. Read the pamphlets. Love you.*

It was as if she had sucker punched me. My mom had done the best she could. That was the lie I always told myself, so I didn't blame her. What good would that do? And I wasn't tormenting myself. I was only doing what was necessary to not become my mother. A woman who was broken by men. And I didn't want to point it out, but Jonah did get divorced, which proved my way of thinking to be correct.

But I never said anything because Jonah didn't move back here for me. I mean, we hadn't even been technically boyfriend and girlfriend. Men didn't move back to a town where they had no family for a woman who wouldn't even let him touch her in public for fear of someone thinking you might be more than what you were. He totally made up for it in private, but that was another story. The story of the best year of my life. Yeah, we had the same best year. That was classified information.

I was happy. Really, I was. I would say it until one day I believed it, or it came true. What more in life did I really need? I had a job I loved that paid the bills with a little extra left over. I had friends and Grandma and Grandpa. And my goldfish. Goldie Hawn and I were tight. We had great conversations in the middle of the night. She would swim in place, intensely staring at me with her big eyes, while I told her all my secrets. See, I didn't need therapy. My fish knew everything.

And, it wasn't like I was a man hater. Once in a while I did agree to have dinner with a member of the opposite sex. I called them appointments instead of dates. You don't accidentally fall in love if you are keeping appointments. Appointments were sterile environments where you never got personal. On the other hand, dates were gateway drugs. That was my problem with Jonah. He had worked his magic on me and I'd spilled my guts to him. The man knew *almost* everything about me, right down to my menstrual cycle. And he still fell in love with me.

Not thinking about it.

I had other things to worry about, like my sick grandma. She called me early this morning, hacking into the phone. "I know it's your morning off and the last thing you want to do is take your elderly, frail grandmother to the doctor this morning, but could you make some time for me?"

Wow, that was over the top. And a lie.

"Grandma, you still run circles around women half your age. You know I'll take you to see Dr. Gibbons. I love nothing more than spending time with you."

She chuckled, sounding better already. "I thought I better be dramatic in case you had any ideas of saying no."

"Why would I?"

"I know how busy the studio gets this time of year."

She rarely came in anymore. She and Grandpa decided to semi-retire now that they were in their late seventies. Grandpa, though, still ran some survival camps in the summer. He sold his wilderness and survival business last year, but the new owners used him from time to time. The old man was still hiking fourteeners.

Speaking of Grandpa. "Not that I don't want to take you, but where is Grandpa?"

"He had some errands to run," she replied.

"Those must be important errands if he left you home sick."

Grandma coughed up another lung. "Are you going to keep making ridiculous observations or are you coming to help an old woman out? Do you hear how sick I am?"

"I'm coming. I'm coming." Sheesh.

"Hurry up." She hung up.

I stared at my cell phone. What had gotten into her this morning? Normally she was more pleasant. I rolled out of bed and threw on some gray sweatpants and the mustard sweater with the small hole in the armpit. I wasn't out to win any beauty contests and all my baggy jeans were still in the wash.

"Good morning, Goldie." I sprinkled some fish food in Goldie's bowl. "Have a good day." She looked up at me and I swore she was saying, "You're going out in public like that? How old are you again?"

"You know what, Goldie? Women should support women." I wasn't even sure Goldie was a girl. But regardless. "So maybe I've let some things go. I always brush my teeth and wear deodorant," I added, heading straight for the bathroom to do just that.

I stared in the bathroom mirror. Dani's sexy black bra hung from its corner next to Kinsley's cute lipstick stain where she kissed it every day. *They* had not let themselves go. I leaned in closer to look at my porcelain skin. It was still smooth. That made me feel a little bit better about myself. But then I looked at my brows. Wow, they could use a good plucking. I didn't have time this morning, though. Maybe later. That's what I always said. Maybe someday I would do my hair and makeup again, or wear clothes that weren't two or three sizes bigger than what I really was, but I never did. I wasn't sure how I got here, but here was comfortable and invisible.

I zipped over to my grandparents'. They lived on the outskirts of Pine Falls in an A-frame house Grandpa had built from a kit he'd ordered on the internet after Kinsley moved out five years ago. I wasn't sure how practical it was since the entire bottom floor was open and the only bedroom they had was in the loft. I worried about them going up and down the stairs, but they were out to defy the odds. If anyone could, it would be them. They were made of a long-ago generation. They were into composting and growing as much of their own food as they could. And if there was ever a zombie apocalypse, Grandpa was your man. The guy had a stockpile of weapons and could live in the wilderness for days with a pocketknife and some fishing line.

Their house was on the same property as their old white two-story house with black shutters, the house I called my "childhood" home. And by that I meant I'd lived there for three years without the worry of being torn away from it. It was now being rented out by a struggling young family my grandparents were helping by charging them cheap rent.

Every time I looked at the place, I felt safe. It was where I'd always longed to be when I was growing up, living wherever the wind blew my mom and her man for every season. I was happy to see two little girls playing on the tire swing Grandma had put up for me on the big oak tree out front. They were happy and carefree, bundled up in their warm coats. It was as it should be; little girls should always feel safe and warm.

It wasn't too much longer on the gravel road until my grandparents' new house came into view. Grandma had the porch decorated in pumpkins and cornstalks. She loved fall and was adamant that no Christmas decorations go up until Thanksgiving had its say. She wasn't fond of all the Christmas ornament classes I was already teaching at the studio. She never understood why people didn't want turkey ornaments.

I walked right in the front door. "Grandma, it's me."

"Up here." She waved from the loft. She sounded much better.

"Did you gargle some saltwater or something?"

She leaned on the railing, looking as she always did. She kept her silver hair long and in a perpetual braid. Though her face was lined, it still had a youthful glow. "Saltwater is for sissies. I went straight for the Jim Beam, that will kill anything."

"It's not even nine yet."

She stood there with her hands on her wide hips and laughed. "When did you become such a party pooper? I'm teasing about the whiskey."

I rolled my eyes and headed for the kitchen, hoping to grab an apple or something. In my haste, I had forgotten to eat.

"Come up here. I have something for you before we go."

"Okay." Who needed food anyway? I climbed up the steep stairs to find Grandma holding a large cream box with a fancy monogram on it that said *M&M'S on Main*. I knew of the clothing boutique in Carrington Cove. It was owned by a customer of ours, Shelby Prescott. She and her group of friends had come in to take one of our classes at the studio. And Shelby had hired us to make a stained glass mosaic for one of the picture windows in her home.

"What's this?" I couldn't imagine Grandma buying clothes from the fancy boutique.

"It's an early Christmas present." She held it out farther.

"What? Aren't you the one who always complains about people skipping Thanksgiving and going straight to Christmas? Besides, you always make my gifts." Grandma was a big believer that gifts should be a labor of love.

Grandma did a sweep with her eyes over my attire. "Honey, I don't know how to say this gently, but you need some help. I bartered some pieces with Shelby for the outfits."

My jaw dropped. I now knew why Grandma had been in the studio working on a secret project. I thought she was making Christmas gifts for us. But that was beside the point at the moment. "What do you mean, I need help?"

She set the box down on her patchwork quilt bed before patting the mattress, inviting me to sit down.

I stood with my arms folded. "I thought you called me over here to take you to see Dr. Gibbons."

She coughed enough to make her face turn red. "I am sick," she said indignantly, "and as soon as you try on these clothes, we'll be off. But first you need to sit down."

Like a child, I trudged over and obeyed.

She sat next to me and took my hand with her wrinkled hand that was beginning to show signs of arthritis. Her fingers weren't as straight as they used to be and the joints were swollen. It panged my heart.

"Honey," she squeezed my hand, "you are such a beautiful woman."

I shook my head no. Maybe I was, once.

She wasn't having it. "You've done your best to hide it, but even though you dress like a slob, you can't hide your gorgeous face and countenance."

I made to disagree with her, but yeah, slob about covered it. It was embarrassing to hear my grandma say it out loud. Tears pooled in my eyes.

"Oh, don't start crying, you know I can't stand to see you cry. And what I have to say is important and I'm going to get through it, even if it hurts you."

I wanted to curl up in a ball, but Grandma held firm.

"Honey," she sighed, "you've been on the run your entire life. First, because of your mom, and when you did finally come home, you had to run from the damage your mom put you through. Then you had to run from your mom's ridiculous notions. Worst of all, you've been running from who you really are." She waved a hand over me. "You know I've never been one to think that clothes make a woman, but Ariana, this isn't you. I know you think if you hide behind ill-fitting clothes no one will notice you. But I'm here to tell you, you are noticed. I notice you. And it's okay if men notice you. And most importantly, *you* should notice you."

"I do," I squeaked.

She patted my cheek. "You notice the person your mom created." She sighed. "I loved your mom more than anyone, but she put a world of hurt on you. It wasn't right, and I wish to God every day I had put a stop to it. Ariana, my love, you are so much more than you let yourself be."

"So, this is what you really think of me?" My voice cracked. Here I thought she was proud of me. After all, she always said it was because of me her business was flourishing.

"No. I think you're a fighter, but you've been picking the wrong battles. You've been fighting yourself and your past. You need to let go and move on."

The tears wouldn't hold back; they spilt over and poured down my cheeks. "I live a good life," I defended myself.

"Honey." She wrapped an arm around me. "I'm not saying you're a bad person. You are one of the best people I know, but you deserve more and I'm sad you're not living your best life. Deep down you know that."

I reluctantly rested my head on her plump shoulder, half offended, half embarrassed. "Did Dani and Kinsley put you up to this?" I wiped away the tears from my cheeks. "Is this an intervention?"

Grandma rubbed my arm. "Call it what you want, kiddo."

"Clothes and men don't make you a better person." I sniffled.

Grandma kissed my wet cheek. "Well, in some cases they don't hurt either, so go try these on for me." She grabbed the box and handed it to me. "By the way, I love you."

I snatched the box from her. "I might still love you."

She cackled. "You're not fooling me."

I begrudgingly stood and marched toward the bathroom.

"Don't be afraid to use my tweezers, and Dani and Kinsley bought some makeup for you. It's on the counter."

I spun around. "I'm not a pet project!"

Grandma stood and surveyed me again. "I hate to say it, but some people take better care of their pets than you've taken care of yourself lately."

My mouth fell open, but no words came out.

She motioned for me to get into the bathroom. "Hurry up, you're going to make me late for my appointment." She started folding towels as if I didn't exist.

I turned back around, humiliated, but not surprised. Dani and Kinsley had been dropping hints lately that it was time for me to get out of my grunge phase. For my birthday six months ago, they got me a gift certificate to a spa, which was odd for two reasons. Dani and Kinsley didn't have a lot of extra cash, and I'd never been to spa in my life. I still hadn't. Also, in addition to the mental health brochures Dani had been leaving around the loft, Kinsley had been leaving her copies of *Cosmo* lying around, strategically left opened to articles about self-care and simple makeovers on a budget.

I trudged into the bathroom feeling like I was wearing the cone of shame. So I had some issues. I didn't know how to be myself, or who that was, even. I didn't want to be hurt, but more importantly, I never wanted to hurt anyone like I had hurt Jonah. But he had gotten on with his life. And I got on with mine. Apparently, though, not as well as I'd thought.

I stared into the mirror while wearing my undies. Yikes. I should probably invest in some new ones—even my bra and panties had holes in them. I took a good look at my body. Besides the fact that my skin could use some moisturizer, it was a nice body. I had forgotten I had curves and lines. I ran a hand across my flat stomach. At least I ate mostly right, and I did yoga on occasion. I hadn't completely let myself go. Somewhere along the way I just got tired. Tired of trying to be someone I shouldn't be—sought after and desired.

I leaned on the counter and looked closer in the mirror. "Who are you, Ariana?" I whispered.

Who do you want to be? My heart whispered back.

That was an excellent question.

chapter four

Grandma kept touching me as we drove to Dr. Gibbons' office. "You look beautiful. That Shelby knows her stuff. She guessed you were a size four, even though you dress like you want to be a spokesmodel for Hefty trash bags. She said she could tell by your bone structure and the way you carried yourself you had a thin build."

"I don't know why I needed to wear a new outfit to take you to the doctor. Dr. Gibbons has known me forever, it's not like I need to impress him."

"We didn't have time for you to change."

I felt overly dressed for the occasion in the skinny jeans, navy striped turtleneck, and bone-colored petite jacket, which I had to admit went nicely with the ensemble—even though I felt like I was in a straitjacket. I wasn't sure when I'd last worn anything so form fitting. At least I still got to wear my Birkenstocks. Grandma thought maybe I should go shoe shopping later.

Grandma smoothed my eyebrow. "You don't look like Grizzly Adams anymore."

I glanced her way before turning onto the street where Dr. Gibbons' office was located. "Listen here, old lady, you should take a look at your wiry eyebrows," I teased.

Her laugh filled the car. "Kiddo, when you're my age, you take all the hair you can get."

I had no idea how to respond to that. "Are you sure you're okay? You're not hiding some disease from me, are you?"

"Why would you ask that?"

"Well, you aren't acting like you have the flu or a cold."

She coughed on cue. "Listen to this cough. I probably have pneumonia."

"Didn't you get your pneumonia vaccination?"

"Yes." She cleared her throat. "But you can never be too careful, especially this time of year."

"I suppose you're right."

"I always am."

I loved the cantankerous old woman.

Grandma took my arm as we walked into her doctor's office. She leaned in, being unusually clingy. "You know I love you, even more than I love your grandpa, right?"

I stopped before we entered the building. "Are you sure you're okay?" She was starting to freak me out. I knew what a fake cough sounded like, having tried to play the sick card many years ago to get out of going to school. I was worried she was trying to ease me into telling me she was dying. Or maybe she wanted Dr. Gibbons to do it.

"Kiddo, I don't plan on leaving this earth anytime soon. I have too much to live for. There's a full moon soon, and your grandpa promised me we would go streaking."

I cringed at the thought of their wrinkly bodies running and flapping all over.

She playfully smacked my arm. "That was a joke. It's too cold. We only do that in the summer."

"You're killing me today." The automatic doors opened and we walked in together.

"Just don't kill me." She rubbed her lips together.

A sense of foreboding struck me. Enough to make me feel ill. Was Grandpa here? Was he the sick one? Yep, that was it. He was dying, and I was about to find out. But why didn't they call Dani and Kinsley? Maybe they were already here. Maybe they thought my mental state couldn't take it, so they were easing me into it. Or maybe this was another intervention. What if they were all waiting at the psychologist's office on the second floor?

While I was trying to figure out how to escape from my family, I wasn't paying attention to where I was going, and I almost ran into an easel with a large sign resting on it in the lobby.

My eyes barely caught what the sign was all about before my brain registered a four-alarm fire in my head. A wave of heat accompanied by a severe case of nausea overtook me. I grabbed onto my traitorous grandma for support. "We need to leave," I struggled to say. My mouth was drier than Death Valley in the summertime.

"Nonsense, I have an appointment with my *new* doctor." She wagged her brows.

"Well great, *you* can see him. I'll wait in the car." I stared at the sign with Jonah's photo and the words, *Pine Falls Medical Center is pleased to welcome Dr. Jonah Adkinson.* There he was in all his boyish-charm glory. His sandy hair had darkened and his face seemed more square, but his beautiful green eyes still sparkled, and he still carried the same aura of goodness. A goodness I could never allow myself to trust. A goodness that made him the most attractive man in any room.

"I gotta go." I was swallowing hard over and over, trying to get some saliva back in my mouth. I turned to leave.

"No. No. No." Grandma held me firm. For an old bird, she was strong. "How can you think to leave your sick grandma?"

"You're sick all right," I tried keeping my voice down so none of the other truly sick patients would hear me. My eyes bore into Grandma's mischievous bronze eyes. "You had me worried something was really wrong with you. You let me think we were going to see Dr. Gibbons. Instead, you were playing dress up with me and deceiving me."

She straightened up, tall and proud. "I've never in my life deceived you. I'll have you know I've had an itchy throat that's been keeping me up at night coughing, and you never asked which doctor I was seeing. You just assumed. And by the way, you should thank me. You've never looked better."

I tried to form a rebuttal, but my head was still buzzing from the fact that Jonah was my grandma's new doctor. What were the odds that he would become a partner at the same office my grandma had been going to for years?

"When did you find out that he was going to be the new doctor here?"

"I got a card in the mail. It was really nice. I'll show it to you when we get home. Our Jonah has been a busy man. Did you know that he regularly donated his time to treating inner-city patients who couldn't afford medical care?"

"No." But it didn't surprise me.

"He's a real sweetheart, and he's looking forward to seeing you. So, let's go."

"Wait. He knows I'm coming? How? Why? When?"

"Honey, none of that matters. What matters is that you're here and you look gorgeous."

"You set me up."

"I had help."

I pinched the bridge of my nose. "Explain," I growled. Grandma pressed her lips together and thought about what she should say. "I want the whole truth," I clarified. I could tell she was thinking of a way to sugar coat it.

Grandma put her hands on her hips, defiant. "Fine. Here it is. We tried to get you on one of those shows like *What Not to Wear*. You know, where they come in and throw away all your clothes and give you a new wardrobe and makeover, but apparently there are worse dressers than you out there and they thought you were too naturally beautiful."

Oh. My. Gosh. "You did what?"

She waved her hand like it was no big deal. It was a huge deal. They had applied, which meant they took pictures, maybe even videos, of me and sent them to strangers who would have humiliated me on TV. Did they all think I was this pathetic?

"Don't worry. Like I said, it was a no-go, but . . ." she hung on to that one syllable like she was humming the alphabet.

"But what?"

"We did our own version."

"What do you mean?" My blood pressure was rising.

Grandma shifted her rainboot clad feet. Not sure she was one to really give fashion advice. "We threw away your clothes. Dani and Kinsley should be filling your closet now with a shiny new wardrobe."

I couldn't believe this. I threw my arms out and knocked over the picture of Jonah. Could this day get any worse? Flustered, I tried to get the picture back on the easel but ended up knocking that over too. It clanged hard against the tile floor, making everyone in the lobby stop and stare at me.

I got the easel up but was so shaky I dropped the picture twice before it stayed put. But even then, it was crooked. "I'm leaving."

Grandma reached for my hand. "Please don't. He really wants to see you."

I stopped, my heart in my throat. "I can't believe you did this." I had to hold back my tears. I wasn't ready to see him. I didn't want to see him. That was a lie.

I couldn't afford to see him. That was the truth.

"Why is this rattling you so much? I thought you said you were only *friends*," she taunted me.

"Don't pretend that you don't know that he asked me to marry him." I was sure Dani and Kinsley had filled her in on that tidbit.

"You should stop pretending that you don't have feelings for him," her voice was filled with tenderness, "and that you don't regret you said no."

A tear escaped and ran down my cheek. I couldn't look her in the eye. "We left things as they should be."

Grandma rested her hand on my cheek, forcing me to look at her. "My love, if that were true, you wouldn't be terrified to see him."

She had a point, but I wasn't admitting it to her. Especially after all the shenanigans she'd pulled with my *ex*-best friends.

"You can do this." She patted my cheek with a grin. "And you never know, maybe he'll repulse you now and you can thank your lucky stars you didn't end up with him."

I stared back at his picture and knew that wouldn't be the case. But that's why I had left things as they were. I never wanted to be repulsed by him. Unrequited love was better than a love that had died.

"I know what you're thinking," Grandma interrupted my thoughts, "and yes, Ariana, there would have been times that you woke up in the morning and stared at him lying next to you snoring and reeking of the onions he ate the night before. And you would have wondered how you could have ever fallen in love with him. But . . ."

I turned from staring at Jonah's picture and faced her.

"But, on the other side of those feelings you would have found a deeper, more passionate love than you could have ever imagined. The only way to get that love is to endure the hard times, the times you don't feel like you love him. Choosing to love and stay in love is far more rewarding than falling in love. Remember that. Now let's go."

I didn't want to let her words sink in. I felt too much truth in them on the surface. Enough for them to make my insides squirm.

"Just so you know, this doesn't mean I'm changing my mind." *Yes, be defiant,* I told myself. "I'm only doing this because I'm a mature adult, and I'm going to ask Jonah about what it will take for me to get you deemed mentally incompetent and committed." I smirked.

"Kiddo, if that's what it would take for you to see how misguided you've been, I'd check myself in this minute."

Oh. I wasn't expecting that. I expected sarcasm. My eyes watered. "I love you," was all I could say.

"I love you more. Now let's get your cute butt in there. It's nice to see it again, by the way."

I let out a deep breath and took her arm. Maybe I was an adult, but I needed someone to hold on to.

We walked across the lobby, Grandma pulling me along to the door that led to the waiting area. While Grandma checked in, I texted Dani and Kinsley. *You are both dead to me.* I couldn't believe they had been conspiring against me. *P.S. If you threw away my* Hold On, Let Me Overthink This *sweatshirt, payback will be hell.*

The brats texted me back with pictures of my closet full of, I hated to admit, beautiful clothing. Everything from jeans and sweaters to slacks and dresses. They all looked formfitting and expensive. Definitely not my usual Wal-Mart sale items. Grandma must have done a lot of bartering with Shelby. It made me feel guilty. But that feeling was quickly replaced with ire when I received a series of pictures of them gleefully cutting my sweatshirts into several pieces and tossing them into the garbage.

Be afraid, be very afraid. I texted back.

In return I received two texts that each said the same thing. *I love you.*

Ugh. I turned off my phone and tossed it in my bag. My old ratty bag. Crap. Maybe I could leave it here in the waiting room. For now, I shoved it next to me in the seat. Perhaps I should have paid more attention to the way I looked and presented myself the last few years. It wasn't like I got up one morning and decided to be a slob, as my grandma put it. It was a gradual descent toward being grungy. It worked really well though. Hardly any men paid attention to me.

Grandma sat next me, grinning from ear to ear. "It should only be a few minutes."

My hands started getting sweaty. I couldn't believe I was going to see Jonah. I wasn't sure why he wanted to see me. Maybe he'd heard I'd let myself go and he wanted to get an up-close view of why he was thanking his lucky stars. Except he wasn't that kind of person. But people changed, as I very well knew. Or was it that people like my ex-fiancé, Kaden, never changed, they were only better at masking who they really were for certain periods of time? I leaned forward and put my face in my hands. I was so confused.

Grandma rubbed my back. "It's going to be all right. You can do this."

What if I couldn't? I felt like I was in a no-win situation. If Jonah truly was as good as I hoped him to be, as he had proved to be when we were "friends," that meant I'd lost out on years. I'd lost *him.* My worst fear would have been realized and shoved in my face. But if I was right about how we would have ended up? Seeing him now would ruin our memories.

The memories I'd cherished and made sure to keep intact. I'd never loved anyone the way I'd loved him.

Sometimes in the middle of the night I would still wake up and think I'd heard him knock on my door just so he could see my face. So he could hold me while he slept. In his arms, I'd never felt such peace. It was if our bodies were contoured precisely for each other. Not once did I ever wake up in those arms and feel repulsed by him. In fact, I'd loved to smell the Skittles on his breath or to hear his heavy exhales. Sometimes he talked in his sleep. It was mostly medical jargon I didn't understand, but sometimes it was about me. I knew he loved me long before he said it while conscious. He'd told me in his sleep a few times. I should have walked away then, but I couldn't. I told myself it was only in his dreams, even when I knew the truth. The way he treated me when he was awake spelled it out for me.

"Kay Kramer," a nurse called out, interrupting my thoughts.

I slowly let my hands drop away from my face and sat back.

Grandma had already jumped up. She was awfully spry for being sick. She gave me a sympathetic look and held her hand out to me.

I wasn't a child, but you know what, I took her hand. Perhaps if I'd had one to hold more when I was a child, I wouldn't be so screwed up. Maybe Dani was right, maybe my mom had emotionally abused me. I should probably read the pamphlet about it that Dani had left on the couch.

"Are you ready, kiddo?"

Um. No.

chapter five

I paced around the exam room after the nurse took Grandma's vitals and asked her to describe her symptoms that probably a throat lozenge and some water would cure. But she was a good little faker and hacked enough for the nurse to be anxious over her non-condition. The nurse's final words were terrifying. "Dr. Adkinson will be in momentarily."

While I paced, I read the posters on the wall. The one about smoking particularly caught my attention. I was always surprised when I saw people smoking. It was clearly bad for you, as in it would kill you bad. But who was I to judge? I had my own addictions—they were all emotional. At this moment my lungs felt as if I had been smoking five packs a day for years. Not a lot of oxygen was getting in and out.

Then I stared at the stirrups attached to the exam table Grandma was sitting on. It was a sad day when I would rather be at the gynecologist with my legs up in those babies waiting to be tortured with a cold metal speculum.

"Relax," Grandma said.

I scowled at her. It was her fault I was here in the first place.

She laughed at me. Amid her laughter a knock came on the door, and I practically jumped out of my skin. I flew into the seat where my grungy bag was, and, of course, I sat on it like an idiot. I was probably going to have to buy a new cell phone after this, and my keys were poking my butt.

Then Jonah appeared. We locked eyes immediately. His green jewels were as bright as I remembered them, his smile just as warm. Maybe his teeth were a tad whiter. Someone had obviously been using some teeth whitening strips or maybe he'd visited his dentist parents recently, but all the same, it was beautiful. He was beautiful. He wasn't necessarily the most physically attractive man ever, though he was handsome. It was his aura.

His eyes were assessing me. I tucked some of my hair behind my ear. Grandma had made me wear it down and styled. Which meant I spritzed some curling spray in it.

He looked well in his khakis and dark blue button-up, accented with a stethoscope. I smiled at the stethoscope, thinking about how many times he had listened to my heart with the one he owned long ago. He used to say, "I've never heard anything more beautiful than the sound of your heart." Then he would put his stethoscope aside and rest his head on my chest. I would stroke his hair until he fell asleep to the sound of my heart beating loudly for him.

"Ariana," he said as if he was catching his breath.

"Hi," I managed to say.

He shut the door and focused on Grandma. "Mrs. Kramer, it's good to see you."

Why didn't he say that to me? Maybe he didn't really want to see me. Maybe Grandma lied about this too. Or perhaps he still hated me for refusing him.

"Call me Kay. It's good to see you too," Grandma responded.

He approached. "Kay, tell me what brings you in today," he stuttered.

Grandma narrowed her eyes at him, annoyed. "Wouldn't you like to catch up with Ariana before we get to business?" Her tone said not to cross her and to stick with whatever plan they had hatched up.

"No . . . I mean, yes . . . I mean…" His ears burned bright. He took a deep breath in and exhaled loudly. "Wow." He ran a hand over his thick sandy hair that feathered back neatly and turned toward me. "I'm sorry. You still get to me. I wasn't expecting to feel like a schoolboy around you, not knowing what to say."

I'd always loved how honest he was. I loved that I still got to him. I offered him a smile. "How are you?"

"Better now."

What did that mean? Better now that he'd seen me? Better now that his ears weren't red anymore? Or was he referring to his divorce? I hoped it hadn't been overly painful for him. But if he was still the Jonah I knew, I would imagine it had been hard on him. Family meant everything to him. He had talked often of wanting a wife and children.

"I'm glad," I replied, though I wasn't sure what I was referring to. But that didn't matter, I was glad he was better.

"How are you?" he responded in kind.

"I'm not really sure." I was always more truthful with him than I wanted to be. There was something about him that brought that out.

He stepped closer. His clean scent tickled my nose and made my pulse tick up. "Anything I can help with?" he asked.

Oh, how I wished he could. I bit my lip and shook my head. "Just make sure my grandma is all right."

He said nothing for a moment. His attention had been drawn to my lips. Did he ache as much as me to feel our lips tangled together? Did he replay the memory of our first kiss over and over in his head as much as I did? It felt like yesterday we were in his car after Thanksgiving dinner at my grandparents' house. Several years before, I had started a tradition of playing hide-and-go-seek with cars. That year, Jonah convinced me we should be a team. We had been flirting a lot, dancing on the edge of our attraction. That night, though, he acted on his feelings while we were hiding behind the grocery store. He'd been staring at me for minutes before he said, "I want to kiss you."

It wasn't a good idea, even though I wanted to kiss him. I knew if we kissed my world would never be the same. I tried to deter him, to keep from deepening the connection I'd already felt with him. "You can kiss me if you strip down to your underwear and make a snow angel in the parking lot," I'd teased him, never thinking he would actually do it. But he hopped out of the car like it was on fire.

He stripped down and stood outside in plaid boxer shorts—his skin whiter than the newly fallen snow—showing off how truly tall and skinny he was. He flashed me a smile before he lay down in the snow and made not one, but three snow angels as a few of the grocery store employees looked on.

When he jumped back in the car, he threw his clothes in the backseat and wrapped me in his cold, wet arms. While he shivered from the cold, I shivered from his embrace, which warmed me in a way I had never felt. When his lips brushed mine, I knew then I was in trouble. From that moment on, we found any excuse to see each other. We snuck around like he was a Montague and I a Capulet. Two star-crossed lovers destined for a tragic ending, even though he believed in happily ever afters.

Now here he was, staring at me like he had that night. Though his shoulders were broader and his facial features more defined, he had the same look in his eye. The look that said, *I would do anything for you, even strip down to my underwear.*

He swallowed hard and blinked a few times. "What did you say?"

Grandma laughed. "Do you two need a minute alone?"

"No," I was quick to say. I had a feeling if given a minute alone, I would find myself right back in his arms, wishing I could always remain there.

My abrupt answer made him flash me a look that said not to expect him to go away before he turned back to Grandma. *Crap.* I was afraid of that.

While Jonah played doctor, I shifted uncomfortably on my keys. I had to stop myself from wincing. While I had a sharp object poking my butt, something else was stabbing my heart. It felt a lot like fear. Dani was right, living in fear was the worst kind of terror. That, and worrying about my keys poking a hole in my jeans in front of my ex, who was never technically my boyfriend because I'd refused to let him give us a title. He used to call us cuddle buddies. I'd found it charming.

Jonah did all the doctor things, from listening to Grandma's heart to checking all her orifices above the neck. Then I heard something disturbing.

"Have you decided if you will be joining us for Thanksgiving or not?" Grandma asked.

I gripped the chair, hoping I'd heard her wrong.

"Are you sure you don't mind if my wife—I mean ex-wife—joins us?" Jonah replied.

What? Did he say his ex-wife was invited too? And when was he invited? I shifted too far in my chair and the keys had their revenge. "Ouch!" I involuntarily popped up.

Jonah and Grandma both whipped their heads my way.

Jonah gave me a pained look. "It's not what you think."

No. It wasn't what he thought. I wasn't jumping up in pain because he was obviously still very much connected with his ex-wife. Maybe even in love with her. *Wife* he'd called her. And did exes typically spend holidays together? Yes, the thought of him still being in love with his wife hurt, but it was also good. It meant no one could put any pressure on us to throw kindling on the fire we'd doused. Okay, the one I'd taken the fire extinguisher to.

But if Grandma knew about him and his ex-wife—enough to invite them all for Thanksgiving, which I was now no longer attending—why did she go to all the trouble to get me here?

I pointed at the chair and my ratty old bag. "I was sitting on my keys and . . ." And I was an idiot. "I'm going to go wait . . . uh . . ." My mind went blank. "You know, in the waiting place, I mean, the waiting room." I headed toward the door, forgetting my bag.

Jonah stepped in front of me, giving me an up-close view of him. Even wearing clothes, I could tell he was more muscular than he used to be.

"Please don't go," he begged. He put his hands out like he wanted to touch me, but he didn't. "There are rules about the kind of contact I can have with anyone in our exam rooms."

I was grateful for that at the moment.

He stepped back. "Let me explain."

"You don't owe me an explanation, other than why you conspired with my grandma to get me to come here in the first place." I gave her the stink eye.

"I thought that would be obvious," he replied.

"It's not."

The corners of his mouth ticked up. "You haven't changed at all. Still beautiful and stubborn."

"There has to be a rule against saying that."

"Probably," he smirked, "but I don't really care. The truth is, I wanted to see you, Ariana."

Yeah, I was afraid of that. "You know where I work."

"I also know you work with sharp objects and solder irons. I thought it best not to surprise you there."

"Okay, I'll give you that one, but you could have just asked to see me. Or called."

"This was more fun, and I need some of that in my life."

I tilted my head. His melancholy tone caught me off guard. "Have you had enough *fun* yet?"

He leaned forward and without touching me whispered, "Not even close."

Shivers erupted. I stepped back, nervously swiping my bangs.

Jonah wasn't backing off. "There's nothing going on between Eliza, my ex-wife," he clarified, "and me. She'll just be in town, and for our daughter's sake, we want to have holidays together as much as possible."

"That's nice." I wrung my hands. Maybe he wasn't hung up over his ex.

"I want you to meet Whitney, my daughter."

"Why?"

"Because we both need some fun in our lives."

Didn't we all?

chapter six

"I'm still not talking to the two of you." I slammed a roll of copper tape down on one of the tables in the studio. I was setting up for *Sip and Solder night*. We were expecting a big crowd. Our Tiffany-style ornaments were all the rage this time of year.

Kinsley and Dani laughed at me.

I hadn't said a word to them since telling them off yesterday when I got back from taking Grandma to her appointment. You know, after I did a fashion show for them with all my new clothes. But after that I'd been giving them the cold shoulder. I didn't care how good I looked.

Kinsley started nibbling on a chocolate cookie.

"Those are for my customers," I growled.

"I made them." She took a large bite and chewed dramatically, making Dani and me laugh.

"Fine, you have a point," I conceded.

Dani reached out across the table and took my hand. "Don't be mad at us. Everything we did was out of love. And see how cute you look?"

I stared down at my form-fitting, soft gray tunic and black leggings that left no doubt I had long slender legs. I even had on some stylish leather booties. My feet weren't loving the constrictive nature of them, but when I was in the studio it was the price my feet had to pay for protection. Glass and heat were a painful combination.

"So how was it seeing Jonah?" Kinsley asked after swallowing. "You never told us yesterday."

"What makes you think I will now?" I suppressed a smile. It was hard to stay mad at them.

"Oh, come on," Dani begged. "If you tell us, I'll tell you what Jonah told Brock about seeing you again."

I grabbed on to the table for support. I wasn't sure how I felt about Jonah talking about me. "What are we, in high school? Do you want me to tell Brant to tell Brock you think he's fine and you would say yes if he asked you out?"

Dani bit her lip. "Please don't."

Ugh. Now I felt bad. I sat next to her on one of the stools and rubbed her leg. "I'm sorry. I shouldn't tease you about him. Is he really bringing a date tonight?"

Dani rested her head on her hand and sighed. "Yep. I gave her my Dani seal of approval." Sarcastic tones oozed through her words.

Kinsley handed her two cookies. "You need to quit torturing yourself like that. Brock's a big boy, he can keep choosing the wrong woman all on his own."

Dani grabbed the cookies, devoured a large bite of one, and took a moment to savor it. After letting out a deep breath, she said, "I gave up hope a long time ago that he and I will ever be anything more than friends." She sat up tall. "Anyway, let's talk about Jonah, who we know wants to be more than someone's friend."

I swallowed hard. "He said that?"

Dani waved her finger in front of me. "Oh no, the deal was for you to tell us how you felt first."

"Please," Kinsley begged while brushing cookie crumbs off her cropped sweater that showed off her tight abs. Food may have been her life, but she worked out like no one's business.

I rubbed the back of my neck. "There's not a lot to tell. I saw him, made a fool of myself, and that was pretty much it." I stood to finish setting up for my class, refusing to mention that he'd followed us out to the parking lot and kissed my cheek before saying, "We'll get together later and talk." I'd mumbled something incoherent like, "What? No. Yes. Okay. I need to go buy bread." It wasn't my finest moment. I don't know what had happened to me. I never used to be so nonsensical around him. He used to call me witty. Now I felt dimwitted.

Dani grabbed me, making me stay put. "You are such a liar. You have Jonah glow."

"Jonah glow?" I questioned.

"Your eyes are twinkling like they used to," Kinsley informed me.

"It's the lighting in here."

They both rolled their eyes.

"Your resistance to tell us only speaks to how much you really care about him," Dani challenged me. "You know he stills cares about you . . . a lot."

I looked down at my shoes. "Is that what he said?"

"Maybe," Dani teased.

I lifted my head and met her devious gray eyes. "Fine. I don't know how to feel about him being back here. It's not like it changes anything. Besides, he's bringing his ex-wife to Thanksgiving, which I'm no longer attending."

"What?" they shouted in unison.

"You can't skip Thanksgiving. Who will sing the Thanksgiving blessing song and organize the car hide-and-go-seek?" Kinsley asked. "And who cares if Eliza's coming?"

"Obviously, I do. It will be awkward." More awkward than if it was only Jonah and his daughter.

"Only if you make it that way," Dani countered. "You don't know Eliza. She's very cerebral and she and Jonah left things amicable."

"The only reason you feel awkward is because you still have a thing for him." Kinsley wagged her brows.

I rubbed my forehead. "You know what? Yes, I still care for Jonah. He's one of the best people I've ever known, but like I said, it doesn't change anything."

"It should," Dani quipped. "Did you read the pamphlets? Make an appointment with the therapist? She's really good with helping people with childhood trauma."

"I—"

"Don't deny it," Dani interrupted me. "Your creepy stepfather, Carl, coming on to you is traumatic on its own; but the unstable environment your mom provided for you and her lack of emotional support, even physical support at times, was enough to mess up any kid."

"You think I'm messed up?" I was offended, even if I knew it was true.

"Uh, yeah," Dani replied with no apology. "Your coping mechanisms are scary amazing. From hiding behind your horrendous clothes to making sure every holiday is full of idealistic traditions, not to mention how you work crazy hours and tell yourself it's because the business requires it, but really it's because you want to make sure you never go without again. And the way you treat each child that walks in this studio like they are your own, because deep down you want nothing more than to be a mother and even a wife. But the thought that you might really be like your mother scares you so bad, you won't even contemplate it. Which is a shame because you would be killer at both. And," she took a breath. "I know it was you who filled the Children to Love donation box I left here. You'd rather save the world than yourself, because somewhere along the way you believed the lies you told yourself, that you're okay. You've done such a good job of it, most people believe it too."

I wiped the tears out of my eyes. "Are you done now?" There was nothing like the knife of truth being stabbed in your heart.

Dani stood and wrapped me up in her arms. "I don't say these things to hurt you. Believe me, I know all about childhood trauma and coping mechanisms."

I knew she did. Her situation growing up had been ten times worse than mine, going from foster home to foster home. Not all of them were stand-up people. She'd had her own Carls. Growing up, Dani had done some things she wasn't proud of to deal with her pain; she even had a brush with the law. But unlike me, she'd sought counseling. She didn't lie to herself.

"I don't know if I can change." I rested my head on her shoulder.

Kinsley came and wrapped her skinny arms around us. "Of course, you can. You've already started by not looking homeless anymore."

I giggled into Dani's shoulder. "Why didn't you guys say anything to me before trying to get me on a TV show?"

Dani leaned away. "We tried to subtly, so we wouldn't hurt your feelings, but you never took the hint."

"Did we hurt your feelings?" Kinsley asked, obviously afraid they had. She was the kindest of us.

"No, but maybe you humiliated me a little. You didn't tell Jonah I was a slob, did you?"

We broke apart, Kinsley and Dani standing back with smirks.

"You care what Jonah thinks about you?" Dani asked smugly.

I waved them away. "I really need to get ready for my class." I headed for the back office to grab more supplies.

"By the way, Jonah is coming tonight," Kinsley admitted sheepishly.

I stopped dead in my tracks, heart beating uncontrollably. I couldn't even look at my traitorous best friends.

"The first step to healing is to face your fears head on," Dani called.

Fear was an understatement. Jonah terrified me. My feelings for him hadn't gone anywhere, but neither had my other anxieties. I mean, Jonah himself was living proof I was right about relationships. If someone like him could get divorced, I wasn't sure how anyone stood a chance. How could *we*?

Why was I even thinking like that? It was presumptuous to think Jonah came back here for me. I wasn't the only person he was close to. And now he was a dad. Maybe he came back for the excellent schools. Though I was pretty sure I remembered reading in one of his family's Christmas letters that his daughter had been accepted to some fancy Ivy League academy for children back in Connecticut where he had moved after his residency. I wasn't even sure why that was a thing. It also made me feel even more insecure. I'd told Jonah he needed a wife with all the right credentials. I bet his parents loved Eliza. I was sure they would still dislike me.

I hustled to get my supplies, trying to think of a way to escape. Nothing was coming to mind, short of me skipping town and changing my name. Too bad I craved stability like a starving vampire at a blood bank. I not only loved Pine Falls, but I think it had gotten to the point where I needed it.

It was one of the many reasons I wouldn't leave with Jonah when he'd asked me. I had been afraid if I moved again, I wouldn't stop. My mom would say, "This time we aren't moving again, I promise." Each time was a lie, until we'd moved back home to Pine Falls for good.

Not only had she changed husbands like they were going out of style, but she'd always chosen ones who didn't have a stable income. We'd been evicted more times than I wanted to remember. I swore that would never be me. Not like I would have had to worry about that with Jonah. But he'd brought other worries, like me not fitting into his world. I wasn't sure I could feel at home in the luxurious places he'd lived.

That thought made me pause and lean against the backroom door. Maybe I was morphing into my mother. I always chose men, with the exception of Jonah, who made me feel good about what I considered my defects. Defects drilled into me all through high school. I'd known what some of the kids said about me, especially the popular kids. My past had followed me along with all the rumors about my mom, which were true. I'd ended up dating guys and having friends who were considered second class citizens in school. No one thought any of us were destined for greatness. Not even my own mother.

Once upon a time I had wanted to pursue higher education. But she'd discouraged me, saying it was a waste of time and money since I already knew I wanted to be an artist and I seemed to have a natural born talent for working with stained glass. Really any kind of art, from drawing to writing my silly Thanksgiving songs I made up every year.

I rubbed the backroom door with my hand. I wondered now if my mom simply hadn't wanted me to be better than her. Maybe she had never believed in me, or I hadn't believed in myself enough. Perhaps I still didn't, in the ways that counted most. In all the ways that kept me from what I'd wanted most in life—someone I didn't have to return. Jonah.

I rested my head against the door and sighed. Why hadn't he stayed away?

chapter seven

Someone or someones, aka Dani and Kinsley, should have mentioned to me that Jonah was bringing his daughter. I needed to prepare for these kinds of things. Like thinking of a good alias and booking a flight.

With all that said, I couldn't help but be mesmerized by Jonah's offspring. Her pictures didn't do her justice; she was even lovelier in person with her long sandy brown hair that looked like it had been brushed a hundred times, making it uniformly straight and shiny. It was her eyes, though, that drew me in. She'd inherited Jonah's sparkling green eyes. But she was different than her father. She was businesslike, which was odd considering she wasn't quite six yet, from what I had gathered in my brief introduction to her before my class started. She was dressed like a mini executive in a smart navy blazer with a white blouse underneath it. Maybe she went to a private school. Wherever she went, they must teach etiquette. I'd never seen a child, or anyone for that matter, sit up so straight.

Her physical appearance had nothing on what was coming out of her mouth. While I was walking around and offering individual help to my class members who were trying to smooth the edges of the stained glass using glass grinders, Whitney was schooling us all on how stained glass was made.

"Stained glass is colored by metallic salts," she informed everyone.

Each class member stopped what they were doing and paid attention to the young genius. I wasn't even sure I could say *metallic* until I was ten, let alone know what it meant.

"And," she continued, "you are lucky that there are fans blowing in here because the solder you are going to use has lead in it." She said every word distinctly and didn't use contractions. Why in the world did this child know so much about the process of making stained glass ornaments?

My wide eyes met Jonah's from across the table. Jonah's eyes said *I know what you're thinking*. I wasn't sure if he did know, because I wasn't sure what to think of the Mensa candidate he was raising. You read about baby geniuses, but you never think you're going to meet one. Or in my case, you never thought your ex (or whatever Jonah was) would raise one. I mean, Jonah was smart, but he wasn't Einstein. I had a feeling his little girl was. She could probably teach us all about the theory of relativity.

"Is there really lead in this solder?" one woman asked me, worried.

I forced my eyes away from Jonah's. It was harder than I thought it would be after all this time. "There are in some types of solder, but not in the kind we are using tonight." I turned back toward Jonah and smiled at his daughter so she knew I wasn't trying to correct her. Whitney tilted her head, studying me like a test subject. I wondered if she knew anything about me.

Jonah wrapped his arm around his daughter and whispered something in her ear that made her smile at me. In that smile I saw her father and the life I might have had. Though I couldn't imagine any children with my DNA turning out as smart as Whitney. My five-year-old would probably be eating finger paints and running around barefoot singing some silly song at the top of her voice.

That thought had me grabbing my stomach. Having a child of my own was one of those wishes that made me ache because I knew a wish was all it would ever be. Or . . . I focused back on Jonah. Did it have to be only a wish? Jonah caught my gaze and opened his mouth to say something. That shook me out of my ridiculous line of thinking. I turned from him before he could speak and focused on the woman next to me who was grinding her piece of stained glass down to nothing.

I berated myself internally for thinking that Jonah had come back here to make babies with me. I took the piece of stained glass out of the woman's hand. "Here, let me help you," I offered, wishing someone could help me. Maybe it was time to seek some real therapy. Or a vacation.

As the class went on, I found myself paying a lot of attention to Whitney and Jonah, from afar that is. His little girl intrigued me—as did her father, but I wouldn't admit that out loud. For as grown up as she looked and sounded, I saw glimpses of timidity within her. She refused to use or be anywhere near the solder iron, even if she wore the protective gloves. She said, "Father, do you know that those can cause third-degree burns?" Jonah lovingly tried to coax her into trying it, but to no avail. She started talking about skin grafts.

How she knew so many medical terms and that solder irons could give you third-degree burns, I had no idea. Was Jonah giving her his medical books? Could she even read them? I had a feeling she could. How was that possible? And why did she call him *father*? She sounded straight out of the Victorian era. Jonah was more of a daddy, not a father.

Brock, who was sitting at the far table, caught me staring at my past. "Why are you avoiding Jonah?" he whispered.

I took the stool next to him. His date had vacated it to use the restroom and "powder" her nose. Who talked like that anymore? If she came back out with any more powder on her nose or more layers of lipstick on her pouty lips, I was going to have to ask her to stay away from any heat sources. How Dani approved of Alexandra, I had no idea. She so wasn't Brock's type. But maybe that's why Dani gave her the green light.

I leaned in close to the love of Dani's life and whispered, "Why are you wasting your time with Alexandra?" I asked instead of answering him.

He swallowed hard while his eyes flickered toward Dani, who was doing her best to act happy with Kinsley. She was laughing louder than she usually did and was purposely not looking at Brock.

"It's complicated."

"Is it?" I said ultra-quiet. "You know how Dani feels about you."

Brock's face flushed red. "You wouldn't understand."

"Try me."

His gaze drifted toward his twin brother, Brant, who was there with a woman named Jill. Jill seemed nice enough, but she wasn't Brant's type. She was more of an understated beauty with mousey brown hair, big brown eyes, and a tiny frame. Brant typically liked his women with curves for days and features that made most women jealous. Women like Dani.

But Jill, from what I gathered, had some serious political connections. She was the daughter of some highfalutin federal officer back in Washington DC. I think she may have even gone to the same private boarding school as Brant and Brock had when they lived back East while their father was serving as a senator. And the rumor was that Brant was planning on running for office in the next election cycle. Or at least, his father was planning on Brant running. John Holland, the retired US Senator, had expectations of his sons, and his sons always met them with flying colors.

Brock fiddled with one of the pencils used to smooth out the copper tape. "Like I said, it's complicated."

"I hope it's worth breaking Dani's heart."

He whipped his head toward me, his jaw pulsing. The anesthesiologist and army reserve major could be quite intimidating. Good thing I knew he had a heart of gold, no matter how stupid he was being.

"Do you think I want to hurt her?" His pain came through loud and clear by the way his voice shook.

"Regardless of whether you want to or not, you are."

He leaned in. "I'm not the only person breaking hearts tonight. You need to talk to him." He nodded his head in Jonah's direction.

"I have talked to him."

"So I heard." Brock chuckled.

My brow popped. "And what did you hear?"

Brock pushed his stool back and stood. "I think I'll let you ask him." He sauntered off in Dani's direction. Dani's face lit up when she saw him walking her way. What a weird mess we were all in.

I stood, ready to walk around and see if anyone needed my help with attaching the hooks to their ornaments, the final step of the process, but Jonah apparently decided it was time I stopped avoiding him. He left his daughter in Kinsley's care and headed my way. In a panic, I darted toward my personal workbench where I made custom orders. Jonah wasn't deterred by my ridiculous behavior.

While staring down at some of the stained glass pieces I had cut earlier in the day, Jonah sidled up to me. His warmth and clean scent hit me like a hurricane. So much of me wanted to get swept away in it, in him, but my fears always prevailed.

"Did you get your bread?"

My head jerked up. "What?"

"Last time I saw you, you said you needed to buy bread." He held his laughter in, but it played all over his handsome face.

I nudged him with my shoulder, embarrassed. "As a matter of fact, I did. Thanks for asking."

"I'm happy to hear that," he teased.

We each seemed to take a deep breath at the same time and let it out slowly. A long, silent pause filled the air between us.

Whitney and Kinsley caught my eye. It looked like Whitney passed on Kinsley's cookies. Odd. "Your daughter's beautiful," I commented.

Jonah looked at his daughter with a mixture of adoration and something else. Worry, maybe? "She is. Thank you. I'm looking forward to you getting to know her better."

I bit my lip. "I don't know if that's a good idea."

Jonah, with no thought for my unsettled state, took my hand as if it was the natural thing to do. Oh, how I had missed his touch. It was like Xanax for my soul. He clung tightly so I wouldn't pull away. We had never touched in public before, except for when my mother was in hospice, dying. No one questioned his motive for holding my hand then. Any friend would have done the same.

"Please don't leave," he begged, as if he knew I was ready to bolt to anywhere he wasn't. He brushed his thumb across my hand, sending sparks through my entire body.

"Jonah, everyone's staring at us." By everyone I meant our friends and his daughter, which made me feel self-conscious. What must his daughter think of this? Her parents hadn't been divorced very long.

"Let them." He turned me toward him, making sure we were eye to eye. He was several inches taller than my five-foot-seven frame, so I had to look up. Being this close to him made me realize Dani and Kinsley were right, there was something missing from his eyes. The playfulness that used to be in them was dimmed. My free hand itched to rest on his stubbled cheek, to caress it until the light returned to his eyes. But it wasn't fair of me. Letting him hold my hand was already pushing it. I didn't want to lead him on, lead him to where I had led him before—a dead-end road.

"Hi," he said as if we were meeting for the first time in a long time.

It made my heart skip a few beats. "Hi."

"I missed you," he easily admitted.

I missed him too, but I wasn't sure how to respond.

"I know you don't know what to say, and you must have a lot of questions for me. I want to answer all of them, but for now, come sit next to me and my daughter. And quit pretending that you don't want to." He flashed me an impish grin.

My jaw dropped. "I haven't seen you in nine years."

"That wasn't my choice."

"You got married," I said quietly. Not that I blamed him. I'd wanted that for him. I'd wanted him to be happy. I still did.

He pulled me a little closer. "I did, but that was past tense. This," he pointed between us, "I'm hoping is present tense."

"Jonah, you don't know me anymore, and you shouldn't assume I want or am ready for—"

He placed his finger on my mouth. "Shh. Don't ruin our moment. You were always good at that."

"Excuse me?" He was much bolder than I remembered.

"Come on." He pulled me back to his table. "We'll talk later."

Dani and Kinsley shot me sly grins as they watched Jonah pull me along. Conflicting emotions coursed through me. It all felt so right, but so wrong. I definitely thought we should talk first. Then I could tell him I was as messed up as when he left nine years ago. Maybe even more so now. I could let him know that he was wasting his time with me. And I would probably mention that his daughter intimidated me.

Jonah pulled out a stool for me next to his daughter. "Whitney, Ariana is going to help you make an ornament."

I wanted to say, "I am?" but the poor thing looked about as nervous as I felt. "I would be happy to," came falling out of my mouth instead.

Whitney pressed her lips together. She looked as if a fierce internal debate raged inside of her.

She wasn't the first kid in here afraid to try, though she was my youngest. The recommended age for my children's classes was eight and up.

"Did you know that a long time ago, stained glass was used to tell stories to people who couldn't read?" I asked her, part of me thinking she probably knew that, seeing as she knew so much about the process already.

Her eyes blinked a few times as if she couldn't believe that people couldn't read. "I can read."

I had no doubt she could. She probably read better than me.

"That's good then, you can make an ornament that helps tell a story. What story would you like to tell?"

She thought for a moment. "I love *Little Women*. I read it last year."

I looked at Jonah to get confirmation. Wouldn't she have been in preschool last year? What preschooler was reading *Little Women*? I didn't read that book until I was in my twenties.

Jonah nodded uneasily.

"What grade are you in?" I asked Whitney.

She sat up straighter, which I didn't think was possible. "Second grade. I want to be in fourth grade, but Father says I am too young."

Jonah kissed Whitney's head. "You are much too young."

She folded her arms in a huff, obviously still put out over it.

I didn't dare get in the middle of a family matter. Instead, I turned her attention back to what she feared. It was probably something similar to my fears, the unknown. I imagined it was even scarier for her—someone who knew so much, probably too much for her age. "What story would you like to tell with your ornament? You could tell the story of the March sisters' Christmas morning. We could make a book or even a tree. Or you could choose something symbolic from the story, like the umbrella or the postbox."

Her eyes lit up. "You have read it too?" She sounded surprised. This child needed to learn how to use contractions. What kind of school was she going to?

"A few times, actually. I relate to Jo." The main character in the book vowed to never marry but does. Oddly, I always found myself upset when Jo turns down Laurie, her neighbor. On the other hand, I'm happy to see her end up with the professor.

Jonah gave me a knowing look.

"Why do you relate to Jo?" Whitney asked.

"She's very stubborn." I grinned. No need to mention my intent on staying single forever.

Jonah nodded profusely. "In the end, though, she comes around," he added in.

I ignored his insinuations. "So, Whitney, what should we make?"

She tapped her finger against her lip. "What does the umbrella symbolize?"

My eyes inadvertently met Jonah's. "Protection."

Whitney turned into her dad and he put an arm around her. "I want to make that one," she mumbled.

"I'm going to need your help cutting the glass." I wasn't prepared to make an umbrella.

She peeked at me, unsure. "Will it hurt?" Her voice trembled.

"I promise it won't." I held out my hand to her. "Let me show you."

Her tiny hand slowly made its way into mine. When our hands met, grief encompassed me. I silently mourned for what could have been.

"I do not want to get hurt," she reiterated to me.

"Me either," I whispered.

chapter eight

I was soldering a chain onto Whitney's umbrella—the final touch—while Jonah watched with Whitney sleeping in his arms. It was just the three of us. The class had ended over an hour ago and our friends conveniently left us by ourselves. I stared at the umbrella, perplexed by the little girl who chose bold purple, red, and blue because they were power colors. When I was five, I chose colors because I found them pretty. I never once thought about the meaning behind them.

"You were good with Whitney tonight. Thank you. I never thought she would break the glass apart after you scored it," Jonah interrupted my thoughts.

It had taken some serious coaxing. I had to show her how to break the glass five times and answer all her questions about the exact properties of glass, and she insisted on googling injuries sustained by stained glass artists. I had to say how impressed I was by how fast she could type into her dad's phone. After her research, she requested goggles and gloves before she would even try. I still couldn't get her to try soldering, even with gloves and my assistance. Maybe next time. Wait. Would there be a next time?

"Can I ask you a question?" I asked Jonah.

"Anything," he responded.

I placed my solder iron back in its stand and took a moment to stare at the sleeping beauty in his arms. "How do you make a kid like her?"

Jonah shifted her in his arms.

"I don't mean that as an insult, by the way. I'm impressed. Maybe a little freaked out."

Jonah gave me an appreciative smile while gently swiping Whitney's bangs. "Sometimes it concerns me too," he admitted. "She was born naturally intelligent, but Eliza and I didn't do her any favors by focusing so much on it. I wish we had let her be a kid. I hate that she's two grades above her age, and according to every standardized test she's leaps and bounds above that, at least in some respects. Emotionally she's still a little girl, even if she doesn't believe it."

"She must keep you on your toes." I settled onto the nearby stool. I had a feeling Jonah wasn't going anywhere.

"Toes and knees, praying that I'm not too late."

I tilted my head. "Too late for what?"

"To undo my mistakes. I wish I would have been more vocal about my concerns earlier on."

"Does your ex-wife," I hesitated to ask, "feel differently than you?"

"Eliza is a good person," he paused, "but she sees life as a series of goals to be completed and milestones to reach. She fears wasted potential like you fear me."

Ah. He found a way to bring it back to us. I clasped my hands together and wrung them fiercely.

"I'm sorry, Ariana. That came out callously."

"I don't think you know how to be callous. And you're right. Which makes me wonder what you're doing here."

He looked between Whitney and me. "At the beginning of the year, Eliza confessed that she felt like marrying me was a mistake."

Whoa. That was harsh. But not unexpected. Isn't that what I had feared for Jonah and me all along? But how could anyone think Jonah was a mistake? You know, except for me. But I wasn't even sure I believed it. Therein was my dilemma. "I'm sorry, Jonah." Truly, I was.

Jonah shrugged. "It was a long time coming. I suppose you would say I should have expected it."

I pushed around some chain scraps on the table. "Honestly, I thought if anyone could beat the odds, it would be you."

"I still plan on beating them."

My head popped up.

Jonah's set facial features said he was issuing me a challenge.

I was more than certain I knew what he meant, but it had been nine years. Nine years since I had broken both our hearts. I cleared my throat. "How do you plan on doing that?"

He leaned forward. "When I left Pine Falls, I meant to do so with no regrets, and at the time I thought I had, even though things between us didn't turn out how I hoped."

The heat rose to my cheeks.

"But after Eliza left me, I realized something. You are my person. You made me who I am, and I regretted not fighting for you."

"Jonah." I pled with my tone for him to stop talking like that. He had no idea the misery and ecstasy he was causing within my heart. I had regrets too, but I was in no state of mind to entertain what it sounded like he was offering me.

"Ariana, I know what you're going to say. You think it wouldn't have mattered, but I don't believe it. You have no idea what it's like for someone to fight for you. Your mother sure as hell didn't, and as much as I love your grandparents, they didn't either. Don't even get me going on your non-existent, cowardly father. You need someone to fight for you. That person is me, so get ready."

I had no words.

All I could think about while staring at Jonah across the table from me at Thanksgiving dinner was what he had said to me last week at the studio. It's all I'd thought about all week as I had done my best to avoid him and his calls. It wasn't surprising that he still had my number memorized. I would have kept avoiding him too, but I was guilted into coming. Grandpa and Grandma laid it on thick, saying this could be their last Thanksgiving and then adding that I was a grown woman and should quit running from my problems.

Little did they know I wasn't running from my problems; I was trying to solve them. I had made an appointment with the therapist Dani had recommended—Goldie Hawn was highly offended I didn't find her helpful anymore—but she couldn't get me in until next week. Apparently, this was her busiest time of year due to the holidays. I only got in because I dropped Dani's name and the therapist had a cancellation.

I figured Jonah at least deserved for me to have my head on straight before we saw each other again. I obviously had high expectations that this therapist could fix me fairly quickly. I needed her to tell me if I was right or wrong about how I approached men, one man in particular. This way I could either tell Jonah I was right and give him sound professional reasons for why he should move on, or I could tell him I was wrong and he still should move on because it was going to get ugly. Like probably a lot of me in the fetal position. There was a better-than-average chance some wailing would be involved and possibly some running—like the marathon kind.

Jonah deserved better than all that. He deserved the well-put-together woman who sat one seat over from him next to their daughter. It wasn't *awkward* at all that his gorgeous ex-wife was there. I mean, it wasn't like she was perfect. Except she was, and this was the most uncomfortable holiday of my life.

Eliza was all I feared she would be and more, now that I saw her in living color. Her dark blonde bobbed hair was impressively shiny, and her facial features were even, as was her smooth peachy skin. She had these alluring aqua eyes, and the perfect body dressed to the nines in form fitting pants and a jacket.

Me? I was wearing yoga pants because Dani and Kinsley had deemed them worthy of not being thrown away since they showed my shape. And for the fun of it, yesterday I bought a turkey sweatshirt to wear for the occasion. It was really classy. It said *Gobble until You Wobble* on it. To top it off, I was barefoot. Ms. Perfection was wearing expensive leather heels.

Jonah stared at me from across the table and nudged my foot under the table. At least I assumed it was him by his grin. If not, my day was getting more awkward because it meant it was Brant, who sat next to Jonah. Brock and Brant, for some reason, always ended up at Grandma and Grandpa's for Thanksgiving, even though their parents lived in Carrington Cove. I think Dani mentioned something about John and Sheridan Holland going out of the country for some conference, so that's why the twins were here. But I was pretty sure it had a little to do with our family tradition of eating pie first, and a lot more to do with Dani.

When I was certain it wasn't Brant who was trying to play footsie with me under the table, I smirked at Jonah. He needed to stop being charming. I was determined to figure out my life before I got him involved. I didn't care how good he looked in his tight jeans and dark button-up or that he was smiling at me as if I lit up his world. He didn't deserve for me to reject him again, and I couldn't handle saying goodbye to him one more time. I knew that left us nowhere. I was smart enough to know that the therapist wasn't a magician. I knew she wouldn't be able to wave a magic wand that would make it so that Jonah and I could live happily ever after, or perhaps more realistically, make me okay with the inevitable break up.

Why wouldn't Jonah just let us be? I still loved him and thought fondly of him. I never wanted that to change. And if he couldn't make it work with Miss Shiny Hair, there was no way we were making it with my turkey sweatshirt.

Grandma stood at the head of the table. "All right, beautiful people, it's time to begin. As you know, we do pie first in this house."

Whitney gasped, horrified. "You cannot eat dessert first. If you eat sugar first it will make you eat more and that is unhealthy."

Each head at the table turned toward the precocious five-year-old who knew way too much for her own good and who seriously needed to learn how to use contractions. Whitney didn't seem bothered to be the center of attention. On the other hand, Jonah cleared his throat and wrapped his arm around his daughter. "Honey, it's okay for one day."

Um. In this family it was pretty much okay every day.

"But Father," she replied, "what about the obesity epidemic?"

Eliza smoothed her daughter's hair. "It is wise of you to be mindful of such things. You do not have to eat dessert first, or at all, if that is what you choose." Her alto voice was mesmerizing almost to the point that I didn't want to eat pie first. But that thought quickly left my brain. I noticed Eliza also didn't use contractions. Weird. I also noticed Jonah give his ex a pointed look. It wasn't unkind, but it was apparent he was displeased.

In response, Eliza took a deep breath and gave him a nod. "Whitney, perhaps it would be good to try a different approach today. I did bring your favorite honey roasted peaches and Greek yogurt."

That was right. I remembered Grandma mentioning that Eliza was health conscious and had asked if Grandma would be offended if she brought her own food. Grandma thought it was odd but didn't see the harm in it. I wasn't so sure it was harmless, judging by Jonah's reaction and the fact that I couldn't be friends with someone who didn't like pie. Not that I thought Eliza and I would become bosom buddies. After all, she'd married the love of my life. And rumor had it she was staying with Jonah. Yeah, that bothered me even though I had no business being jealous. The exes were free to shack up as much as they wanted and do whatever they pleased.

"Would it really be all right to eat that first?" Whitney asked her mother, too concerned for such a little girl.

"I believe for today it will be," Eliza responded as if she were pleased with herself for making an exception.

I looked between Dani and Kinsley who were sitting on either side of me to see if they thought this was as weird as I did. Their vacant stares said we were all on the same page.

Grandma turned the attention back to her. Her uneasy smile said she too wasn't sure what to make of it all, but she soldiered on. "Before pie, though, Ariana will perform her annual Thanksgiving blessing song." She turned toward me. "Take it away, honey."

Before I could reluctantly stand—I was a little embarrassed in present company to perform the song I wrote every year for this occasion—Whitney had another question. "What is a blessing song?" she asked Jonah.

"It's the best part of Thanksgiving," he informed her before throwing me a wink.

"I thought the best part was when we read George Washington's proclamation about Thanksgiving Day and then eat butternut squash stuffed with rice," Whitney responded with no guile.

Jonah's ears turned red. "Well—"

"Whitney," Eliza interrupted, "each family has their own traditions. It is important that you appreciate people's differences and perhaps incorporate them into your life." Eliza gave me a meaningful look. Almost as if she was giving me permission into her daughter's life. Did she know Jonah's intent? If so, Jonah must not have told her how messed up I was or how reluctant I was to be in any sort of relationship where I was afraid it would end bitterly. That included one with her daughter. Don't get me wrong, I liked Whitney. In some ways I even understood her. She used her intelligence to hide her fear and I used any means possible to hide mine. The question was, what was Whitney afraid of? Part of me ached to know so I could ease it.

I stood and headed for the bench near the front door where I had left my ukulele. Even with my back turned, I could feel every eye in the room on me. I had a feeling those who knew what I did every year were anxious to see how I incorporated each person at the table into my song. Like I said, this was going down as probably the most cringeworthy holiday in my existence. And that was saying a lot since one of my stepfathers used to eat Thanksgiving dinner in his boxer shorts. He figured why unbutton your pants when you could not wear them at all. I was still disturbed by it.

When I returned to the table, I swallowed hard and refused to look at anyone for fear of losing my nerve. Usually I loved this part—I was the one who had started the tradition. Dani was right, I made up several holiday traditions in hopes of recapturing what I wanted so badly growing up—innocence, peace, and happiness.

"Please hold your applause to the end," I teased before I began. "However, I will accept money thrown my way at any time."

Everyone laughed. At least, I think everyone did, since I wouldn't look up. I mostly heard Jonah because he was the loudest and I was still attuned to him after all these years.

"Here goes nothing." I plucked out a few notes. "It's that time of year we gather round to feast and let our guards down. For only goodwill and cheer and maybe a little beer will—"

"Beer is bad," Whitney whispered to her parents.

I didn't hear their responses before I carried on with my silly tune. "—dwell among us. For we are always grateful for those who join us, even if sometimes Brant annoys us. Please no talk of politics tonight, for we all know you plan to run and all our votes you've already won." I got brave and looked at Brant who was thankfully smiling at me while everyone else laughed.

"Now for Brant's brother, our American soldier, we give thanks to you and your Army crew for keeping us safe and making sure we can continue to give thanks for this great land in which we live. Speaking of living, there are two among us who have lived a lot of days and we wish you many more. But Sam and Kay you should watch your ways. Your girls love you more than words can say, but we hope and pray you'll stop your meddling ways."

Dani and Kinsley snickered and looked at Brant, who Grandma had mentioned on occasion would make a fine catch for Kinsley. I disagreed, as I knew he had feelings for Dani, and from what I'd gathered over the years, I knew Brant would marry who his father deemed worthy, which meant it would be a strong political ally. There was no way John Holland would find Kinsley worthy—an orphan who was in debt up to her eyeballs, doing her best to live her dream of running her own restaurant. Unfortunately, I think Kinsley had kind of taken Grandma's comments to heart by the way she blushed at Brant when he smiled at her. Poor Kinsley didn't need any more love triangles in her life. The one she had with her business partners was more than enough.

Dani looked to her left where Brock sat, close but never close enough. Grandma had made sure that Brock sat next to her. A looked passed between them that pained me. It was as if each was staring into a mirror that showed them their deepest desires, but it was always a reflection, never a reality. I had to move on with my song or I was going to start tearing up. I related too much to the unrequited love that brewed between Dani and Brock.

I strummed a few more chords before I went on. "Now that the old folks have been warned." I smirked at my amused grandparents. "I'd like to call Dani and Kinsley to attention. The next time you cut up my clothes, be ready for it to come to blows."

Dani waved away my warning. "Please," she called out, "you look hot now. Well, not so much today." She pointed at my turkey sweatshirt.

"I like the sweatshirt," Jonah gave his two cents, making me blush. I didn't want him to compliment me in front of his ex-wife and daughter. It felt sacrilegious somehow.

I continued my song to hide my embarrassment. "Now that I'm all out of warnings, I'd like to extend a welcome to those who are new. Eliza and Whitney, thank you for joining our motley crew, we hope it doesn't feel too much like a zoo. That leaves us with our long-lost friend." I swallowed. "There's no need to pretend that you were not missed. But it's time for me to say goodbye. Now pass the pie."

Everyone clapped and laughed, Jonah being the loudest. Everyone, that is, but Whitney, who still seemed confused about our weird family traditions. She was looking tentatively at all the pie on the table. Every kind from pumpkin to Dutch apple.

I sat back down at the table and let my ukulele rest on my lap, nervous to look across the table, but I could feel Jonah's gaze on me. When I braved looking in his direction he mouthed, "I missed you too."

Heaven help us.

chapter nine

"I hope you do not mind that I followed you out here," Eliza's sultry voice startled me.

I dropped the trash bag I was holding before turning around in the cold night air. We had just finished cleaning up and I was taking the trash out to the bins behind Grandma and Grandpa's house. I needed a moment alone after the cozy way Jonah had helped me fill the dishwasher. If he touched me one more time tonight, I was going to self-combust. Did he know how hard it was to resist him? Probably.

I turned around to see his gorgeous ex-wife shimmering in the moonlight in an expensive looking cashmere overcoat like some model. I wasn't sure if I minded that she followed me out here. Was she looking for a catfight? Did Jonah's flirting bother her? Was she abhorred by the gluttony she witnessed while she ate her perfectly portioned vegan Thanksgiving wrap? Was she mad that Jonah chose to eat our meal even though she brought him a wrap too?

I didn't know how to respond to her. Instead, I rubbed my arms through my thin sweatshirt.

"I apologize, you must be cold," she noticed, "but I wanted to talk to you alone tonight and this is probably our only chance."

I dropped my arms and stood still, intrigued by what she had to say. "What would you like to talk about?" If she was going to try and get me to give up sugar, I was out of there. Sugar was seeing me through until I made it to therapy.

Eliza stepped closer.

I wrung my hands.

"Please do not be nervous around me," she pled. "I am very happy that I finally have the pleasure of meeting you."

"Really?" I couldn't help but ask.

She chuckled. Even her laugh was alluring. I could see why Jonah was attracted to this woman.

"Yes," she responded. "I wanted to know the woman who stole Jonah's heart."

I choked and turned to cough into the night. "It was a long time ago. Nothing is going on between us," I stuttered. My breath played in the cold air between us.

She touched my arm. "You are taking that the wrong way. I am happy for Jonah. He deserves to be happy. And I know I did not make him happy." The regret in her tone was apparent.

"Are you sure?" I knew Jonah wouldn't have married her if she didn't make him happy. If he didn't love her.

She squeezed my arm. "I am sure. He is a different man than when I first met him and I wish I could say it was for the better, but I know I siphoned the life out of him."

He probably hated the way she didn't use contractions. It was driving me batty. But it didn't take away from what she was admitting to me. I felt sorry for her. I could tell she still loved him. It was something we had in common.

I tilted my head, confused as to why she was sharing this with me. I was so perplexed I had forgotten I was freezing.

"You are wondering why I am telling you this," she said.

Great. She was a mind reader too. I nodded without thinking. I swore her voice had magical properties. She would be a great salesperson.

"You see, when I met Jonah, he matched my profile for the perfect life partner. He is equally successful and as intelligent as me. Our families have similar backgrounds, and he," she paused, "I believe he mistook my ambition for adventurousness. I think he wanted to see that. He was missing you."

My jaw dropped.

"Do not act so surprised. Of course we talked about you. I do not believe this nonsense that you should not talk about previous relationships. Those relationships make you who you are. And you profoundly shaped Jonah. He spoke fondly of the woman who was not afraid to take hikes in the middle of the night or make up songs to help him with his shelf exams. Honestly," she looked down at her feet, "I was jealous of you. I still am, but I made my choice, as difficult as it was." She raised her head slowly. "As terrible as it sounds, my first love is my career."

My eyes bugged out before I could stop them.

"I know. I know." She didn't seem upset that my facial expressions were judging her. "It sounds awful. It probably is, but as much as I love Whitney and Jonah, I am who I am. And who I am was slowly killing my husband and possibly my child." She choked as if she hated to admit that.

"You don't need to tell me this," I said.

She stepped closer and took my hand. She obviously had personal boundary issues. "Oh, but I do, because Jonah has every intention of making you part of his life, which means you will be part of my life and Whitney's. And I want you to know that I welcome you. After everything

I have put Jonah through, he deserves to be happy. I do not believe I have ever seen him as happy as I did tonight."

"I think it was the turkey and the pie."

She laughed deeply. "I think you might be right. He is a good husband. He was," she corrected. "He indulged my dietary preferences. He indulged all my preferences." She sounded ashamed.

"You still wish he was your husband." It wasn't a question. And part of me didn't like that one bit.

She shrugged. "I will always love Jonah, but I loved him enough to let him go. Please do not make me regret that."

My brows skyrocketed. "I don't know what you know about me, but the odds for Jonah and me ending up together are slim."

She squeezed my hand. "I probably know more about you than you would like. But this I know for sure, Jonah is a patient man and he loves you," she stuttered. "He always has."

I squirmed and pulled, but she wouldn't let go. "It is okay that he does. He never treated me less because of it. You did not hang over our marriage. I did. Please," she begged, "try for him. Do what I could not do."

I stood in shock for several seconds. This little powwow was more than I had bargained for. The tears in her eyes got to me. Jonah got to me. "I'll try," I whispered.

"Thank you." She wrapped her arms around me and hugged me tight. "Will you do me a favor?"

What more could she want? She had already asked me to face my greatest fear by trying to strike up a relationship with her ex-husband. Did that sound odd to anyone else? "Um, what do you want?" I asked.

"Please share yourself with Whitney. She needs someone like you."

I leaned away from her. "I'm not sure if that's true. She's way smarter than me, and I'm pretty sure I disturbed her by the amount of whipped cream I put on my pie."

Eliza laughed. "It is good for her. You will be good for her. She told me about the stained glass umbrella you helped her make. Thank you for helping her come out of her shell."

"I just got her to break some glass."

"You do not know what an accomplishment that is for her."

"It's not that I don't like Whitney—I do—but I don't know if it's a good idea for me to try and get to know her when I'm so unsure about not only Jonah, but myself."

Eliza took a moment to think. "Whitney and Jonah are a package. Jonah loves her more than anyone. To know and love one is to know and love the other. And maybe," she paused, "you will find yourself by helping Whitney discover who she is."

I wanted to say that was her job, not mine, but I think she knew that. And, like she said, she had made her choice.

She hugged me once more. "I hope we will become good friends."

"Uh." Insert awkward pause.

"It is all right. I know I can be a lot." She let go of me.

I studied her for a moment. I admired her honesty, but she was right. She was a lot. A lot different than I thought she would be. "If we're going to be friends, I'm going to need you to start using contractions when we talk."

Her laughter pealed through the night air. "I will . . . I mean, I'll try."

So would I.

We walked back in together to the stares of everyone. I didn't make eye contact or offer any explanations to what I was doing out there with Eliza. I was too numb from the cold and the promise I had made to Eliza. I headed straight for the fireplace to warm up. Not surprisingly, Jonah joined me.

"You look overwhelmed. Everything okay?" he asked.

"Not yet."

"Anything I can help with?"

"You mind staying away from me?" I half teased.

"Yes," he wasn't teasing at all.

"That's what I figured." I held my hands out in front of the fire, hoping to get some feeling back in them.

He nudged me. "I guess that means we're going to be hide-and-go-seek partners tonight."

"Actually, I was going to see if Eliza wanted to be my partner."

He wrapped his strong arm around me and whispered in my ear, "That's a pity. Eliza is taking Whitney home. She wants to spend some time with her before she heads out tomorrow. And before you try to choose anyone else, they all have partners already."

"So you're saying we're stuck together?"

"Like glue, baby."

Looks like things were going to get sticky.

chapter ten

Each pair in each car had ten minutes to hide anywhere within Pine Falls' city limits. Grandma and Grandpa were the seekers this go-around. I loved that they still wanted to play my ridiculous games. Every pair was supposed to message the group chat when they were in their hiding spot and give two clues to where they could be hiding.

Jonah and I were in his car. His boring, safety-rated Volvo, I might add. I missed his old Mustang, which only had lap belts and seats that leaned way back. He suggested we hide behind the grocery store, the first and last hiding spot we had chosen together. The first place we kissed.

"It will be too obvious," I objected. And I didn't need any more reasons to want to kiss him tonight. I was planning on keeping my lips to myself until I figured myself out.

"Okay." Jonah sounded disappointed, but quickly made another suggestion. "What about the old drive-in movie theater? That's within the city limits, right?"

"I think so, but Mr. Udall hates when people trespass, especially in the fall and winter months when it's closed." I knew this from experience. I might have snuck in with a few friends to engage in some underage drinking a long time ago. Though we had deserved to get caught, we were all fast runners. It wasn't my proudest moment. "And I'm not even sure we could get in. We would be sitting ducks out in front." I was pretty competitive when it came to vehicle hide-and-go-seek, or basically any game I played.

Jonah patted my leg. "Don't worry. I've got a plan."

"You do?"

"Mr. Udall is a patient of mine."

"Oh. Did you ask him for permission?"

Jonah squeezed my leg. "Something like that."

"Mind elaborating?"

"Just message the group, 'But now, the only thing he can't do is walk away.'"

I scrunched my nose. "What kind of clue is that?"

He glanced my way before turning down Orchard Street toward the drive-in. "You don't remember? That hurts."

I thought for a moment, and a memory of us watching TV came to mind. I had never seen Jonah get so excited as when they announced what was playing next. "Is that part of the tagline from *Rocky IV*?" Jonah loved all the Rocky movies, but that was his favorite by far. I had watched them all with him.

Jonah grabbed my hand. "You do remember. It's very apropos don't you think?"

I bit my lip. "Is that how you feel?" That the only thing he couldn't do was walk away?

"It's exactly how I feel."

I looked out the window at the leafless trees. I felt as stripped bare as they looked. "Jonah, you can't even know if you like me anymore. Nine years is a long time."

He ran a finger down my cheek, leaving a trail of long forgotten desire behind as he went. "It is a long time, but it hasn't changed how I feel about you. Did you think I would leave here and magically get over you?"

"You got married," I spoke into the window.

"Yes, I did. I've been lucky enough to love two women."

"Do you still love Eliza?" I wasn't sure I really wanted to know.

"Of course I do. She's the mother of my child and a good *friend*. But that's all she is to me."

As he pulled into the entrance of the drive-in, I turned toward him, wondering if that was really true. He threw his car into park and faced me.

"What do you want from me?" is all I could ask.

He reached out and rested his warm hand on my cheek. His thumb gently swiped my skin. "I want you to watch a movie with me and eat popcorn and Skittles."

"Right now?"

He leaned in. "I have a confession to make. We aren't playing hide-and-go-seek."

"We aren't? Where did everyone else go?"

"I don't know, and honestly, I don't really care." Our foreheads met. His warm breath tickled my nose. "All I care about right now is us in this moment, getting to know each other again. So what do you say? Will you go to the movies with me?"

"I made an appointment with a therapist," I blurted like an idiot.

"For right now?"

"No," I laughed.

"Then you're free to watch the best movie ever made on the big screen."

"We're watching the movie here at the drive-in?"

He leaned away with a big goofy grin on his face. "I told you, Mr. Udall is my patient. And apparently a closet romantic, but don't tell Mrs. Udall. He doesn't want the expectations."

"You know, you could have just asked me out."

"This was a lot more fun, and I was pretty sure you would have said no."

"It's not that I want to say no; it's just the right thing to do. I don't want to hurt you again. I need to figure myself out. It's why I'm seeing a therapist."

"Ariana, I'm not in any rush. I just want to spend some time with you. I want to talk to you. I want to look at you and touch you." He brushed my hair back. "You're so beautiful."

"I'm wearing a turkey sweatshirt that says, *Gobble Until You Wobble*."

"And I love it. It's so you."

"I'm not sure what that says about me."

"It's says you're still the same woman I shouldn't have left nine years ago."

"No, Jonah, you did the right thing. Don't you see? The way we left things meant never hating each other. It means we can sit here with no malice and only good feelings." I needed him to understand.

"You're looking at it all wrong. We missed out on nine years of loving each other and growing closer together," he countered.

"You don't know that. For all we know, you could have been introducing me as your ex-wife tonight, and I can't bear that thought. I don't want to return you."

"Then don't. Let's take it a day at a time. Please," he begged. "I'm not asking you for a commitment. I just want to watch a movie with you."

"Uh-huh. I've heard that line somewhere before." It always ended up with us not watching anything but each other and our lips being tangled up. That wasn't a complaint.

He moved in closer, our lips dangerously close.

"Jonah," I could hardly breathe with him so near, "we shouldn't kiss." I hoped he didn't hear the longing. Because while we shouldn't, every part of me wanted to grab his shirt and erase the distance.

"You think I want to kiss you?" He moved in a little closer, so close I could practically taste the mint he'd popped into his mouth before we left the house.

"I want to kiss you," I admitted.

"Mmm," he groaned and almost sealed the deal.

I backed up and placed my finger on his expectant lips, internally convincing myself we shouldn't all while my body begged me to. I outlined his soft lips. "If we kiss, it will only muddy the waters."

He kissed my finger. "Perfect. We'll swim in them together. I love getting dirty with you."

Oh, this man. I pushed him back. "We can't until I figure out my head, and heart, for that matter."

Jonah let out a deep breath of disappointment. "Okay. We'll wait. Can I at least negotiate holding your hand?"

"I'd like that."

"I'll take what I can get." He sat up and drove us through the entrance where Mr. Udall waited for us. Jonah rolled down his window. "Are we all set?"

Mr. Udall tapped the top of Jonah's car. "You're ready to go. Just tune your radio to 90.9. I'll come back later to close up, so the place is all yours."

"Thank you, sir. I owe you," Jonah responded.

"Ah," the old man waved. "You don't owe me a thing. There's nothing like young love."

Jonah and I weren't exactly young. But we were still in love. I wanted to say it shouldn't be possible, but it was exactly how I wished it. I wanted to always love him. I didn't want him to leave me for another woman or grow tired of me and discard me. I always wanted to say his name and be able to smile.

"Best thing around," Jonah agreed before heading toward the middle of the empty drive-in.

It was until it wasn't, though. Maybe Jonah was right, I should take it a day at a time. The problem was, I had never been able to live that way. My life experience taught me that when things went good it only meant that something really bad was going to happen. I could never truly enjoy the happy times. I was always waiting for the other shoe to drop.

Like when my mom brought home a kitten when I was eight, I thought I could have died of happiness. Snowball was a puffy white dream. But then Tom, one of my mom's husbands, got mad when she scratched him, and he'd killed her. I'd watched him throw her against the wall. It still made me sick to my stomach. More nauseating was that my mom didn't leave him for that. Instead, she told me I should have kept Snowball in my room.

No wonder I had issues. Jonah was right. No one ever fought for me. Even when my mom left Carl because of what he wanted to do to me, it became all about her. I'd never wanted to admit that. My eyes teared up.

Jonah was ever observant. He slammed on the brakes, which barely jolted us since he was driving so slow. "Did I do something wrong?"

"Not yet."

Jonah reached over and took my hand. He held it between his own, gently caressing it. "I know you're waiting for me to mess up. And guess what, I will, and you will too. When that happens, we'll work through it."

"I'm a mess, Jonah."

"A beautiful mess." He brought my hand up and kissed it.

With my free hand, I wiped my eyes. "You ready to watch your movie?"

"I always thought of it as ours."

"People battling it out in the ring to the point of death. That sounds about right," I teased.

"I will fight for you, Ariana."

I wanted to believe him. "We'll see."

"You will." He squeezed my hand before letting it go and tuning the radio to the right station. The car was suddenly filled with the song, "Eye of the Tiger."

Goosebumps erupted on Jonah's neck. "I forgot how much I loved the soundtrack to this movie." He pretended to play the drums on the steering wheel.

"How long has it been since you've seen it?"

He gave me a sly look. "Around nine years." He reached behind the front seats and grabbed a canvas sack filled with a bag of white cheddar popcorn and the biggest bag of Skittles I'd ever seen. I swore Jonah's eyes misted when he pulled out his beloved candy. "Oh, how I missed you." He kissed the bag.

I tilted my head. "Didn't they have Skittles in Connecticut?"

"They did but . . . Eliza doesn't like refined sugar, or really anything that tastes good." He grinned. "She had my best interests at heart," he added in.

"I believe that. She seems nice."

"Did she scare you tonight?" Jonah asked lightheartedly.

"She caught me off guard. I thought she might want to rumble or something."

Jonah's laughter filled the car. "You don't know her. Eliza doesn't believe in physical violence at all, which is why she never watched Rocky with me. Come to think of it, I don't think she ever raised her voice the entire time we were together."

"You sound disappointed."

He ripped open his bag of Skittles with gusto. "A man wants his woman to have some passion in her, especially for their relationship. I don't think she ever really cared enough to fight."

"I'm sorry, but she does love you."

Jonah grabbed a handful of rainbow candy. "In her way she does." He tossed several candies in his mouth. "Mmm," he let out a blissful sigh.

"Do you need a moment there?"

"You have no idea how much I missed this." He closed his eyes to savor the moment.

"I think I do. I don't even think you need me around."

His eyes popped opened. "I'll lean these seats back right now and show you how much I missed you."

The temperature in the car shot up about a hundred degrees, and somehow it became a vacuum seal too. There was no air to breathe. "Uh . . ." I stuttered, "maybe later." He had no idea how tempting he was.

"I'm going to hold you to that." He grabbed another handful of candy and popped it in his mouth. The pleasure I expected to see never came, instead his brows knit together. "Wait, something tastes different. Where's the lime flavor?"

I laughed. "Didn't you know they replaced the lime with green apple?" I remembered when that happened a few years ago. I'd thought of Jonah and how disappointed he would probably be about it. The green ones were his favorite.

"What?" He grabbed the bag and scanned it with a look of horror on his face. "Why would they do that? I'm calling to complain, or start a petition."

I smiled at him, holding back my urge to run my hands through his hair and take him up on his offer to lean the seats back. Instead, I took his hand. "Maybe that can wait. Why don't you tell me about the last nine years?"

He set the Skittles on the console between us. "You want to know about Eliza."

"Yes, but mostly about you. You've changed."

"I suppose I have. Fatherhood does that to you. And," he hesitated, "not being true to yourself."

"I might know a little something about that."

He tapped my nose. "Regardless, you're still irresistible."

I bit my lip. "We're focusing on you."

"All right, but I expect you to do the same for me. Deal?"

"Okay," I whispered.

He turned down the volume to the movie we weren't paying attention to. "What do you want to know?"

I thought for a minute. "If it didn't work out with someone as put together as Eliza, why in the world do you think it would ever work out between us?"

He pulled my hand up to his heart and held it firmly against his defined chest. I could feel the steady rhythm of his heart. "First of all, Eliza may be more put together in some respects, but not in all the ways that count. She's careful to the extreme, as I'm sure you've noticed. And she struggles to see outside of herself—to love those she's closest to."

"Just like me."

Jonah's face scrunched. "Not at all. You easily love others more than yourself. Your problem is you don't believe you deserve to be loved, which is absurd. But I get it, considering who your mother was and that your father abandoned you."

"So why did you choose Eliza?" I wanted to deflect any comments away from my own issues. At least for now. I was waiting to get a professional opinion.

He stared out into the distance at Rocky, who was now in bed with his wife, handing her an anniversary gift. A *nine-year* anniversary gift to be exact. Weird to think it could have been our nine-year anniversary. "Because in some ways she was like you. She's beautiful and she sees the world differently than most; she has a zest for life, but in a different way than you. But mostly, I chose her because she was different than you. She's a planner, as in a hyper planner, and at the time I needed someone to help me not focus on you. Looking back, she took me on a ride, and I got caught up in it, in her. She can be persuasive."

I believed that. Her voice alone would convince me to follow her.

"And honestly," he added, "she really helped me focus on my career goals and catch a vision of what I could accomplish."

I pulled my hand away from him. I was feeling more and more like a loser. Like I said, our offspring would be the kid licking the finger paints and eating Play-Doh. "I'm happy she helped you reach your goals."

He took my hand right back. "Please don't take that the wrong way. I may have been making more money than I'd hoped, but I wasn't happy."

"Are you now?"

He tucked some of my hair behind my ear. "Always, when I'm with you."

"Why?"

He played with some tendrils of my hair, which drove me wild. Did he have any idea how wonderful he made me feel inside and out?

"Ariana, I don't know how to explain it other than when I'm with you, I feel like anything is possible. I remember the first night I met you at that hole-in-the-wall Mexican place Dani and Brock love."

I did too. I thought about it every day.

"You," he continued, "were unimpressed that I was a med student."

I laughed, remembering how I'd rolled my eyes when we were introduced.

"You sealed our fate there. I was determined to make you like me." He paused. "But I had no idea how much I would come to like you. That night, I knew I was in trouble when our server informed us they had run out of sopapillas, and while everyone else was getting bent out of shape that a Mexican restaurant would ever run out of sopapillas, you suggested we go to your place and make them."

"Everyone else thought it was too much of a bother, except you," I said.

He wagged his brows. "I was no idiot. I wanted sopapillas and . . . I wanted to be alone with the beautiful woman who'd purposely ignored me all night. I liked that you didn't care that I was going to be a doctor."

I'd almost rescinded my offer when it ended up being only him, but he'd said something to me that night no one had ever said before. *Thank you for helping me see life in a different way tonight. I like your attitude.* It was a simple thing, but it made me like him. Made me change my attitude about him. He made me feel like I was more than a pretty face that needed to be conquered.

He leaned in. "Remember, we talked all night while listening to your old Carly Simon vinyls?"

"I do remember. I was appalled you didn't know who she was."

"I do now, thanks to you." He paused. "You bring out the best in me, do you know that? You bring out the dreamer in me. I love how your world is gray because it lets you love everybody. I love that you sing silly songs and lick the batter out of the cake bowl. I love that you watch Rocky with me and will eat half this bag of Skittles, minus the awful green apple ones." He smirked and I giggled.

He cupped my face and drew it closer to his own. He had no idea how much I missed his Skittle breath. "And I love that you took time for my daughter. She knows she's not her mother's priority."

Oh. That hit too close to home.

He pressed a kiss to my forehead and let his lips rest against my skin that was aching to be touched by him. "You make me happy in a million different ways. Please believe me."

"I'll try."

chapter eleven

I'll try was becoming my mantra. I supposed it was better than not trying. I had to say, though, I wasn't thrilled about trying while I filled out the patient questionnaire at Dr. Morales's office first thing Monday morning. It was . . . uncomfortable. Questions like: *Have you ever been emotionally or verbally abused?* I was having a hard time circling yes. Why didn't I want to admit that? Maybe because it made me seem weak and like I was blaming my mother for my problems. I didn't want to be that person. A victim.

I skipped ahead, but the questions only got more uncomfortable. *Has anyone in your family ever attempted suicide?* The answer was, *I think so.* I'd found my mom unconscious once surrounded by two empty pill bottles. Her boyfriend at the time, Weston, told me not to worry about it. He carried her out of the house. I assumed he'd taken her to the hospital. When she returned home a few days later, she'd said she had the flu. She'd lied. A lot.

The next set of questions made me cringe in my stiff waiting room seat. *Do you find it hard to be open with people? Is it NOT important to you to be in a romantic relationship? Do people often call you stubborn?* Holy hell. Had some-one followed me around and devised this questionnaire based on my life? I will say, though, that one of the last questions made me laugh, even if it probably shouldn't have. *Does anyone in your family have a history of mental illness?* I wrote in, *Does blowing up your wedding dresses count? If so, yes.*

I was worried that after seeing my responses Dr. Morales might want to commit me on the spot. Which might not be so bad. Then I wouldn't have to make any decisions about Jonah while I was in there. Knowing him, though, he would find a way to come visit me even if he had to break in.

I hadn't seen him since Thanksgiving night. He'd said he knew he was coming on strong and would give me some space. Emphasis on *some*. He planned on contacting me today after my therapy session. He was the only person I'd told about it. I wasn't sure why. Maybe because he got me like no one else ever had, and he wouldn't be pushy about it. Or maybe it was because as much as I was afraid to admit it, he was my person, like I was his. That one person I wanted to tell everything to. The person who made me more me.

If only I knew who *me* really was. I suppose that was why I was sitting in the simply decorated waiting room, painted in calming blues, about ready to crawl out of my skin. After that questionnaire, I was even more afraid to be called back. In fact, I jumped when they called my name. I swore everyone in the waiting room gave me a look like *we understand, friend.*

I slowly stood and smoothed out my blouse. I'd dressed extra carefully today in slacks and a fitted peasant blouse, so I looked like someone who was well put together. As soon as I was done here and before I opened the studio, I would be getting into some yoga pants and possibly the Christmas sweatshirt I bought with my Thanksgiving one. It said, *Naughty but Nice, I'm a Multitasker.*

I followed Dr. Morales's assistant, flexing my fingers as I went and trying to take deep breaths without making it seem like I was on the verge of hyperventilating. I don't know what I was so afraid of. I already knew I was a mess. But there was something comforting about not having it clinically diagnosed. That way I could pretend I didn't have issues.

Dr. Morales's stark white office was off-putting. It reminded me of those solitary confinement rooms on TV shows where they put psychiatric patients. You know, the patients in straitjackets. I scanned the room quickly to see if I could spot any of the restraining devices. All I saw were some large plants and two comfortable chairs, one of which was occupied by Dr. Morales. She stood when I entered. She was a short, welcoming Latina woman with the darkest brown eyes I had ever seen. Like wells filled with wisdom. I could only hope she had some for me.

"You must be Ariana. Welcome." Dr. Morales held out her hand and greeted me like a colleague instead of a patient. I liked that.

I took her hand. "It's nice to meet you," I sort of lied. I wished I was anywhere but here, but I was trying, and she had a comforting air about her.

"You say that now," she quipped.

My eyes widened.

She laughed. "I'm teasing."

I laughed nervously along with her.

"Have a seat." She waved to the chair across from her own. "Feel free to kick off your shoes, if you like, or curl up. Whatever makes you most comfortable."

Did she know I didn't like shoes? I didn't remember writing that down on the questionnaire. If she had ESP, I was out of there.

"You look worried."

"I am," I admitted.

"That's natural. Let's see what we can do to put you at ease." She took her seat.

I did kick off my ballet flats, and when I sat down on the poufy white chair, I curled my legs under me.

She smiled at my behavior. “I hate shoes too, but believe me, you don’t want to see my gnarly toes.”

She made me laugh and put me a bit at ease.

“So,” she began, “I looked over your questionnaire, but since you know you best, I want you to tell me why you’re here. And if you don’t mind, I might ask you some questions, even take a few notes. Is that all right?”

I nodded.

“Great. You can begin when you feel comfortable.”

“We could be here a long time then,” I joked, sort of.

“Take your time. I bill by the hour.” She winked.

I liked her. I rubbed my lips together. “Well, I guess I’m here because…” I tried to think of how to put it into words. “You see, I had this super crazy childhood. But I thought I came out unscathed and had life all figured out, and then I didn’t, and I’m afraid of losing the people I love because it seems like I’m never meant to keep them. But there’s this man who I really, really love and I thought we were over because I made sure of it, but now he’s back, and after everything I’ve done to push him away, he still wants me, which makes him the crazy one, but, honestly, I want him too, but that scares me more than anything.” I was pretty sure I sounded nuts after that. I couldn’t even look at Dr. Morales for fear of what she must think of me.

“Why don’t you tell me about your childhood and why you feel it was crazy. I’m curious about the blowing up of wedding dresses you mentioned in your questionnaire.”

I met her smiling eyes. I didn’t see any judgment there. And she wasn’t reaching for any straitjackets yet, so I proceeded. I told her all about my mom’s plethora of husbands, including some of the sordid details about almost becoming a sexual assault victim and watching my cat be killed. She handed me a tissue when I teared up. We covered the blowing up of wedding dresses and we ended on my father, who I never knew but got a mysterious letter from every year that I didn't open. I knew that piqued Dr. Morales's interest, but she didn't say anything about it.

Dr. Morales wrote down a few notes. "Why do you think your mom married so many times?"

I clasped my hands together. "I think because she was searching for the happiness she had with my dad, but she could never find it."

"Did she tell you this?"

"No, but my grandma said my mom was never the same after a phone call in which we assumed my father rejected her."

"But you don't know that for a fact."

"No."

"And how long did your parents know each other before she became pregnant with you?"

"I can't say for sure, but maybe a month or two."

"You're positive Roger is your father?"

I wasn't sure I liked her line of questioning. It was like she was making me rethink my entire existence. "I have a picture of him and there's a fair amount of resemblance. And my mom gave me his last name and every letter that comes has his name on it."

She tapped her pen against her paper. "Yes, the letter. I have to say I find it interesting that you've never opened one. Aren't you curious?"

I let my legs drop to the floor and sat up. "Of course I am, but I promised my mother I would never open it. And why would I care to know what's in it when," my voice began to raise, "he knows where I am and he's never tried to help me. He should have protected me!" I covered my mouth. It was as if this massive epiphany struck me. Jonah was right. No one ever fought for me, and deep down I ached for it.

She leaned forward with a warm smile. "You're right, a father should have. Why didn't your mom want you to open the letter you get every year from Roger?"

It wasn't lost on me that she didn't call him my father. Could that be true? I'd never considered the possibility that my mom had lied to me about it all those years. Which was foolish, considering all the times she had lied to me. But the picture. We had the same eyes.

"I don't know." I wiped my eyes. "She wouldn't ever tell me."

"Ariana, from what you've told me today, I would say that your mother was a manipulative individual. She may have even suffered from borderline personality disorder—I can give you a pamphlet about it, if you would like. I think it would be beneficial for you to search out the truth for yourself. I know it sounds cliché, but the truth can set you free. Or at least put you on the path to healing. I'm going to give you some homework. First of all, I want you to open that letter when it comes this year."

I grabbed my heart.

"I know it might feel like opening old wounds, but your wounds have never healed. Which is why I also want you—this next week before we meet again—to find a quiet place every day and choose a situation from your past to relive. A time when you didn't feel safe and protected."

That sounded awful. The horror must have shown on my face.

"I know it sounds difficult, because it is, but you need to allow yourself to let those past feelings percolate. Explore every emotion and sensation that comes to you. Once you've done that, acknowledge them. Then love all of those feelings, no matter if it's anger, terror, or sadness. Love that you are allowing yourself to own them. Afterward, choose someone you trust to share those feelings with. Then let them go."

I leaned back in the chair and let out a heavy sigh. "I'll try."

"That's a start."

chapter twelve

I think I cried all the way to the loft. Once the floodgates opened, I couldn't stop. I replayed telling her about all the times I saw my mom break down and how frightened I was when I did the same thing after Kaden left me. My worst fear had come to life—that I would end up like my mother, used and abused by men. I refused for that to be me. Hence, all my life choices since.

I had blabbered on about how I'd privately mourned Jonah and even my father. Basically, I came out of there more of a mess than when I went in. To make it worse, I had promised her I would continue the misery and relive all my worst memories over the next week. Couldn't she just give me a pill to fix my problems? I couldn't believe I was paying for this torture.

Before I made it home, Jonah called. I'd promised him I would no longer ignore his calls. He had even given me a special ring tone like it was 2006. You guessed it, Rocky's theme song, "Eye of the Tiger."

"Hello." I sniffled.

"Are you okay? You sound like you've been crying."

"Therapy is a real killjoy."

"Do you want to talk about it?"

"I think I've talked enough today, but maybe later. Actually . . . I need a favor from you."

"Anything," he was overly eager.

"I need someone willing to let me . . ." Wait, what was I doing, asking him to be my safe person already? It just seemed natural, but I couldn't. Shouldn't? But he was the only person who knew I was seeing a therapist. That was telling. But I couldn't just yet. "Um, never mind."

"Ariana, I'm here for you."

"I want to believe that."

"I'll see what I can do to prove it to you. In the meantime, I was going to ask a favor from you."

"Okay."

"Our office offers 24-7 care and I'm on call tonight. It's not likely I'll have to go in, but if I do, can you watch Whitney? My babysitter came down with bronchitis."

Uh, that seemed like one giant leap for mankind. Or my kind.

"Ariana?"

"I'm here."

"Whitney likes you, and as you might imagine, she doesn't take well to everyone, and they don't take well to her." I could hear the distress in his voice. "It would mean a lot to me on the off chance I need you. I can even bring her to your place if coming to my place feels like I'm pushing the envelope."

How could I say no to that? "Sure. I would be happy to."

"Thank you. You know, if I don't get called in, we could all do dinner together."

"What happened to giving me space?"

"You just agreed to watch my daughter; I think we are past giving each other space. Besides, it's been forever since I've seen you."

"It's been four days."

"It's been a long four days."

I felt the same way. "Where are we going for dinner?"

"Would you mind if we went to Porters? They have a lot of healthy options for Whitney."

"Healthy is probably a good idea. I've been eating pie for breakfast every morning since the day after Thanksgiving."

He chuckled. "Can I pick you up at six?"

"You can."

"I can't wait."

"I'll see you tonight."

"Ariana."

"Yes?"

"I'm proud of you. I know how hard this is for you."

"Jonah, therapy and you coming back isn't going to magically fix me. You know that, right? Dr. Morales said I shouldn't contemplate the future until I deal with my past."

"All I want right now is your present. We'll fight for the future later. Together."

He always said the loveliest things. "You sound so sure."

"I am. I'll see you tonight." He hung up, leaving me feeling tipsy.

When I arrived home to change before heading back downstairs to the studio, I was surprised to run into Kinsley. Both she and Dani were usually long gone before me every day. In fact, I was sure they were both gone by the time I left for my appointment this morning, which is how I planned it. No need for them to ask me where I was going, especially dressed like I was late for a board meeting.

I set my keys in the decorative bowl near the front door. I had a clear shot of the kitchen from where I stood; basically, it was a clear shot of everything except the bedrooms and the bathroom.

"What are you doing home?"

A startled Kinsley in a white chef's jacket popped her head out of the refrigerator. Her eyes looked like they had shed more tears than mine. The chocolate frosting on her lips from a large brownie she was holding spoke volumes.

I rushed over to her. "Kinsley, what's wrong?"

More tears leaked out of her pretty brown eyes.

I took the brownie out of her hand and set it on the counter before wrapping her up in my arms. Her head fell on my shoulder, as did her tears.

"What happened?" I rubbed her back.

"Do you ever feel like," she hiccupped, "it will never be your turn?"

"What do you mean?"

She sniffled and shuddered against me. "It's just, my entire life I feel like I've been left out. It's what happens when your parents are poor."

I knew she spoke of her biological parents, who Kinsley always spoke fondly of even though they had very little. They had left twelve-year-old Kinsley with nothing when they both died in a car accident. It's how she had come to live with Grandma and Grandpa.

"And," she continued, "even now, when I've worked so hard and sacrificed everything for my dream, it's been more like a nightmare."

I leaned away from her. "What do you mean, honey?"

She broke away from me, grabbed the brownie, and shoved almost the entire thing in her mouth. She closed her eyes and let the chocolate settle her soul while she chewed slowly. When she finally swallowed and sighed, she opened her eyes and faced me.

I pointed to a big blob of chocolate frosting on her lips. "You might want to get that."

She licked her lips with a sad smile.

"Tell me what's going on?"

"You're going to think I'm stupid."

I reached out for her hand. "That's impossible."

She took my hand and squeezed before letting it go. She looked up to our steel beamed ceiling. "I think Carter and Giselle are seeing each other. I know you and Dani told me not to open a restaurant with them, but we promised each other we would remain *friends* and the restaurant would be our priority. Lately though, I've noticed the stolen glances between the two and I can't seem to do anything right in their eyes. They're both constantly vetoing my new menu ideas even though my dishes are more popular, and they think I don't manage people very well. They think I'm too soft."

"You're not soft, you're kind. That's a huge difference. And they're jealous that you're a better chef than the two of them put together." The anger bubbling up in me had me wanting to go to Carrington Cove and go big sister crazy all over Gisele and Carter. I knew it wasn't a good idea for her to go into business with those spoiled rich brats. All their investment capital came from their parents, while poor Kinsley had to take out a huge business loan that required the fatted calf, a sacrificial lamb, and the blood of ten virgins.

"I don't know what to do." She put her face in her hands and cried. "I can't back out or I'll have to declare bankruptcy, and there's no way I can buy them out. But going to work every day is becoming miserable."

I removed her hands from her face. "Have you confronted them?"

"You know I'm terrible at that sort of thing. I faked my period starting so I could come home and take a break from the two of them."

"Ah, Kins, do you want me to go back with you and get all confrontational? Because I will."

"No. This is my problem. You have your own to worry about. But why," her voice hitched, "can't anyone ever choose me? Why am I always the leftover or the sloppy seconds?"

I knew she wasn't talking about work. She was talking about love. "You can do so much better than Carter."

"It's not only Carter." Her face shined red.

"Who else?"

She waved her hand in front of her. "Never mind. No one." She wiped the tears from her cheeks. "How's it going with you and Jonah?"

"Kinsley," I wasn't going to let my last question go unanswered, "did you meet someone?" A thought popped into my head. A thought of her and Brant pairing off together for vehicle hide-and-seek on Thanksgiving. I saw the way she had smiled at him when he opened her car door. "Is it Brant?"

Her wide eyes looked as if I'd electrocuted her with his name. "Why would you say that? There's nothing going on between us."

Wow. *The lady doth protest too much, methinks.* "You can tell me anything."

She grabbed what was left of her brownie. "There's nothing to tell." She shoved the rest of the brownie into her mouth. "Are you and Jonah working it out?" she asked with her mouth full.

I knew I wasn't getting anything else out of her. I couldn't blame her. I had kept my relationship with Jonah secret a long time ago, or at least I thought I'd kept it secret. And I had my own secrets now. "We're taking it a day at a time. Actually, I might have to babysit Whitney tonight here, if that works for you and Dani." I wasn't sure if I was ready to go to Jonah's yet. At least with Dani and Kinsley here, Jonah and I couldn't get too cozy.

Kinsley finished chewing and swallowing. "Of course. That's kind of a big step—watching his daughter."

I rubbed the back of my neck. "Well, it might not happen. If Jonah doesn't get called in, we are going to dinner."

Kinsley gave me a crooked smile. "That's a big step, too, for you."

"I suppose it is."

Kinsley tilted her head. "By the way, why are you dressed like that? It looks like you had a job interview."

I pursed my lips, thinking about what to tell her. "I'll tell you where I went if you tell me about Brant."

She walked out of the kitchen as fast as her legs would take her.

"I'm here for you," I called out.

"I know," she responded in a mouse voice. "Have a good day."

I was going to *try*.

chapter thirteen

"I'm sorry about dinner." Jonah walked into my apartment holding a timid Whitney's hand. She looked around our urban loft with wide eyes. It made me wonder if she was thinking about building codes and safety violations. I wouldn't be surprised if she was. Or maybe she was put off by all our mismatched furniture. That burnt orange couch was an eyesore, but you couldn't beat free. Or maybe she was afraid I would torture her with solder irons. Jonah said she liked me, but I wasn't so sure. She had to know there was something going on between her dad and me. That couldn't be easy on her, no matter how young she was.

"No problem." I smiled at Whitney. "We'll have a great time while you're off saving lives."

Whitney hid behind her dad's legs. I didn't think she agreed with my assessment.

Jonah put his arm around Whitney. "I shouldn't be too long."

I knelt so I was eye level with Whitney. "Do you want to help me make spaghetti?"

"Are the noodles whole grain?"

Oh crap. Could enriched flour noodles be considered whole grain? I mean, they obviously came from wheat grains somewhere along the way. "Yep." I was an awful person. Guess who was hiding the freaking spaghetti box? I held out my hand. "Should we get started?" I was hungry.

She stared at my hand like I had the plague. "Did you know that tattoo ink can be toxic?"

I almost laughed. Her dad had said the same thing to me when I got my "real" tattoo on my shoulder. I'd tried to convince him to get one with me, but he'd cited that tattoo ink could be found in people's lymph nodes and I should be cautious. I pulled up my sleeve to show Whitney my henna tattoo. I was proud of the flower and leaf pattern I had drawn on myself yesterday. "This is a henna tattoo. It will be gone in two weeks."

"Henna? What is that?"

"It's a dye made from the plant Lawsonia inermi."

Whitney leaned back like she was surprised I knew such a technical name. Then she scrunched her cute button nose. "Is it safe?"

"For most people, yes."

She hesitantly reached out and with her tiny fingers she brushed my arm. "It is pretty."

"Thank you. Maybe," I looked up at Jonah, "if it's okay with your dad, I can draw one on you."

Jonah flashed me a smile before we both focused on a horrified Whitney.

"I could not do that."

I thought she might cry. "I promise I won't make you." I felt awful for even bringing it up.

Jonah knelt next to me and took Whitney's hand, sweetly kissing it. For that she gave her dad a little smile. It eased some of the tension lines on Jonah's face. He obviously worried a great deal about his little girl.

"Honey, please try and have fun tonight." It sounded like he was begging her.

Her doe eyes said she wasn't sure if she could. That was heartbreaking, but it offered me a challenge that I was going to take seriously. Whitney was going to leave the loft a happier little girl. And she was going to be a little girl tonight, if I had any say in the matter.

Her lip trembled as if she didn't know what fun was, you know, outside of reading George Washington addresses. "My books and computer are at home," she replied.

Jonah smoothed her straight-as-a-pin hair. "I promise you don't need those things to have fun."

Her eyebrows raised in alarm.

Jonah kissed her brow. "You can do this. I love you very much." He stood, and before I knew it, he was kissing my cheek before whispering, "Save some fun for me."

I had a feeling he wasn't talking about henna tattoos. He had me wishing he was kissing more than my cheek. I had to take a moment to catch my breath. I felt like a silly schoolgirl all flummoxed over a kiss on the cheek, but it was more than that. Jonah's tenderness with his daughter and me was flutter inducing all on its own. "I'll see what I can do," I flirted back.

"I look forward to that."

I smiled to myself, thinking he had no idea I meant we would color together or something innocent like that. I took Whitney's hand. "We'll see you later."

Jonah's eyes sparkled at the sight of Whitney's and my clasped hands. He had to have known, though, that her hand was limp in mine, as if I was forcing her to hold hands.

"I'll be back as soon as I can. Thank you," he said to me.

I opened the door and waved him out, acting braver than I felt about the prospect of watching Whitney. But what was the adage of children being able to smell fear? I was trying to hide the stench of it brewing within me. Once Jonah was gone and the door shut, I turned to my charge. "Are you ready to make dinner?"

She swallowed hard. "Okay. May I wash my hands first?"

"Of course." This was good. It would give me time to ditch the pasta box. Yeah, I still felt bad about deceiving her. But would some empty carbs really be all that bad for her? Her dad used to love them. If anything, empty carbs made you happier, so there you go, I was doing it for her happiness. Wow, I was really stretching it. I should feel ashamed, but I was kind of proud of my logic. I showed my little charge to the bathroom before I ran to the kitchen and tossed the pasta box. I also set up a stool next to me near the counter.

Whitney came out with her hands up in the air as if she was ready to be gloved for surgery. "The hand towel in that bathroom looks dirty. Do you have a clean towel I may use?"

The kid had a point. The bathroom hand towel was more like a makeup wipe. "Sure." I ripped off a couple of paper towels and handed them to her.

"Are these recycled?"

"Yes." At least I didn't have to lie about that.

She looked relieved that I was environmentally conscientious and that she didn't have to use a dirty towel.

I took the used towels from her and threw them in the recycle bin. "Hop up on that stool. I'm going to teach you how to make the best spaghetti sauce ever."

She tipped her head to the side. "How do you know it is the best ever?"

"Because my grandma told me so."

She pressed her lips together skeptically.

"How about this? After you taste it, you can tell me," I offered.

She nodded as if that was a reasonable request.

"Oh, I almost forgot. You need an apron." I didn't want her to stain her cardigan and pleated plaid skirt. I thought Jonah had said she went to public school, but she had the whole private Catholic school vibe going on, right down to her patent leather Mary Janes. My bare feet cringed for hers.

Kinsley had several different aprons hanging on the pantry door. I grabbed the one with snowflakes on it. It looked to be the smallest and cutest. "Let's get this on you and get to cooking."

The poor thing looked resigned as she stood abnormally still and straight. She got an A+ for posture. I slipped the apron over her head and got a whiff of her hair, which smelled like strawberries. It gave me some hope there was a little girl in her somewhere after all.

"All right, kiddo, on the stool you go."

She climbed up like she was hiking Mt. Kilimanjaro and never expected to return.

"Do you know how to measure ingredients?" I asked her.

She shook her head no, to my ever-living surprise. I thought this girl knew how to do everything.

"We have a meal service that delivers our food. Except Father does not like it anymore," she informed me.

I so badly wanted to get her to use contractions. I felt like I was talking to a stuffy old royal. "Why doesn't he like it?" Maybe if I used contractions regularly, she would catch on.

"My mother says that he never liked them, but he wanted to make her happy. Can food make you happy?"

What? Uh. YES! And I was going to prove it to her. "How about we have ice cream for dinner and watch a movie?"

She about fell off her stool. I had to steady her.

"Ice cream is not dinner and it is full of bad cholesterol, which can make you have a heart attack and die."

This kid knew too much, but I knew a thing or two as well. "Ice cream makes you happy and happy people live longer."

"Is that true? May I use your phone to google that?"

I tapped her nose. "You may, while we watch a movie and eat ice cream."

She squirmed in her seat. "My mother only lets me watch National Geographic and documentaries."

I was going to have to talk to Jonah about that. "Okay, but we'll have to do it in a blanket fort." If I had to be bored to tears, I would enjoy it more in a blanket fort.

"What is a blanket fort?"

Jonah was seriously getting a talking to. How could his child not know what a blanket fort was? It was a rite of passage for every child. And, hello, her dad and I made one once. Best. Date. Ever.

"I'll show you."

Whitney watched me as I pulled all the table chairs out and arranged them in a square. Then she watched me drape several blankets over them. She wasn't impressed with my Santa Claus comforter. Because guess what? The girl didn't believe in good ol' Saint Nick. Yes, Jonah and I were going to have a lot of words when he returned.

When I finished, I pulled back the fort door. "After you." I waved her in.

She peeked inside the fort that I'd filled with pillows, blankets, and my laptop since we didn't have a TV. If Dani, Kinsley, or I wanted to watch anything, we had a mini projector we could hook up to our laptops to project the show on the white brick wall that ran the length of our loft.

"Don't be shy. Get comfy while I get the ice cream. And if you still want to, I left my phone in there so you can google anything you'd like."

Wait, I should probably add a caveat to that. There were a lot of things she shouldn't be googling. "I mean, you can google about happiness."

That got her to go in. She went straight for my phone.

While the girl genius did her homework, I made ice cream sundaes that would make you cry tears of joy, or hopefully in Whitney's case, at least crack a smile. Kinsley had made a batch of vanilla ice cream made with Tahitian vanilla beans. It gave it a cherry chocolate flavor. I made a quick cherry sauce to drizzle over it and then added some chocolate wafer cookies. Kinsley would be so proud. I would have taken a picture of the sundaes and sent them to Kinsley, except Whitney was using my phone, doing her best to prove me wrong in the fort of happiness.

"This study here says that older people who are happier live longer, but it could be because of well-being. And well-being is tied to having good social relationships," her voice faded.

I ducked under the blankets holding two big bowls full of happiness to find a quivering lip and watery eyes. "What's wrong, honey?"

"I am going to die young."

What in the world? I set the bowls down outside the fort and crawled in to take Whitney in my arms, if she would let me. She did without any resistance. I held her close to me and stroked her hair. "Whitney, you're not going to die young."

"I am, because I do not have any friends."

Oh. My heart thudded and then dropped. "Honey, you just moved here. You'll make some friends."

"I will not. I never do. Everyone thinks I am weird, and I talk funny. They call me a know-it-all or a freak," she cried.

"You're not a freak. There's nothing wrong with being smart. You should be proud of that."

"That is what my mother says, but I want friends too. How do I make people like me? I tried what google says. I ask other kids questions and I listen to them. But they do not want to talk to me."

Oh, Jonah was getting more than an earful. I wasn't prepared for these kinds of life-altering questions, especially when I couldn't figure out my own life. But I knew I had to soothe her, help her if possible.

I pulled her closer to me. Her little body curled against me. I kissed her head. It felt warm and wonderful, like it was what I was meant to do. "What kind of questions do you ask the other kids?" I thought maybe that was a good place to start.

She shuddered against me. "I ask them what their favorite documentary is."

I stifled my laugh.

"One girl said, 'You are so dumb. What is a *dog men Terry*?' I tried to tell her what a documentary was and tell her my favorite one is called *Walking with Dinosaurs*. She said I was boring and only boys like dinosaurs."

"That's not true. I love dinosaurs. Did you know we live near Dinosaur National Monument?"

She sat up, her eyes brighter. "We do? Can you take me there?"

"Yes, but not tonight. You need to go during the daytime." What was I doing promising this girl outings? I didn't know, but I wasn't sorry for it.

"Oh." She fell back against me.

"Whitney," I rubbed her arm, "can I tell you something?"

"Okay," she squeaked.

"Most of the time when someone is mean to you, it means they're either afraid or jealous of you."

"Why? I am a nice girl."

"Yes, you are, but you're very bright for your age. And very pretty. That probably makes a lot of kids jealous. My guess is that they don't understand you."

"How can I make them understand me?"

"Well, maybe you can help them when they don't understand their schoolwork."

"Like with math problems?"

"Yes. Or sounding out new words."

"I can do that."

"I know you can."

"But they might not want me to because they say I talk funny. Why do they think that?"

Yikes. How did I put this? "Do you know what contractions are?"

She nodded against me. "My mother said contractions are forbidden in academics."

"I think she meant higher education, like college, and probably when you're writing dissertations or something." It wasn't like I knew a lot about that sort of thing. "But when people speak, especially children, we use contractions. Like, I bet your classmates would say something like *don't* do that, instead of *do not* do that."

"But the second way sounds more commanding. My mother says it is important to command an audience."

I had no words. Who tells their five-year-old that? "Well, in your mom's job, I'm sure that's important, but would you want your classmates to command you?"

She thought about it for a second. "No. But I am not trying to be mean," she cried.

I smoothed her hair. "I know that, honey. But maybe since your classmates don't know that, you can try using contractions to see if that will help."

"Maybe I can write some sentences out and practice them," she suggested innocently.

Oh, this girl. "Maybe later. Let's eat ice cream first and watch some National Geographic." I never thought I would say those words.

"Can we watch the show about Egypt?"

"Whatever floats your boat, kid."

She looked up at me with a crinkled brow. "I don't have a boat."

I squeezed her tight. "You just used a contraction."

"I did?" She sounded astonished.

"You did."

"But I still *don't* have a boat."

I ruffled her hair. "It's a figure of speech that means whatever makes you happy."

"I want to be happy." She said it as if she didn't know that was a possibility.

"Me too. Let's eat some ice cream."

chapter fourteen

"They're under there," Dani whispered.

I had asked her to get the door. I looked down at my lap where a beautiful sleepy head with chocolate stained lips rested peacefully. Whitney had been that way for a good two hours, leaving me to watch her show about the wonders of Egypt alone. It wasn't half bad.

Soon Jonah peeked his head in the fort, all smiles even though his eyes were tired. It had been a long day and night for him. It was ten and he had been gone for five hours.

He looked between me and his sleeping beauty. "I don't think I've seen anything more beautiful in my life." He crawled toward me and kissed my lips without warning. It was over and done before I could process his lips grazing mine. "I'm sorry. I know you don't think we should kiss yet, but I highly disagree. And how do you expect me to refrain when you are making me the happiest man in the world?"

I sat stunned for a bit before I could answer. "Exactly how am I accomplishing that?"

He sat close to me, not leaving an inch between us. He brushed my hair back with a look of pure adoration. "In one night, you got my daughter to go in a blanket fort, and, from the looks of the two empty bowls, eat ice cream. You're a miracle worker."

"She did insist on watching National Geographic and eating some fruit and vegetables, just to be safe." I glanced at the fruit and veggie tray Kinsley had kindly brought to us.

Jonah chuckled, making Whitney startle, but not to the point of waking up. He kept his voice down when he said, "I've tried to convince her that she doesn't have to be learning something new every minute of the day and that eating treats in moderation is okay, but it's been a hard sell."

"I bet."

"Thank you, Ariana, you have no idea what this means to me. What you mean to me."

I bit my lip.

"I know. I'm moving too fast. Could you try and be less irresistible?"

"What would you have me change?" I grinned.

"Not a thing."

His deep, sexy voice was going to have me accosting him. Time to change the subject. "How's your patient?"

Jonah undid the top two buttons of his shirt. "It was a night. I ended up having to admit him and his wife. They both had pneumonia. The wife was in worse shape than him."

"That's awful."

"Honestly, I'm not sure if the wife will recover. She's well into her eighties and isn't in the best of health to begin with." Defeat laced his words.

I reached out and took his hand. "I can't imagine how hard it is for you to lose a patient."

"Unfortunately, she won't be my first or last."

"I know this doesn't fix anything, but do you want some ice cream?"

"I thought you would never ask. I've only eaten two protein bars since lunch."

I looked down at Whitney, who was sleeping so peacefully on my lap. Such emotion swelled in my chest for her. "If I move her, will she wake up?" I had been afraid to move, which was why I was now well-versed in all things Egypt.

"She's usually a sound sleeper," he informed me. He reached over and lovingly swiped her bangs.

"We can move her to the couch while you eat," I suggested.

He looked around the cozy fort, lit up only by the glow of my laptop. "I vote we stay in here."

I was afraid he was going to say that. Like I said, the best date ever had happened under a blanket fort. "Don't get any ideas," I half teased.

"I have all the ideas," he wagged his brows. "But those will have to wait until we are alone again."

A thrill went down my spine. *Deal with your past, Ariana,* I had to remind myself before I did something we would both regret. I gently moved Whitney and laid her on a pillow next to me. I covered her with an old quilt my great-grandmother had made. "She's lovely," I commented.

"She is," Jonah agreed.

I turned with the intent to exit the fort, but Jonah caught my hand. He held it up and traced the henna tattoo with his finger, sending tingles down my arm. "Do you still have the tattoo on your shoulder?" He trailed soft kisses down my arm.

I couldn't speak or breathe, so I nodded.

His eyes locked with mine. "Can I see it?"

Before I thought about it, I pulled down the sleeve on my peasant blouse—I had decided against the sweatshirt since I was going to see Jonah. I wanted to look pretty for him. For me. When my bare shoulder was exposed, Jonah let go of my hand and moved closer. His finger began outlining my tattoo that said, *Sometimes you have to fall before you can fly.* A tiny bluebird was inked close to the quote.

"I remember the night you got this," Jonah whispered in my ear. "I wished I was adventurous like you. I contemplated getting a tattoo to complement yours that said, *I'll catch you if you fall.*"

"I wish you would have," I said in hushed tones.

"I overthought it and I was too busy wanting to punch the artist for making you wince, but more because he was admiring you. I wanted to be the only man who looked at you that way. I still do."

I felt not only his warm breath against my skin, but his desire. My own, as well, burned inside of me. "Jonah," I breathed out.

"Please don't push me away."

"I don't want you to go away, but I don't want to hurt you again."

His lips skimmed my shoulder, making goosebumps erupt. "You didn't hurt me—"

"I didn't?" I wasn't sure if I should be relieved or offended.

"You didn't let me finish. I hurt me . . . us."

"No. You did the right thing. You got Whitney, and I got what I'd asked for—all fond memories of you and us."

Jonah closed his eyes and sighed. "We could have had Whitney. We could have had lots of babies. We could have had more than memories if I'd just stayed and taken the residency position here," he trailed off.

"What?" I was in shock. "You could have stayed?"

His eyes crept open. "Yes," he said, ashamed. "I didn't tell you because I thought if you were willing to go with me to Michigan, I would then give you the option of staying. I was offered an obstetrics and gynecology residency here, but it wasn't my first choice. I didn't want the kind of on-call hours an OB/GYN has. But you were my first choice, and I would have stayed if you had wanted me to."

"Why didn't you tell me?" I was flabbergasted by the news. I wasn't sure if I should feel angry or sad. I wasn't even sure I deserved to feel either way. I made him go.

"Would it have made a difference?"

I thought for a moment "No." *Maybe. We'll never know.*

"You're wrong. I should have stayed and fought for you. Instead, I proved you right. I left you because you'd wounded my pride."

"I told you not to ask me. I should have ended it before it went so far."

He took my face in his hands. "Don't say that. I loved every second. I would do it all over, even if I knew we would never see each other again."

Tears filled my eyes and flowed over, dripping onto his strong, capable hands.

He leaned in, allowing me to breathe in his breath.

"I think you had more than protein bars," I whispered.

He chuckled low. "You and Skittles are my weakness."

"I don't want to be someone's weakness, I want to be their strength, but I don't know if I can."

"You are so much stronger than you think you are. You gave me courage to come back here. To change my life."

"How?"

"First, because I missed this." His lips swept mine, leaving me aching for more. So, for once in a very long time, I threw caution to the wind and pressed my lips against his until they melded into one. He groaned with pleasure before pulling me onto his lap. Once securely in his arms, his lips urged mine to part. I wrapped my arms around his neck, bringing us closer together. His hands trickled down my back like a waterfall of pleasure. His tongue danced between being entangled with my own and prodding as deeply and urgently as it could. Oh, how I'd missed the taste of Skittles on his tongue.

He kissed with such intensity, as if to assure himself this was real and it was truly me he was kissing. Finally, he sighed and the kiss slowed into a steady rhythm until his lips glided off mine, only to kiss the corner of my mouth. From there he planted soft kisses across my cheek, speaking beautiful words in between each kiss. "You are my hero, Ariana. After everything you've been through, you persevered. You make everything and everyone around you thrive. I'm more alive when I'm with you."

My head fell against his shoulder. "How can I be your hero? I run from life." *I ran from you.* I didn't have the heart to say that to him.

"No, you run your life. From what Brock says, you run the studio better than your grandma ever did, and you helped Dani get Children to Love up and running. And . . . no one, not even me, could have gotten Whitney to eat ice cream in a blanket fort, except you."

"Jonah, it wasn't me. She only did it because I told her people who eat ice cream are happier and they live longer. She had to google that, of course, and what she found scared her. She thinks she's going to die young because she doesn't have any friends."

Jonah stiffened. "Not even one?" His heart sounded broken.

"None. Didn't she tell you?"

"She likes to talk about what she learned at school and her teacher, whom she seems to like a great deal. Whitney says she often sits with her at lunch," he choked out. "I feel like I've failed at my most important job."

I snuggled in closer to him. "Believe me Jonah, you're doing a good job. The mere fact that you've provided her with a stable, loving environment puts her ahead of the game. And more importantly, you want what's best for her. She's a lucky girl to have you as her dad."

He rested his chin on my head. "More than anything, I want her to be happy and well-adjusted. I want her to see past her own brilliance."

"She did use a contraction tonight, and she asked for more chocolate cookies to go with her ice cream. She's on her way to becoming a juvenile delinquent," I teased.

Jonah's muted laugh rumbled in his chest. "Thank you for taking such good care of her tonight. You don't know how much it means to me. To have you both together is incredible."

"I hope you don't mind, I promised her I would take her to Dinosaur National Monument."

"I don't mind at all. We should make that a camping trip."

"Maybe we should wait until it's warmer for that. I love to camp, but not when it's ten degrees at night."

"I have ways to warm you up," he groaned against my ear.

"I thought we were taking this a day at a time."

He kissed the top of my head. "You're right. We should take things slow. A lot has happened to Whitney and me this year. She knows I like you, and that her mom and I aren't getting back together."

"How does Whitney feel about that?"

"Honestly, I don't know. She only repeats Eliza's talking points back to me, as if it was all a sterile business transaction. I'm afraid for the time when she does start to feel the weight of the divorce. I think it hasn't hit her because Eliza was gone more than she was at home. Honestly, things aren't a lot different other than we live in a new house and she goes to a new school. A school of my choosing this time. I want her to have a normal upbringing."

I drew circles with my finger on his taut chest. "I wanted nothing more than to be normal growing up, but now I'm not even sure if there is such a thing. Honestly, I don't think Whitney is meant for *normal*, but there is nothing wrong with that as long as she's *safe*," my voice betrayed me and hitched.

"I'll always do my best to keep her safe." Jonah's arms tightened around me. "I wish I could have kept you safe. I wish you would let me now."

"That might be kind of hard considering the person you would be keeping me safe from now would be myself."

"You are scary," he joked.

I playfully smacked his chest.

"Honestly, though, you need to stop fearing yourself. If you could only see yourself like I do, you would know how amazing and capable you are. You would know you aren't your mother."

I desperately wanted that to be true. And more than anything, I wanted the truth. "Jonah," I whispered, "my therapist thinks I should open my father's letter this year."

Jonah's heartbeat ticked up. "Are you going to?" I knew he thought I should. When I'd told him about it all those years ago, he thought it was weird I never had. And he'd never trusted my mom's motives. He was smarter than me.

"I'm thinking about it, but I'm scared. Dr. Morales said some things today that made me wonder if my entire life has been a lie. What if Roger Stanton isn't my father?"

"It doesn't matter who your deadbeat father is," Jonah spewed angrily. "Your life isn't a lie. Your life is your own. Now you just have to decide what do with it." He paused. "I have some suggestions."

"I bet you do."

chapter fifteen

It was like déjà vu waking up in Jonah's arms, except we weren't on my old couch and his daughter was in my arms. I wasn't sure how that happened in the middle of the night. The last thing I remembered was Jonah and me eating ice cream and watching *Creed*, which was part of the *Rocky* saga. I had no idea the storyline had continued.

I also had no idea what time it was because it was especially dark in the fort. But what I did know was I felt safe and warm, snuggled between Jonah and Whitney. It got me thinking about a lot of things, but especially about the qualities my therapist said my safe person should have—steady, nonjudgmental, trustworthy, willing. Most importantly, someone I felt comfortable with. I didn't know why, but I'd never felt more comfortable than when I was with Jonah. And he certainly met all the other criteria. At least I thought so. Jonah was trustworthy. Wasn't he?

"Good morning," Jonah kissed my cheek. His morning scruff tickled and startled me. I didn't know he was awake too, as my back was to him.

"Good morning, at least I hope it's morning or we're all late," I replied.

Jonah lifted his arm and checked his watch. "It's just after six." He pulled me tighter against him. "I missed this."

"Me too." I took a deep breath and let it out at a snail's pace. "Jonah, do you know what being someone's safe person means?"

"Of course. Do you . . . need one?"

"Yes. Apparently, Dr. Morales thinks it would be good for me to relive all my bad memories on a daily basis and then share my feelings with my safe person. Me, not so much, but I promised her I would try. You know . . . there are things the safe person might not want to know about my past. It's not pretty. It could make that person think twice about me." Which I guess would make my decision about Jonah easy.

"Ariana, I meant what I said last night about wanting to keep you safe. I want that in every regard—mental, physical, emotional. There's nothing you can tell me that will change how I feel about you."

I kissed Whitney's head before gently letting her go and turning toward her father. I needed to look in his eyes, try and gauge the truth if I could. That was one of my problems, though; I had major trust issues. Being lied to repeatedly for a good portion of your life will do that to a person. Especially when it was the people you'd loved the most. People like your mother and fiancé.

Jonah's smile awaited me when I faced him. My fingertips brushed his strong jawline, enjoying the feel of the stubble that had grown overnight. "Jonah," I whispered, "my mother did some pretty unspeakable things. Things I don't like to think about, much less say out loud. And I saw things no child should. I even did things I'm not proud of just to survive mentally, sometimes physically." Tears pooled in my eyes.

Jonah kissed my forehead and lingered there while tears trickled down my cheeks.

"Ariana, I know who you are. I don't care about your past other than how much it pains you. I'll do anything to help you overcome that."

"You realize some of the pain of my past involves you, right?"

He drew me closer to him. "I know, and we'll work through it together."

I burrowed my head into his chest, wondering if we truly could. If perhaps there was hope for us, for me.

Jonah ran a hand slowly down my back. "As much as I would love to lie here with you all day, Whitney has school and I have patients to see." He leaned away and tipped my chin before his lips came down on mine, pressing hard, but never parting them. It reminded me of the last kiss we shared before he left for his residency. He was trying to convey how he felt about me to the point of begging me silently to believe him. I pressed just as hard, hoping he knew how much I wanted to. That was enough of an invitation for him to part my lips—until a tiny body stirred next to us. We broke apart faster than a Nicholas Cage marriage.

I sat up and ran a hand through my hair. Jonah did the same as we watched Whitney stretch and come to life. When her eyes drifted open, she blinked them several times as if she were disoriented.

"Hi, sweet girl," I said, hoping to jog her memory of where she was.

She popped up and looked down at her clothes. A look of great anxiety filled her tiny features. "I slept in my clothes and I did not brush my teeth. How could this happen?"

I guess she didn't know that the year I'd known her dad he slept in his clothes probably every night. The life of a med student was anything but glamorous.

Jonah reached across me, picked up his little girl, and set her on his lap. "Good morning, Winnie." He kissed her cheek.

"Father do not, I mean don't call me that." She flashed me a sideways grin.

Jonah wasn't having it. He tickled her. "You will always be my Winnie."

She giggled. I wasn't sure she could do that, but it was a beautiful sound. "I am not Winnie," she protested through her fits of laughter and wiggling.

Jonah stopped tickling her. "I'll make you a deal. You start calling me Dad again and I won't call you Winnie anymore."

I'd wondered when she'd started calling him Father. Her mom probably told her it sounded more commanding. That came off snarky and maybe a little jealous in my head. I honestly didn't think Eliza was a bad person—perhaps misguided and, let's be honest, strange—but I think she had good intentions.

Whitney had to stop and think for a moment about Jonah's proposal. "You promise to never call me that again?"

"I promise."

"What if I accidentally call you Father?" She sounded like a miniature attorney.

"Then I might accidentally call you Winnie." He gave her a squeeze.

"Okay," she sighed "I agree."

This girl killed me. But I found myself wanting to know everything about her. I wanted to ease her pain.

"We better get home and get you ready for school," Jonah announced.

Her beautiful eyes widened. "I did not practice using contractions," she cried. "I cannot, can't," she corrected herself, "go to school today. The kids will hate me." She turned into her dad.

Jonah stroked her hair while his eyes begged me to know what to do.

How should I know? I didn't have any children of my own and I was a mess myself. But just as I thought that, a memory slammed into me like a wrecking ball. A memory of me as a seven-year-old, wearing the same dirty outfit day after day because we'd run out of money again and we didn't have a working washer or dryer in the hellhole we were living in. I'd begged my mom not to make me go to school. I had already been teased about wearing the same thing every day and about my greasy hair. All she told me was it was better if I wasn't at home and I shouldn't care what anyone said about me. There was no love or sympathy. But I remember being afraid about what she was doing at home while I was gone. I'd seen some strange men come and go, so I went to school for another day of humiliation. I wasn't going to let that happen to Whitney.

"How would you like to come to work with me today? We'll work on contractions all day."

Jonah's brows raised, as did the corners of his mouth. Maybe I should have asked him if that was all right first, but his facial expression said he could kiss me for it, so I think I was safe in assuming he was okay with it.

Whitney sat up and wiped her eyes. "Will you make me break glass and use a solder iron?"

"Not unless you want to."

"I do not think I will."

"That's okay with me."

"Can we eat salad with protein for lunch?"

"I think I can manage that." I smiled.

"Then I will stay with you." She looked up at Jonah. "We must go home so I can change and get my notebook." She was the cutest old lady I'd ever known.

Jonah shook his head as if he was astonished at the turn of events. "Okay," he said, coming out of his daze. "Let's go home." He faced me and mouthed, "Thank you."

We all crawled out of the fort to find Dani and Kinsley, both dressed in flannel PJs, coming out of their shared bedroom and smirking at us.

"Well, good morning," Dani sing-songed.

"Good morning," Jonah answered like it wasn't unusual for two grown adults to come crawling out of a blanket fort with rumpled hair and clothes. He turned to me and pecked me on the lips. "We'll see you later."

"Goodbye, Ariana," Whitney said before taking her dad's hand and, with her shoes in the other hand, marching him out of the loft like a tiny woman on a mission.

I headed to the kitchen to make coffee. My two best friends followed me, still wearing smirks.

Kinsley leaned across the counter, looking too cute for six in the morning with her blonde hair up in a ponytail. "Sleepovers already?" she purred.

I threw her a *you're not funny* look. "It wasn't a sleepover. And hello? His daughter was with us the entire time. What kind of people do you think we are?"

Dani jumped up on the counter. She too looked like she had been up for hours. Was she wearing lip gloss? "I would say, from the looks of it, you're *lovers.*"

I tossed a coffee filter at her. "Who says words like lovers? We're friends."

"Kissing friends," Kinsley chimed in.

I cleared my throat and flipped the water on. "Friends can kiss."

"Oh, we heard," Dani claimed.

I turned and stared at them with my mouth agape. "You were spying on us?"

"I wouldn't say spying." Kinsley grinned. "It was just hard not to notice Jonah's groans of pleasure."

"We were afraid we might have to rescue Whitney when we heard you gasp a few times," Dani playfully added in.

Did I really gasp? I didn't remember that. My cheeks reddened. "So, we were a little overzealous last night." It had been forever since we'd kissed. And a long time since I'd kissed anyone. Man, had I missed it. Especially his kisses.

They burst out laughing.

"You're both immature." I finished filling the coffee pot with water.

"Don't be mad," Kinsley said. "It's just you've never brought a boy home before."

"He's a man, thank you very much."

"A man you tell all your secrets to." Dani folded her arms.

"What do you mean?" I poured the water into the coffee maker.

"Just that we heard you tell Jonah about your appointment with Dr. Morales. Why did you keep that from us?" Dani's tone bordered on hurt and proud.

I set the coffee pot on the counter and sighed. "I didn't want anyone to make a fuss over it or get too many peoples' hopes up. And, you know, I would miss all the pamphlets you keep leaving for me around the loft." I tried to weave some lighthearted sarcasm in there.

They rushed me unexpectedly and put me in an Ariana sandwich.

"Look at you bringing home boys, dressing like an adult, and going to therapy," Dani said in a way that let me know she wasn't too upset I'd kept my appointment a secret from them.

"You must really love Jonah," Kinsley said, "if you're willing to go to therapy."

I did really love him. "It's not for him, exactly. Unless you count scaring him away once and for all when I find out I'm certifiable." And when I tell him some other ugly truths about my past.

Dani leaned back. "From the way he looked at you this morning, I don't think you have anything to worry about."

Kinsley let go of me. "Yeah, what was all that about this morning? His daughter seemed awfully determined."

"That's one word for her." I chuckled. "But she doesn't fit in very well with her peers and I'm going to help her work on that today."

"You like her," Dani said as a statement, not a question.

"I do. She's an interesting girl, but there's something about her that tugs on my heart. Makes me want to help her be happy."

"I think we can all see some of ourselves in her," Kinsley wisely observed. We had all been on the outside in more ways than one during different times in our lives. I think we all still felt that way in some ways.

Dani grabbed coffee cups for all of us. "I guess it proves that it doesn't matter how rich or privileged your parents are, they can still screw you up."

I leaned against the counter. "I'm not sure if that makes me feel better or worse."

Kinsley swiped her favorite pink mug from Dani. "It makes you wonder how anyone survives."

Dani handed me my cup. "I'll tell you how we survived—we survived because we're fighters who have each other's backs." She looked me squarely in the eyes. "You have to fight for Whitney."

"I plan on it."

chapter sixteen

Whitney was happily building a dinosaur model with one of my friend's daughters in the corner of the studio. Grandma stared thoughtfully at her while she helped me cut glass for a custom project I was working on.

"She and Tabitha seem to be getting along well," Grandma commented.

"They do, don't they?"

I thought it was a stroke of genius on my part to ask Kara if Tabitha could have a playdate. I had known Kara for a long time. She'd been bringing her kids here for years on fieldtrips. She was a strict believer in homeschooling and had raised the smartest kids I had ever known, until I'd met Whitney, that is. Although, I would say Kara's five kids were more socially adept than Whitney. Tabitha was Kara's youngest child, at eight years old. She was also kind, brilliant, and loved dinosaurs. I'd been listening to her and Whitney chatter for over two hours while they built a large wooden replica of an Amargasaurus, which, according to the girl geniuses, was a sauropod, and only one skeleton had been discovered of the rare dinosaur, in Argentina.

It was about all I understood of what they said. Those girls knew bigger words than a dictionary. But I had to say, I was proud of Whitney for using as many contractions as she could between her ridiculously complicated words. So maybe she still had to look at her notebook from time to time to remind herself of some of the phrases we had written down together after Jonah had left her in my care this morning, but it was progress.

Her notebook was filled with sentences like:

Isn't that funny?

I can't wait for recess.

What's your favorite food?

I'm so excited for math. I didn't help her with that catch phrase. I wasn't sure how many points that would score with her classmates, but she insisted she needed a friend who liked math as much as she did. I wasn't sure that person existed.

I was thankful Tabitha didn't mind at all that Whitney would halt their conversation to write down new phrases with contractions to use. Tabitha even helped her come up with some. Girls like Tabitha would make this world a better place; we needed more inclusive people like her.

Grandma set down the pair of flat pliers she was using to help break the scored glass. "Dani called me this morning," she whispered, though I wasn't sure why. Whitney and Tabitha were far enough away and chatting nonstop, so they probably hadn't heard a word we'd said. And Crystal, who ran the storefront for us, was not only busy with customers, but on the other side of the wall that divided the workshop/classroom area from where we sold our goods. Since we didn't have any classes scheduled for today, we were virtually alone.

"Do you want me to whisper too?" I teased.

Grandma took the glass cutter out of my hand and set it next to the beautiful aqua-colored glass I had been cutting into flower petal shapes.

She took my hand between her own and started patting it. I'm not going to lie, it kind of freaked me out. It wasn't that Grandma wasn't affectionate, but not like this, especially in the workshop. Normally we would have cranked up some Fleetwood Mac or Led Zeppelin and sung our hearts out, but I didn't want to frighten Whitney. First, we would get her to master contractions, then sugar, then classic rock. Baby steps.

Then I noticed tears in Grandma's unusual bronze eyes that were looking pale.

"What's wrong? What did Dani tell you?" My mind began to race.

"She said you were going to therapy."

I tried to pull my hand away—somewhat annoyed that Dani would divulge that without asking me for permission—but Grandma gripped tighter.

"It's no big deal," I responded, knowing it was a lie. But I didn't want to make a fuss over it, and it had Grandma in tears. Or at least that's why I assumed she was crying, but you know what assuming makes you—a big fat butt.

"Did you tell your therapist how awful your grandpa and I are?" she tossed out there.

I jumped back, shocked. "Why in the world would I tell her that?"

Grandma reached into her total mom jeans pocket and pulled out a tissue before dabbing her eyes with it. "Because we are terrible people. We should have put a stop to your mom's madness and gotten custody of you. Your grandpa always said we would regret it, but," she sniffled, "I told him you were resilient, and that Joanie was a good girl who was having a hard time and she needed you. I wanted to believe that so badly." Her voice shook while she spoke.

I pulled away from her and grabbed a stool so she could sit down. I had never seen her so distraught, not even when my mom died. According to Grandpa, she'd mourned deeply but privately.

She sat while I grabbed another stool so I could sit next to her. This time I took her hand in my own. "Grandma, I'm okay. I survived."

"You shouldn't have had to *survive.* Why didn't you tell us things were so bad when you visited?"

I shrugged. "I was scared, and I guess because in some twisted way I thought I was protecting Mom." And I had been embarrassed. So embarrassed.

"She should have been protecting you."

"I agree."

"I know you're still keeping things from us. I don't blame you. I'm glad you're talking to someone. You probably don't trust Grandpa and me after we betrayed you like we did."

"Don't say that. You didn't betray me. I know you were in a difficult position."

"Don't try and make me feel better. It was you in the difficult circumstance." She paused. "I've been thinking about this a lot lately. I sacrificed you so I could maintain a relationship with my daughter. I knew Joanie wasn't telling us the truth. And for a while I thought I was right—you seemed to do so well when you moved back here. You had friends. You found love."

"With an idiot."

"But you tried, despite your mom's brainwashing, and that was a good thing, until it wasn't. Your grandpa was right. Your mom did a number on you and it had never been properly dealt with. She had never been dealt with."

"There was no dealing with her." I tried to keep the bitterness out of my tone. When Joanie Kramer decided on something, no one could change her mind.

"We should have at least tried." Grandma slapped her free hand on the wood worktable.

"Grandma, I really am okay. Yeah, I'm a bit screwed up, but honestly, things could have been far worse."

Grandma shuddered. "You don't know how sick that thought makes me."

Me too.

We both sighed at the same time. I wasn't sure what else to say.

Grandma looked back over at Whitney, whose smile lit up her face as she helped Tabitha click in a piece of the dinosaur.

"I wished you would have smiled more like that when you were growing up. A smile that says all is right in the world."

I wasn't sure all was right in Whitney's world, but at least she knew she was going home to what I assumed was a beautiful house, given Jonah had bought a place in the Creekside development. She knew her dad loved her and would always make her his priority. She had a lot going for her, though she lacked the peer connections every child needed and desired. But I would say she'd made a friend today by the way she and Tabitha giggled when the tail of the dinosaur fell off.

"Grandma, for a long time I was naïve enough to think my childhood wouldn't affect me. I thought I was better than my mom, and maybe I didn't want to deal with it because I was angry with her and I felt guilty about that. I thought I would just show her up and prove to her how wrong she was and how much better I was—until I wasn't. I don't want to be like her. And that still makes me feel guilty, despite everything she put me through," I admitted through a few tears of my own.

Grandma gave me a side hug. "I'll let you in on a little secret. You are better than your mom. You've taken responsibility not only for her choices, but your own. And you've always tried to help others. Your mom most often thought of herself."

"I picked a cheater, just like her."

Grandma kissed my head. "You also let a winner go."

I bit my lip. "What if he ends up being a loser?"

"Do you really think that's going to happen?"

"No, but that thought frightens me. I've been fooled before. What scares me more is what if it's me? What if I end up screwing us up? I don't want to return him."

"Honey, love isn't something you buy and then take back to the store if you're dissatisfied. It's hard work and a pain in the backside." She laughed. "And I hate to break it to you, but you're going to screw up and so is he, probably more often than you. But that's where real love is born and made. It's a love you'll never know until you're willing to risk becoming a *loser.*"

"That makes me feel so much better."

"You know what I mean, kiddo. Life is full of risks. Sometimes we come out winners and sometimes we come out on the losing end. But if you don't try, you'll always lose."

"My mom tried plenty. It never worked out for her."

Grandma tilted her head. "Did she really try? Do you think she really thought those men she chose were going to give her what she really wanted or needed?"

I shrugged. "Then why?"

"I ask myself that all the time. I've wondered if we didn't do enough for her as a child. She obviously had some need she wanted to fill. She loved attention. It was cute when she was younger, not so much as she aged. I mean, look at her artwork. It was provocative and edgy—it garnered attention, both good and bad. She thrived off it." She rested her hand on my cheek. "You're nothing like that. And Jonah is nothing like the men she chose, not even Kaden was, if you don't mind me saying."

"I kind of do," I growled.

Grandma laughed. "Well, honey, he was well employed, polite, he didn't drink in excess or do drugs, or have any criminal record. Obviously, he ended up being a louse, but that was his problem, not yours. I hesitate to say this, but good people can make bad choices. It's unfortunate that they affect those they love."

"I don't know if Kaden ever loved me," I contradicted her.

"That man loved you. Not as well as he should have, but honey, you took a risk. How were you to know how it would end, given what he presented to you upfront?"

"He did flirt with me when he was on a date."

She waved her hand around. "Do you know how many good marriages started that way? My parents' story began that way and they were some of the best people I've ever known."

I blinked several times, dumbfounded. "Really?"

"Yes, kiddo."

"So, what you're saying is, Jonah," I whispered his name so as to not alert his offspring, "could turn out to be a jerk and leave me even more devastated than Kaden?"

She let out a heavy breath and hung her head. "You're missing the point."

"And what is that?"

"The point is that you're a *loser* if you don't try."

My eyes narrowed.

She flashed me a sly grin. "Don't tell me you don't regret letting him go."

"I . . ." *I didn't*, that's what I always told myself, at least. "Well, we got a happy ending."

Her nose crinkled. "I don't know what fairytales you've been reading, but if you call him leaving and marrying another woman happily ever after, then you better get some new books."

"My mom never read to me," I blurted without thinking. I didn't know about fairytales until I started school. I made up my own, but they never came true. No one ever rescued me.

The tears were back in my grandma's eyes. "No wonder you wanted me to read so much to you when you visited. And you were so adamant about your traditions."

I wiped the tears from my own eyes. "Yeah, I know, I've been trying to recreate something I never had."

Grandma looked at Whitney. "Honey, you've created some magical times for us, but if you choose, you can use your magic to create something even better for your own family."

I swallowed down the lump in my throat that always formed when I thought about having a family of my own. When I thought about having a family with Jonah, I couldn't respond. The lump was having a hard time going down.

Grandma rested her hand on my arm. "Think about it. Talk to your therapist about it. And if you ever want to talk to me, I'm always here for you," her voice cracked. "I know you might not believe it, but I am. I hope you can forgive us."

I hugged her fiercely. "I never blamed you. There's nothing to be forgiven. I love you."

She bathed my shoulder in her tears. "I love you more than life itself. I hope you believe that. And while there is no such thing as fairytales, there are such things as happy endings, and if ever anyone deserved one, it's you. And even you have to admit that Jonah returning after all these years is the start to a pretty damn good story."

It was, but how would it end?

chapter seventeen

I tucked some hair behind my ear. Jonah wouldn't stop staring at me from across the table at Porter's where he had taken Whitney and me for dinner. Whitney sat next to me, talking a mile a minute about her day with me and Tabitha.

"Dad, you should meet Tabitha. She knows more about dinosaurs than you."

Jonah took a staring break and chuckled. "I'd love to meet her. Why don't you invite her over one evening this week?"

Whitney's eyes widened as if she had never thought of such a concept. "Do you think she would like to come over?"

"I'm sure she would love it," I jumped in. "I can arrange it with Kara, if you would like?" I asked Jonah.

Jonah reached across the table and took my hand. "That would be great." He turned to Whitney. "Would you like that, honey?"

"Yes!"

I had never heard her so animated.

"I can show her my fossil collection." She set down her fork and turned thoughtful for a moment. "Dad," she paused, "I think I should get some new clothes."

Jonah tilted his head. "All right. What would you like?"

She looked down at her child power suit in navy. She let out a heavy breath. "Tabitha said I dress like a grown up. I think I want to look like a kid."

"I think that's a good idea." Jonah looked as if he were suppressing a smile. I could also see some relief wash over his face. "Do you want to go shopping now?"

"After I finish my Brussels sprouts." She grabbed her fork and her knife and daintily cut her disgusting vegetable of choice into bite size pieces, and she actually enjoyed eating them. The child was a freak of nature, but I was beginning to adore her and her quirks.

"Do you have time to go shopping with us?" Jonah asked me.

I really should be home finding a quiet spot and reliving one or more of the worst moments of my life. I was already a day behind. I should have visited my own personal hell last night, but I was busy helping Whitney through some of her own problems and learning that ancient Egyptians used moldy bread to help fight infections and that they loved their makeup—both the men and the women. The responsible thing for me to do would be to go home, but Jonah began using his finger to outline the henna tattoo on my hand, sending shivers up my arm. His smolder wasn't helping me want to be responsible, either.

"Please come," his sexy voice implored.

"Okay." Hell could wait.

Jonah held up his hand to flag down our server. "Check, please."

Porter's was located at the local outdoor mall, which made the impromptu shopping trip convenient but cold, as it was the first week of December. However, the scenery and walking hand in hand with Jonah more than made up for the chilly temps. The shopping center went all out this time of year with thousands of white lights hanging between the buildings and hundreds of decorated trees, including a thirty-foot-tall tree in the center square where there was also an ice-skating rink. There were even carolers singing "God Rest Ye Merry Gentleman" under lamp posts. It was a scene right out of a Christmas card.

I had a love/hate relationship with this time of year. I truly did love Christmas and my traditions. Especially the one I was currently working on. Each year I picked a theme for my Christmas tree and made my own ornaments. I had been having a hard time choosing, but Whitney had inspired me. I was going with a *Little Women* theme this year. I had started making clothespin-doll ornaments of the March sisters, and I made some more stained glass umbrellas and a few post boxes. Dani, Kinsley, and I would pick out a tree this weekend and decorate it while watching *Miracle on 34th Street*—the old black and white version. That movie spoke to me on so many levels. A lonely little girl given the gift of believing in magic again, in something she couldn't see, but knew was true in her heart. In some ways I still was that little girl.

Jonah pulled me closer as we walked toward one of the children's boutiques, weaving between the flurry of holiday shoppers. Being with him felt magical, especially since I never thought we would see each other again. My heart desperately wanted to believe he was true, but this time of year also brought out my worst fears and memories. My earliest memories of Christmas were of being lonely and forgotten. I was lucky if my mom remembered to fill my stocking with the gifts Grandma had sent. Most of the time she'd just ended up handing me the shipping box on Christmas day, after my childhood hopes and dreams were crushed waking up to nothing on Christmas morning. Christmastime was also when I wished the most that Roger would come rescue me, that instead of a letter on Christmas Eve, it would be him. Each year I was disappointed. He never came to whisk me away to his beautiful castle that I just knew he lived in. I was really disappointed, too, because I had really wanted a tiara.

It's why I went overboard as an adult on the holidays. I had to make my own magic. My eyes drifted and landed on Whitney, who was leading the way, bundled up in her wool coat and a cream scarf with matching gloves. Maybe I could help her believe in the magic of Christmas, or at least show her how magical it could be.

"If I haven't said it already, thank you," Jonah interrupted my thoughts.

He had already thanked me quite thoroughly when he'd arrived at the studio to pick us up for dinner, while Whitney was using the bathroom. He'd picked me up and kissed me so deeply I could still taste the Skittles.

I gazed up at his happy face. "You're welcome . . . again. I had a great time with her today."

She really was the best part of my day. Well, except for waking up in the arms of the man I loved. But there was something about Whitney. Maybe it was her determination or her precious innocence. I don't know, but I really did enjoy spending time with her. She made me laugh and smile, though I didn't think she meant to. That was endearing all on its own. And she had a thirst for knowledge. She followed me around the studio asking about everything from how stained glass windows were installed to how much money the studio made each year and what types of advertising I was doing. She made sure to use contractions while she peppered me with questions. She also touted that her mom could make me more productive.

I had no doubt, but I was busy enough and I liked the setup I had now. Besides, I was still trying to sort out how I felt about Eliza. I knew if Jonah and I continued down this uncertain road, she was part of the package. But we didn't have anything in common, except we loved the same man. Honestly, that was disconcerting for me. It was nothing like high school where two girls liked the same boy. This was real life, and Jonah and Eliza would forever be connected by Whitney.

And there was the fact that Eliza and I obviously had different views on parenting. Granted, I wasn't a parent, but if I was, I knew I would want to be with my kids as much as possible. And I wouldn't dress them like miniature adults. I wouldn't even let them have a computer or really any electronics at this age. They would be licking finger paints to their heart's content, or until they threw up the non-toxic stuff.

"Why do you look so concerned?" Jonah was always good at reading my mood.

I blinked a few times and took a deep breath of cold air, shaking myself out of my thoughts about his ex-wife. "Just thinking."

"Care to share?"

"I will later." We had arrived at Charlotte's Children's Boutique. I could tell the place was pricey from the window display of mannequins dressed in fine clothing surrounded by mounds of gold-and silver-wrapped presents. At least the clothes were more age appropriate for Whitney. The one mannequin was wearing a darling sparkly gray sweater with a pink turtleneck underneath and a cute pair of jeans. My favorite, though, was the matching beanie. Whitney would look adorable in it.

"That's a cute outfit." I pointed out to Whitney before we walked in out of the cold.

"I will have to try it," she said matter-of-factly.

We walked in and immediately took off our hats and gloves. The store was toasty and cozy and filled with lots of shoppers, so it felt abnormally warm. It didn't take long until our coats came off too.

"I'm going to need your help," Jonah admitted while we browsed. "I'm not really good at this sort of thing."

I wasn't either, but I figured I could at least make Whitney look her age. "I'm on it."

He kissed my cheek.

I knelt near Whitney, who was looking at the sweaters from the mannequin in the window display. I pulled one off the rack I thought looked like her size and held it up. "I think this would look very pretty on you."

"Does it look too grown up?" She bit her lip.

"I think it looks very girlish, but why don't you try it on and you can tell us what you think."

She nodded and took the sweater. We also found several other pieces for her to try on. I hoped Jonah didn't mind spending a small fortune because the price tags were giving me heart palpitations. One of the sweaters alone was $75. I had never even spent that kind of money on a sweater for myself. Granted, I was wearing a sweater that probably cost at least $150, but that was only because my grandma was a sneaky old broad who knew how to barter.

The dressing room was something else. It reminded me of the fancy ones in movies, where not only did they have fine furniture for you to sit on and wait, but each dressing room was the size of a small bedroom with hand painted benches in it and cute sayings on the mirror like, *Leave a Little Sparkle Wherever You Go* and *Be Your Own Kind of Beautiful.*

Whitney read them out loud. "I don't think I sparkle."

"Sure you do." I bent down and kissed her head. "Your eyes light up a room."

"They do?"

"I promise." I hung up her clothes on the hooks at her level. "I'll be right outside waiting with your dad. If you need any help, let us know. Come out and show us once you've tried something on."

"What if I do not, I mean, don't like the outfit?"

"Then try something else on and show us."

"Okay." She didn't sound too sure.

I wondered if she had ever done this before.

I closed the door and sat next to Jonah on the loveseat in front of Whitney's room. He put his arm around me and we waited.

"Did her mom ever take her shopping?" I whispered.

"Eliza belongs to one of those online personal shopping services. It was more efficient."

"Oh." I settled against him.

"You think it's weird."

"Who am I to judge?"

"I wouldn't blame you if you did."

"I'm trying not to." I really didn't want to judge the woman, but everything in Whitney's life seemed so sterile and regimented.

"We messed up," he said quietly.

I did kind of agree with him. "At least you're trying."

He didn't respond right away, which made me feel horrible. I sat up so I could look at him face-to-face. "Did I upset you?"

"No, Ariana." His eyes drifted toward the door that his daughter was behind. "She needs someone like you in her life."

I rubbed my chest and swallowed hard.

"I know that scares you, but I knew—I knew you were the person we both needed. Wanted. At least me, but it won't take long for Whitney to feel that way too. You have that effect on people." He grinned and tapped my nose. "I don't expect this to be a one-sided relationship. I plan to offer you an array of services."

My brow popped. "That sounds illegal."

I laughed while he sputtered, "I meant . . ." He sighed. "Hell, I'm rusty at this."

"It's okay." I rested my hand on his chest. "I get what you're saying."

Thankfully, Whitney came out and saved us from our awkward selves. She looked adorable in the outfit from the window display. I jumped up and went to her, straightening the pink beanie on her head. "You look beautiful. What do you think?"

She shrugged her shoulders. "The jeans feel funny."

I looked down at them. I thought they looked great, but I asked, "Are they too big?"

"No. I've never worn jeans before."

I didn't dare look at Jonah. I didn't know there were any kids in America who hadn't worn jeans at least once. "Well, I think they look perfect on you."

Jonah joined us and knelt next to his daughter. "I love it. I love you." You could hear in the timbre of his voice that he hoped with all he had that Whitney knew that.

Whitney's face shone. "Okay. I think we should buy the outfit." She went to turn around but stopped mid turn and faced back toward us. "Dad, I love you too."

Jonah was a puddle of goo after that. I had a feeling he didn't hear those words often from her, which broke my heart. It's probably why we came out of Charlotte's with five bags. Jonah didn't even bat an eye at the $1500 price tag. I about threw up in my mouth over it. We lived in different worlds. Which was another concern, but one that would have to wait for another day.

Whitney had one more surprise for us that night. She stopped us in front of one of those tween jewelry stores. "Tabitha has pierced ears," she said out of the blue.

Jonah pressed his lips together as if he wasn't sure what he should say.

I nudged him and tugged on my pierced ear, hoping he would get the hint.

He stared blankly at me, totally not getting it.

I guessed it was up to me. "Honey, do you want to get your ears pierced?"

Jonah stepped back like I'd elbowed him.

Whitney touched her ear lobes with her tiny gloved fingers. "Does it hurt?"

"Not really."

She looked at my ears. My left ear had two lobe piercings and a helix. My right one only had the double piercing.

"How come you have so many?" she asked.

"I like the way it looks."

"I don't like that. I only want one in each ear."

I wasn't offended at all. I was more shocked she was even considering it.

Jonah finally came to. "Do you really want to get your ears pierced?"

"Maybe," she responded uneasily. "They make dinosaur earrings, right?" she asked me.

"I'm sure they do, but you typically have to start out with a tiny stud. After your ears have fully healed, you can get whatever kind of earrings you want."

She shifted her feet, unsure.

"What if your dad got his ear pierced to show you how easy it is?" I grinned evilly at Jonah.

Jonah's jaw dropped so far I had to tip it up for him.

"You always said you wanted to be more adventurous," I taunted him.

"Would you, Dad?" Whitney asked so sweetly.

Jonah rubbed the back of his neck while giving me a look that said he wanted to wring my neck. "I . . . I," he stuttered. "I think Ariana would like to get hers pierced again."

I tugged on my ears. "Sorry, I would, but these lobes are as pierced as they can be." I smirked at Jonah.

Jonah ran his hands through his hair, trying to think of a way out of this.

"I like a guy with a pierced ear." That was true. I found it sexy, but I figured in present company I should leave that tidbit out.

"Do you now?" Jonah didn't sound convinced.

"Cross my heart." I crossed my heart as best I could over my poufy coat.

"Please, Dad. If you do it, I *won't* be so nervous." She had to think about that contraction, but she was getting better at using them naturally.

That sealed the deal.

"All right," he groaned, "but I might not keep it. What will my patients think?"

"I'll tell you later." I winked.

That at least got a smile out of him.

When we walked into the shop together, Jonah whispered in my ear, "Don't think there won't be payback for this," he teased.

"It will be worth whatever it is you come up with to see you do this. I'm thinking a big diamond stud for the stud. What do you think?"

"You think I'm a stud?"

Uh. Yeah. "Maybe." I smiled. I could kiss him breathless right now if we weren't in a crowded store with his innocent daughter as a witness. Honestly, the crowded store wouldn't be much of a deterrent; Whitney, on the other hand . . .

He wrapped his arm around me and gave me a squeeze. "Life will never be boring with you." He sounded so confident that we would have a life together. I didn't disagree out loud, not even in my head so much. But I wasn't sold yet.

Whitney and I perused earrings while Jonah called Eliza in Japan to see if she was okay with Whitney getting her ears pierced. I think Jonah was hoping she wouldn't be. I thought she might not agree, with how long the call was taking. I had no idea what was being said as Jonah was across the store in a quiet corner. Meanwhile, Whitney and I struck gold.

"Look," she held up the pack of not one, but three pairs of dinosaur earrings. There were pink brontosauruses, silver stegosauruses, and dinosaur footprints. "I want these," she squealed.

"I love them." Now I only hoped her mom agreed. Not only for Whitney's sake, but I really, really wanted to see Jonah get his ear pierced. I picked out the perfect onyx earring for him.

Jonah walked back, shoving his phone in his pocket. I wasn't sure by the disgruntled look on his face if she'd agreed or not.

"Everything all right?" I asked.

He nodded, still not giving me the warm fuzzy feeling he usually invoked. I had a feeling there was a story there I would have to ask about later.

"Dad, look what I found." Whitney held up her treasure. "Did Mother say I can get my ears pierced?"

"If that's what you really want?" His tone said, *please say no.*

"It is." She held the earrings to her chest.

Jonah let out a heavy breath of resignation.

That's when I held up the sexy pair of onyx earrings. "I'm thinking this for you."

He grabbed the earrings. "That's subtle." He didn't hide his sarcasm.

I took them back and held them up to his ear. "I like. I like a lot."

He pecked my lips. "Fine. Let's get this over with."

I looped my arm through his. "I think it would help if you were a little more enthusiastic," I gently reminded him under my breath.

"You're right," he reluctantly agreed. He bent down and picked up Whitney. "You ready for this?"

She nodded, not one hundred percent sure.

"You're going to be great. Both of you," I encouraged.

Jonah shook his head at me as if to say he couldn't believe he was doing this. Neither could I, but I couldn't wait. It was like Christmas had come early for me.

I held Whitney's clammy hand while Jonah filled out the paperwork for them. You would have thought he was getting a kidney transplant with all the forms he had to sign. By the time he got in the chair, poor Whitney was looking pale. She didn't like the look of the piercing gun.

I knelt next to her while we watched Jonah.

"Does it feel like a shot?" Her little lips trembled.

"No. It's more like a tiny pinch that's so fast you hardly feel it." I was drawn to Jonah, whose ears were turning red since it seemed like the entire patronage of the store was watching this grown man get his ear pierced in a tween girl store. I found it quite attractive. I grinned up at him and mouthed, "You're so sexy."

That at least got a smile out of him.

"I do not want to get hurt." Whitney turned into me at the precise moment her dad's ear got pierced.

I held her to me. "Honey, it doesn't hurt, but no one will make you get your ears pierced."

She snuggled into me. "Do you think the kids at my school will like me more if I get my ears pierced? Lots of girls at my school have their ears pierced."

Oh. Is that what this was all about?

I leaned away from her and looked into her pretty green eyes. "You listen to me, Whitney Adkinson. You don't have to change a thing about you. You're wonderful just the way you are. Now if you want to get your ears pierced because it's what you really want, you should do it; but if you don't, that's okay too."

She looked at the cute dinosaur earrings in her hand. She thought and thought some more.

"What do you ladies think?" Jonah appeared, sporting his pierced ear.

Whitney's head popped up. "I don't want to get my ears pierced."

Jonah's deer in the headlights look was priceless. "What?"

"Surprise!" I laughed. Best. Night. Ever.

chapter eighteen

I couldn't help but look around in amazement at Jonah's home as I sat on his leather couch, waiting for him to finish tucking Whitney into bed. Even in the low light from the fireplace, his house looked grand. There were windows for days and those expensive touches like custom crown molding and a stone fireplace with a rustic mantle that would be right at home in a five-star resort. Don't even get me going on the gourmet kitchen I got a peek of. Kinsley would be in love. I was kind of in love too. But it was intimidating. I knew Jonah saw us here. He didn't say it out loud, but when we walked in, he gave me a look that said he hoped I was pleased with the home he'd chosen—for us.

I'd never imagined living in such a nice home, unless you counted when I'd thought my father was a prince and would come and take me away to his castle. But aside from that, I'd only ever wanted a small place to call mine. Jonah's home was anything but small. An L-shaped staircase led to the upstairs, where I bet there were at least five bedrooms. I'm not sure why he thought he needed all the room. Maybe he was still serious about having five kids. Nine years ago, that had been his plan. I used to tease him about it, but secretly I wanted to be the mommy of those babies.

I still did, but I needed to work through my past, if I could. It was why I was sitting here. Before Jonah had dropped me off at home, he'd convinced me to follow him back here. He said it would be quieter here and we would have more privacy for me to work through my issues. That was true, considering Dani was having a guy friend over in her feeble attempt to pretend she didn't need or want Brock.

I stared into the fireplace, mesmerized by the flames. I knew soon I would be feeling as if I had jumped into them. Dr. Morales, and even Jonah, assured me I would feel better once I allowed myself to feel the pain and let it go. But I couldn't see how that was true. I'd been feeling the pain for years. I'd felt like I'd already walked through the flames and there was no salve strong enough to repair the scars. But I would try. I promised myself I would.

Jonah jumped over the back of the couch like he was twelve and landed next to me, making me jump. He wasted no time pulling me into his arms, and there I found myself with my head resting on his chest, listening to the steady beat of his heart.

"How's Whitney?" I asked. She was somewhat distraught over not getting her ears pierced. She wanted to so bad, but just couldn't do it.

"She's okay. She made some big steps today, thanks to you."

"I didn't do much."

"Are you kidding? You spent your entire day with her, not to mention you helped her make a friend. And you tricked me into getting my ear pierced," he growled. "I think I'm going to take it out."

I sat up out of his arms. "Don't you dare. Deep down she wants to get her ears pierced, so you have to keep it. Besides, I love it."

He tugged on my sweater and pulled me closer. "Do you now?"

I reached up and touched his earring. "It's very sexy. Now you just need a sleeve tattoo and I'll never keep my hands off you."

"Is that a promise?" He skimmed my lips.

"We both know you'll never get one," I whispered above his lips.

"Did you ever think I would get my ear pierced?"

"No." I laughed.

"You think you're funny." His lips teased my own.

"I think I'm hilarious."

He took me into his arms, then his lips came crashing down on mine. For a moment I gave in and parted his lips. I missed the taste of Skittles and him. Always him. But I pulled back before I got swept away and lost my nerve to do what I needed to do.

"Jonah." I placed my hands on his scruffy cheeks. "I want nothing more than to kiss you all night, but you need to know everything about me, and I need to let you." Tears filled my eyes.

He kissed the corner of my eye. "I know all I need to know, but I'm here for you."

I slid off his lap and sat next to him. He offered me his hand and I gladly took it.

"I don't even know where to begin."

"Why don't you start slow. Rate your experiences by pain levels and start with a lower level."

He sounded like a therapist, which made sense considering he was a doctor and had taken several psychology classes. I even remembered him doing his clinical rotations in the psychiatric unit at the hospital.

"Okay," I breathed out. I looked around the darkened house. Something hit me and triggered my own bad memories. "You don't have a Christmas tree. Or stockings."

Jonah let go of my hand and leaned forward, resting his arms on his legs. He stared out into the fire. "Eliza didn't believe it was good to fill Whitney's head full of fairytales and commercialized holiday nonsense. She believed in giving Whitney experiences. We always took a trip during the holidays."

"Are you this year?"

"No. I wanted to be here for the holidays. For obvious reasons." He nudged me. "Eliza will be joining us."

"Will she be staying here?" I wasn't sure that came out as nonchalant as I wanted it to.

"Does it bother you?"

"No," I said, way too high-pitched.

He gently turned my head toward him. "There's nothing remotely going on between us, other than we are parenting our daughter."

I wanted to believe that. "Why were you unhappy when you spoke to her tonight?"

"I thought we were talking about you tonight."

"We are, but you first."

He kissed the side of my head. "Fine. I don't like that it was so easy for her to go on with her life."

I stiffened next to him.

He took my hand and held it between his own. "You're taking that wrong. I mean in regard to our daughter. It angers me for her to be so dismissive now after how much she insisted on Whitney being raised the way she was. Her favorite thing to say whenever I call her about Whitney is, 'You do as you see best.' It's like she wants none of the responsibility for Whitney's future or for the repercussions I'm dealing with because of my failure to be more vocal. To be the kind of father I always thought I would be." He leaned back against the couch and ran a hand over his face.

I joined him and rested my head on his shoulder. "I can't imagine how difficult that is, but . . . you did get your ear pierced for her. If that doesn't say father of the year, I don't know what does." I giggled.

"You just wait, payback is coming."

"I'll be ready."

"Are you ready now?"

I knew he wasn't talking about payback. And no, I wasn't ready. "Promise me something."

"Anything."

"We'll get Whitney a Christmas tree and you'll play Santa Claus."

"Did you say *we*?"

"I suppose I did."

He squeezed my thigh. "I promise, Ariana."

"Okay." I let out a deep breath. I couldn't stall any longer, well, I could, but I supposed I shouldn't.

I took Jonah's hand and closed my eyes. For a moment, I focused on the way his thumb glided across my skin. It felt nice. I wanted to stay feeling that way, but I knew I couldn't.

Okay heart, where did we begin? My mind shifted from Jonah to my father. I was ten, and it had been two years since I'd known about the letter Roger Stanton sent every Christmas Eve. I wanted to see what was in it, so I waited by the door all morning on Christmas Eve until there was a knock. I went to answer the door in the dingy apartment we were living in, but my mom was there in a second, only wearing a holey t-shirt, pushing me out of the way. She went outside and wouldn't let me come out. When she came back in, I begged her to tell me what was in the letter. She grabbed a cigarette and lighter from her bra and lit it before she said, "Don't you ever open that letter. Your daddy never wanted you. I'm the only person who will ever want you. Don't you forget that." She left me alone, in tears. I sank to the dirty tile floor and cried and cried. In my head, I kept telling myself it wasn't true. Roger was my only hope and I knew he loved me. He had to. Who else was going to save me?

I leaned forward and wiped the tears off my cheeks. Jonah didn't say a word, he only applied reassuring pressure to my hand, letting me know I wasn't alone. But I had to live, breathe, and feel the ugliness of that Christmas Eve so long ago. I had to own how much I'd hated my mom in that moment. Why was that so hard? I easily mourned for how desperately I'd wanted my father. I ached for the piece of hope my mom had chipped away in that moment. She would eventually steal every last bit I'd had, but foolishly, at ten, I had still hoped, despite the odds, that she was just a liar. That someone truly loved me. It's all I'd ever wanted—to be loved. That's when the hate came. I hated her. Not just then but now. I hated her for everything she took from me. Guilt crept in because I did love her. She was my mom, after all. *Own the hate,* I kept telling myself.

"I don't want to hate her," I said out loud.

Jonah sat up. "Own your feelings, Ariana."

I nodded and tried to focus on that moment. My ten-year-old self called out to her at that moment, "I hate you!" I screamed in my head.

"I hate her," I whispered. "How am I supposed to love these feelings like Dr. Morales said?" I asked Jonah.

"You don't have to love the feelings. Love that you are allowing yourself to own them and feel them."

"That sounds so smart, but I don't love that I'm allowing myself to feel them either."

He chuckled softly. "You're doing great."

I gripped his hand tightly. It felt so odd for me to tell myself to feel the hate, but I had to. "What if I can't stop hating her?"

"You're asking yourself the wrong question. The question is, can you afford to not let yourself hate her? Not allowing yourself to all these years hasn't done you any good. Be true to yourself, Ariana, own what you're feeling now. When you can be true to your feelings it will allow you to know the truth of others' feelings for you."

I turned toward him. "Wow. That's profound."

He swiped my bangs. "No, that's truth."

"My mom told me when I was ten years old that no one but her would ever love me or want me."

Jonah clenched his fist and composed himself before he spoke. "That was a lie."

"I didn't believe her in that moment because I wanted so much to believe that my dad loved me and wanted me. He just couldn't be with me. As I got older, I had no choice but to believe her. My dad never loved me. Kaden didn't love me."

"I loved you, Ariana. I still love you." Emotion bled through his words.

I wasn't ready to hear those words, even though I knew that's how he felt. And how I felt. "You left me too." My hand flew to my mouth. "I'm sorry, I didn't mean to say that. You were right to leave." I had rejected him and practically begged for him to go. That one was on me.

"Dammit. Don't say that. It wasn't right. I should have told you about the residency here."

"You didn't owe me that. I wouldn't even acknowledge that we were in a relationship. I'm surprised you stuck around for as long as you did."

He shook his head in frustration. "Will you listen to yourself? Stop thinking you don't deserve the best someone has to offer. That you deserve to be walked all over."

"You didn't walk all over me. If anything, it was me who walked all over you."

He gently grabbed my arms. "Ariana, I never saw our relationship that way."

"How did you see it?"

He pulled me closer, making our foreheads meet. "Every day I would wake up and my first thought was always about you and how I could arrange my schedule to see you. I didn't care if it meant losing sleep, because you energized my soul. I didn't mind the sneaking around, because it meant I had you all to myself. And I thought if I loved you enough, you'd come to trust me. But then I gave you every reason not to by leaving." He pecked my lips. "I am sorry. If I could go back and change that moment in time, I would."

"Please don't apolo—"

"Shh." He rested his finger against my lips. "It's okay for me to be wrong. And it's okay if you're hurt by my actions, and your mother's, and father's, or anyone else's for that matter. Don't fear your feelings."

I kissed his finger before removing it and holding his hand. "I don't want to be afraid anymore."

"Then let it all out."

I took in a deep, cleansing breath and let it out. "I hate my mom. I hate that she never put me first and she put me in harm's way. I hate that she hated you. I hate all the lies she told. And I hate that I hate her," I cried.

He took me in his arms and let me sob until there were no more tears left to cry. I soaked his shirt and probably left some ugly makeup stains on it. He stroked my hair while I shuddered against him time after time after time. After a good half hour, I sat up and wiped my eyes. "Huh. I do feel better."

Jonah gave me such a tender look. "I'm glad."

"Are you sure you want to keep being my safe person? I have a feeling it's going to get uglier before it gets better."

He cupped my face. "Ariana, I'm not going anywhere ever again unless you come with me, so bring it on."

I hoped he remembered that he asked for it.

chapter nineteen

"I helped make all the clothespin doll ornaments," Whitney made sure to tell each person decorating the tree. Which ended up being more than I thought. When I'd asked Dani and Kinsley if they would mind if we moved our decorating party to Jonah's, they thought it was a great idea. They didn't even mind me using the ornaments I had planned for our tree for Jonah's and Whitney's tree. After all, Whitney was the inspiration. And, like she was telling everyone, she had helped me make several of the ornaments. Well, mostly.

"I did not use the hot glue gun. No way. Ariana glued on all the heads. But do you see how pretty I painted her hair?" She held up a likeness of Jo March for Brock to see.

"You did a great job," Brock praised her, making Whitney beam.

"What a crafty little girl you are," Alexandra, Brock's date, added in.

Oh yes, we had a house full of awkward dates. Because nothing says Christmas like fake relationships. Brock was there with the Dani-approved Alexandra, who had to go powder her nose like five times. I was beginning to think that was a code word for something else and I was more than a little worried.

Dani's date wasn't much better. He had a love affair with himself. I don't know how many times I caught him staring at his reflection in Jonah's stainless-steel appliances, but it was an unhealthy amount, to be sure. I mean, yes, Scott was handsome with his chiseled jaw and wavy dark hair, but I wanted to tell him he still looked the same as he did ten minutes ago. When Scott wasn't ogling himself, he was perusing Dani while always making sure to have his arm around her, which made decorating the tree a little hard. Not that a lot of decorating was getting done. Brock and Dani kept looking at each other—when the other one wasn't looking their way, that is. It was like a cringy rom-com.

Then there was Brant and Jill, who took awkward to a new level. Jill obviously liked Brant more than he liked her. He was nice to her, making sure she was well supplied with Kinsley's homemade wassail and Christmas cookies. I'm pretty sure the poor woman had already eaten about a dozen herself, since Brant kept bringing them to her, and sadly, she seemed desperate to please him. She kept reaching out and touching his hand or the lapel of his jacket, all while he kept feeding her, never reciprocating the physical affection.

That left us with Kinsley and Ethan, who she'd met at her restaurant. Apparently, he'd been in several times to flirt with her and had finally worked up the courage to ask her out. Why Kinsley thought this was a good first date, I didn't know, but Ethan didn't seem to mind. He had a kind, goofy demeanor to him and was happy to help Kinsley with whatever she needed, from arranging cookies on the platters to hanging ornaments. He was super tall. I would say at least six feet, four inches. He and Kinsley looked kind of odd together since she was only five feet, four inches. But Ethan seemed enamored with our Kinsley, who, unfortunately, kept sneaking glances at Brant. I think I was the only one who noticed. Brant seemed overly interested in Ethan too, peppering him with all sorts of questions as if he was Kinsley's dad. *Where do you work? Where did you graduate? Who's your family?*

Ethan good naturedly answered—he was an accountant from California who'd just moved here not too long ago. Brant made sure to throw in that he was an attorney and a Holland. Ethan didn't know the Holland name, which made me smile. I wasn't sure what Brant's deal was. I'd never seen him throw his name around like that before. Not that he really had to. Everyone around here knew who the Hollands were.

It was an anomaly that I had the most normal relationship of the night. I smiled up from my seat on the couch where I was finishing the red bows that would adorn the tree. In my line of sight, Jonah was holding up Whitney to place one of the umbrella ornaments I'd made toward the top of the ten-foot Fraser Fir the three of us had picked out last night at the tree farm.

Whitney had insisted on walking the entire lot to make sure she was picking out the best of the best. She really was the most determined little girl I had ever known. She was also working her way right into my heart. So was her daddy. Though I'm not sure he had ever vacated his place there.

After this week, Jonah deserved a gold star. The last several nights after Whitney helped me make ornaments and Jonah put her to bed, it was therapy time. I was right, it had gotten uglier. We'd delved into the world of Carl. We even visited my fears that my mom was selling her body to make ends meet. The hardest part was admitting I had shoplifted food and, a couple of times, clothes. I never got caught. In a way, I wished I had. Maybe it would have alerted the authorities to my situation. Maybe my grandparents would have been forced to take me. I still felt awful about it. You do things you normally wouldn't do when you're desperate and hungry.

I felt better, though, after Jonah helped me write letters to the places I had stolen from, including enough cash to repay my debt with the letter.

Jonah had suggested it even though he didn't think I had anything to feel guilty about. The more I spilled my guts to him, the more I think he was glad my mother was already dead. He didn't bad-mouth her, but I could see in his eyes how much he loathed her. Honestly, Jonah didn't really say much of anything while I vomited my past, night after night. He just listened and held me. Amazingly, I hadn't scared him away yet.

In fact, Jonah looked positively giddy tonight, picking up Whitney to help her place the ornaments on the majestic tree that looked perfect in his twenty-foot-tall great room. I loved the smell of the Christmas tree and the way the multicolored lights twinkled and reflected in the large windows. I loved watching Whitney be happy, even if she would only eat one cookie, saying that was her sugar limit for the day. Five-year-olds shouldn't have sugar limits, especially at Christmastime.

At least she'd dressed her age tonight in a rose cable knit sweater with matching plaid leggings. She was adorable, even if she acted like she was thirty. According to her, she hadn't made any real friends at school yet, but she had organized a math study group for the kids in her class that needed help. She was the leader, of course. And one girl told her she liked her pink beanie, so there was that. Baby steps. Thankfully, she and Tabitha were getting along famously, seeing each other every weekday.

Whitney admitted to Jonah that afterschool care was awful for her and where she felt the most alone. I mentioned it to Kara, Tabitha's mom, and she came to the rescue, offering to pick Whitney up after school and watch her until Jonah was done at the clinic. It was the perfect setup. Kara ran her home like a school, and she didn't believe in TV or sugar-filled snacks. It was basically like Disneyland for Whitney.

Jonah caught me smiling at him as he set Whitney down. He made his way over to me and slid into the spot next to me. He pecked my lips. The light in his eyes had returned full force.

"You're happy," I commented.

"This is the best Christmas I've had in a long time."

"Me too." It really was. Looking around Jonah's beautiful home reminded me of a cheesy Hallmark Christmas movie. It was honestly like a Christmas dream come true. I wanted all the cheesy things. Christmas music was playing on the surround sound while a cozy fire burned in his fireplace. People were smiling and laughing, even if some of it was fake. But it was fake in those cheesy movies too. And there I was, making Christmas ornaments, sitting next to the man I loved. I had to stop myself from thinking that something was surely bound to go wrong because moments like these weren't meant to last. At least not for me. But maybe they could? Right?

"By the way, nice earring, doc," Brock teased Jonah. I was surprised no one had noticed before. I didn't say anything about the infamous earring because I knew it embarrassed Jonah and he was only keeping it for Whitney's and my sake.

Jonah's ears pinked while he inadvertently touched the onyx beauty in his ear. That drew the attention of everyone. Suddenly, there was a congregation of people around us gawking at poor Jonah.

"It's totally manly," he said, like he needed to defend his honor or something.

I reached up and played with his earring. "It's very manly."

Dani sat down on the other side of Jonah and got deep into his personal space to peer at it. "I didn't think you had it in you, Jonah. This looks like the work of Ariana."

Everyone laughed, especially those who knew Jonah and me, because Dani was right.

"Just wait until I convince him to get a tattoo."

Whitney dropped one of the clothespin ornaments onto the hardwood floor. "No, Dad, you can't. It is dangerous." At least she got one contraction in there. She was using them more naturally and frequently now.

"Don't worry, Daddy isn't getting a tattoo." Jonah tried to calm down a fretting Whitney.

Oh, poor naïve Jonah. He was totally getting a tattoo—tonight, unbeknownst to him. I'd brought my henna supplies with me. Seriously, that earring was a turn on, and I totally dug tattoos. And I felt if Jonah saw how good a henna one looked on him, I might be able to convince him to get the real deal. Of course, he would have to get it where Whitney would never see it, lest she have a heart attack or spend a night googling how to safely remove tattoos.

"I wouldn't bet on it," Kinsley said under her breath so the munchkin in the room didn't hear her. She knew me too well.

Jonah stood, obviously uncomfortable with the direction of the conversation. "Let's make a toast." He walked to the kitchen and began pouring the adult wassail in mugs for everyone but Whitney, who got water because, you know, wassail had a lot of sugar . . . and Kinsley's version had rum. I stood and helped Jonah in his quest to not talk about tattoos or the jewelry he was sporting.

Once every person had a drink in their hand, we gathered around the tree. Whitney stood in front of me. I had one arm around her while holding my drink in my free hand. I loved the way the twinkle lights reflected on everyone, except for maybe Alexandra, whose sequined shirt was giving me a headache, as was the way she had an iron grip on Brock. Stupid, stupid Brock, who was causing Dani to cling tightly to the moron she'd brought who, yup, was trying to look at his reflection in the shiny red mug I'd handed him. What a tool. I would tell Dani that later. But I was pretty sure she knew.

Jonah raised his mug. "To Ariana," he said, surprising me.

My eyes drifted up to meet his. Those intense green orbs made me weak in the knees.

"Thank you," he continued, "for this beautiful night and your beautiful soul. How lucky we all are to know you."

"Here, here," Dani said the loudest.

While everyone raised their glasses to me before partaking, all I could do was stare up at the man who had just owned me with his words and heart. I stood on my tiptoes and kissed his cheek. "Wait until I get you alone later," I whispered in his ear.

He raised his glass. "Merry Christmas to me."

That was my plan.

"You choose where it goes, but we are totally doing this." I held up the alcohol swab, ready to clean his skin. "How about your neck?" I suggested for the tattoo.

"How about I grab more wassail for both of us and we get comfortable in front of the fireplace while I show you how happy I am that we're finally alone?" He took the swab and unceremoniously tossed it before pressing his lips against mine and pushing me against the couch.

His offer was hard to refuse, which was why I played along for a while and ran my hands through his hair, thoroughly ruining that swept fringe look I loved. Though it was considered a retro cut, it still had a modern flair to it. And it was all Jonah.

Jonah took his time exploring my mouth while his hands caressed my cheeks. He always made me feel adored and wanted. I especially loved it when he trailed soft kisses down my neck. I may have gasped a few times when his warm breath played against my skin.

With every kiss, I almost forgot about the tattoo. Almost. I did one more brush of his hair and gave him another long slow kiss that said just how much I was enjoying reveling in the taste of the spices and rum on his lips.

"As fun as this is," I rested my hands on his chest, "you are getting inked tonight."

"Ugh," he groaned against my lips. "Why is this so important to you?"

"You said you regretted not getting one when I did, so I'm remedying that." I batted my eyelashes innocently.

"Nice try. You just think they're hot."

"I think you're going to look hot with one."

"Do you know how many patients commented on my earring this week?" He didn't take a breath or let me answer. "All of them."

I suppressed my laugh. "All compliments, I'm sure."

"If you consider, 'Did you lose a bet or something?' a compliment, then sure, I got a lot of those."

I broke into fits of laughter. "I would say I'm sorry, but I think we both know that's a lie. But if it makes you feel better, I love it."

He pressed a kiss to my lips before settling next to me. "It's the only reason I'm keeping it. Well, until Whitney gets hers done, then it's coming out."

"I can't allow that." I touched the earring lovingly.

Jonah tilted his head and swiped some of my hair back. "Are you afraid of me?" he asked out of the blue.

"In what way?"

He grimaced. "In any way."

I swallowed hard. "Why are you asking?"

"When we're alone together, you always seem to find a way to physically keep yourself from me."

I bit my lip, wishing he hadn't noticed. "It's just—"

He held up his hand. "Ariana, let me put your mind at rest. Even if you begged me right now to take you to my bed, as difficult as it would be, I wouldn't do it. I would never make love to a woman who is afraid of me, in any way. Especially you. We aren't taking that step until you know what you want, and you freely commit yourself to me—forever."

Forever seemed like, well, forever. And like a dream. Do people happily stay together forever? Could we? Could I?

"Jonah," I eked out, "I know you would never take advantage of me."

"Do you? I know your past, Ariana. I'm not any of those men."

"I know that. It's . . . it's just . . . I'm afraid of feeling too much for you to only have it end. I don't want to hurt you and I don't want to get hurt."

His thumb glided across my cheek in slow motion. "I don't know what to do to prove to you that I'm not going anywhere, other than to show you day by day, but you're going to have to find a way to trust that."

"I know," I whispered.

The corners of his mouth lifted. "I think I know what tattoo I want and where I want it to go."

"You don't have to." Just like he would never make me do something that was truly uncomfortable for me, I would never force him to do anything he didn't want to.

"I want to." He began unbuttoning his shirt.

My heart started to race. Like, sprinting. "What are you doing?" I thought he said we weren't going to take this step yet. But I couldn't help but stare at his chest that, with each undone button, was becoming more and more visible to me. Mmm. Like, so yummy. Holy, holy, holy. I didn't know what his workout regimen was like, but *hello*. His chest was a beautiful sight of defined muscle and lay-your-head-on hair. I wanted to reach out and touch it.

"I meant what I said," his voice drew my eyes upward. "You're safe with me." He slid his shirt off.

I wasn't sure I was safe from the thoughts stirring around in my mind. I reached out and brushed my fingers along his broad shoulders. I loved the feel of his skin. I loved how it raised under my touch. "You're beautiful, inside and out. Thank you, Jonah."

"Don't thank me for behaving like a decent human being. Contrary to popular belief, men can control themselves. Though," he leaned in and kissed my forehead, "you do make it difficult."

I breathed in his intoxicating breath that lingered between us. "The feeling is mutual. So, where do you want that tattoo?"

He leaned away. "I want it to say, *Fly with me.* And I want it here." He pointed to his heart.

My eyes filled with tears thinking of my own tattoo, *Sometimes you have to fall before you can fly.* I felt like I had been falling forever, trying to find my wings. I rested my hand on his good heart. More than anything, I wanted to keep it. Keep him.

He covered my hand with his own. "Fly with me, Ariana."

chapter twenty

"Tell me what you've learned this past week," Dr. Morales said in her soothing voice.

I curled my legs under me on the comfy white chair across from her. It had been quite the week. I had learned Jonah looked fabulous with a tattoo, which didn't surprise me at all. But I didn't think Dr. Morales wanted to hear about the "Fly with me" tattoo that I'd adorned with two turtle doves since they were known for their lasting bonds and all things Christmas.

"Um . . ." I tucked some hair behind my ear. "Well, I hate my mom," I reluctantly admitted. "I mean, I love her too, but I hate her."

Dr. Morales leaned forward. "You feel guilty about that."

"Shouldn't I? She's my mother, after all."

"Just because someone gives birth to you doesn't mean they automatically deserve your loyalty, though yours is admirable." She smiled. "This is good."

"It's good that I hate my mother?"

"It's good that you recognize it. But you will feel better when you own it and let it go." She wrote some notes. "Were you able to share these feelings with anyone this week?"

"Yes, Jonah."

Dr. Morales's head popped up. "Jonah. Interesting choice for your safe person."

"Why?"

"I just find it interesting that you would choose someone who is so recently back in your life, someone you have conflicted feelings about. Why him?"

I rubbed my lips together. "I guess because I want him to know the truth, and I love him."

"Does he know that?"

"I've never said it."

"Why?"

"Because then he can hurt me."

Dr. Morales nodded. "I see." She thought for a moment. "When you were a child, did you often feel helpless?"

"All the time. I felt like no one could or would save me."

"You wanted your father to save you?"

"Yes."

"Do you see Jonah as a father figure?"

"Not at all. He's not like that."

"Tell me more about him."

I thought she wanted me to explore my past before I thought about my future, but I guess choosing Jonah to be my safe person said I was already skipping ahead. Maybe that wasn't a good thing. "Was it wrong for me to choose Jonah as my safe person?" I had to ask.

"Ariana, I'm not judging your choices. The reasons you chose him are valid ones, but you don't need me to tell you that. It's important that you're confident in your choice." She set her notes to the side. "So, tell me about Jonah."

I wasn't sure where to begin. "What do you want to know?"

"Whatever you want to tell me." She leaned back and waited.

"Well, he's a doctor. He's divorced and has a daughter, Whitney."

"You smiled when you said his daughter's name. Why is that?"

Wow, this chick was invasive. "I like her. I like her a lot."

"Does she like you?"

I nodded. "We have a good time together."

"You spend a lot of time with her?"

"Yes. We see each other almost every day."

"Where does her mother fit in the picture? Am I correct to assume that is Jonah's ex-wife?"

I inadvertently squirmed in my seat. She tilted her head. "I've hit a nerve." The dang doctor was observant.

I clasped my hands together and twisted them. "Eliza is Jonah's ex-wife, and mother to Whitney."

"How do you feel about her?"

"Honestly?"

She grinned. "I want all your honest feelings."

"In that case, she intimidates me." Especially after the conversation Jonah and I had last night while I drew on his skin. I was hoping it would have been more romantic than it was, but I'd wanted to know more about Eliza and Jonah had obliged.

Dr. Morales waited patiently for me to continue.

I looked up at the stark white ceiling with the crystal chandelier I thought was odd for a doctor's office. "Eliza and I are very different. She's a powerhouse corporate woman who knows exactly what she wants in life. She was the one to pursue Jonah."

"That bothers you." She was so perceptive.

"Only because he really loved that about her. It makes me feel guilty for pushing him away a long time ago, and even now for being afraid of my feelings for him. I worry he'll want her back or she'll pursue him again when she stays with him."

Dr. Morales held up her hand. "She's staying with him?"

"During Christmas, so she can be closer to Whitney."

Dr. Morales pressed her lips together and thought for a moment. "Are you comfortable with that arrangement?"

"Not exactly, but I don't feel like I have a say in the matter."

"Why not?" Dr. Morales seemed surprised. "Have you talked to Jonah about how you feel about it?"

"Not really."

She scooted her chair closer to me. "Ariana, part of being in a solid relationship is not only being honest with your partner, but with yourself. You need to stop feeling guilty about your feelings."

"Please tell me how to do that," I begged.

"It's not easy, but one suggestion is to look for evidence. Meaning, do you have valid reasons to feel the way you do? You can also look for the emotion behind your feelings of guilt. Are you masking your emotions?"

"All the time," I laughed softly, though there was nothing funny about the situation.

"Let's see what we can do about that." She picked up her notes and scanned them quickly. "I think a lot of this goes back to you feeling helpless. You need to recognize that you're not helpless anymore. You don't need your father or anyone else to save you." She reached out and patted my knee. "Ariana, you saved yourself. You survived, and despite the circumstances of your childhood, you're a productive member of society. That is a pretty incredible feat, given your background. You need to give yourself credit for that."

I sat up a little taller.

"Don't let past traumas define your relationship with Jonah. You need to be honest with him so you can trust your feelings, and even his."

"That's what he said."

"He sounds like a smart guy."

"He is."

She grabbed her pen and notes and wrote while she spoke. "Your homework for this week is to keep working on those past traumas. Also, any time you start to feel helpless, I want you to remind yourself you're not that little girl anymore. List in your head what you have going for you, like your job, home, friends, family. All the things in your life that you created. I also want you to be cognizant of your feelings of guilt. Maybe even write them down in a journal and analyze them. Look for evidence to support your feelings and search out those underlying emotions beneath the guilt. If there is no reason for the guilt, let it go. Also," she looked up from her notes, "I want you to tell Jonah how you feel."

"You want me to tell him I love him?" I choked out in a panic.

She pursed her lips together. "I wasn't talking about that, though you should be working toward that if that's how you honestly feel. Feelings like those don't keep well inside. I was talking about his ex-wife."

"Oh." My heart rate slowed a bit.

"Can you do that?"

I nodded.

"You're doing a good job. I think you're making progress. I'll see you next week."

Great. Now all I had to do was tell Jonah I didn't want Eliza staying with him. That sounded like a lot of fun. Maybe I should start spending my money on something more fun than therapy, like a Brazilian wax job. That would be less painful than this.

"Dinner was great. Thank you." I reveled in the feel of our clasped hands swinging between us as we walked in the cold toward the comedy club, High on Laughs.

Jonah tugged on my hand, bringing me closer to him. "I'm glad you agreed to come out with me tonight. I wasn't sure if you would say yes if Whitney wasn't part of the package."

Whitney had been tentative when we'd dropped her off with my grandparents. Until Grandpa brought out his fossil collection and Grandma announced they were having stuffed zucchini for dinner. Whitney was pretty much in heaven. It was weird how much I missed her, though.

I nudged Jonah with my hip. "As much as I adore Whitney, there is something to be said about being alone with her father."

"Are you sure? You were quiet during dinner."

"I wasn't quiet. I was enthralled with a day in the life of Dr. Adkinson. It's not every day a seventy-year-old woman hits on you. I told you that earring was sexy." I laughed, thinking about Jonah's tale of the older woman telling him he would make a great fourth husband for her.

Jonah wrapped his arm around me and squeezed. "I told her I was saving myself for someone special."

"Is that so?"

"Most definitely." He kissed my head. "But . . . you were quiet during dinner. Did something happen in therapy today?"

I had been waiting for Jonah to bring up my therapy session. I knew it was probably a great segue into talking about my feelings, which I was awful at. But I was taking courage from Dr. Morales's words today. I wasn't helpless. If I wanted saving, I was going to have to do it myself. "It was a good session, but I do want to talk to you about something."

Jonah stopped and peered down at me concerned. "Should I be worried?"

I bit my lip. "Maybe."

He went pale. "Are you breaking up with me?"

"I didn't know we were going steady." I smiled.

He pulled me off to the side. My back ended up against a sandwich shop's brick wall. Jonah's body was dangerously close, shielding me from the cold. Passersby probably thought we were getting too cozy for public. I rested my hand on his chest.

"Ariana," he whispered, "whatever it is, we can work on it together. And if you need me to ask you to be my girlfriend, I will. I just assumed."

"Jonah," I rubbed my hand across his wool coat. "I'm not asking you for a title and I'm not 'breaking up' with you. I just need to tell you how I feel about some things."

The creases in his forehead smoothed while he let out a breath of relief. "But you want to be my girlfriend, right?"

"Will that make you feel better?" I couldn't hide the smile in my voice.

"It's a start."

I supposed we should start somewhere. It was a big step for me. I hadn't had a boyfriend since Kaden. "Maybe you should hear what I have to say before you decide if you want me to be your girlfriend. Does girlfriend sound juvenile?" I wasn't sure what one should call someone at this age.

"I can think of a much more mature title I would love for you to have." He brushed my cheek. "But I see by the color draining from your face we have a ways to go before we get there."

"Uh," I squeaked, trying to catch my breath. Wow, was he bold. It wasn't bad. In fact, I wished I could be so certain. I was working on it, which brought me back to that conversation we needed to have. "Why don't we talk when we get to the comedy club. I have a feeling we're garnering a lot of attention. I wouldn't be surprised if we ended up on some social media posts."

He leaned down and brushed my lips. "I would be happy to give people something to post about."

I pushed against his chest. "Dr. Adkinson, I don't think that would be in your best interest."

"I suppose you're right." He reached down and took my hand. "Let's go sort out your feelings together."

Together. I liked that.

chapter twenty-one

Jonah and I slipped into the back row of the comedy club, hoping to have a bit more privacy before it filled up. I'd never been here when it wasn't a full house. Tonight, they were doing sketch comedy, and the hilarious owners, Brad and Jenna, were headlining. Weird that people I went to high school with could draw such a crowd. I looked around the club decorated in movie memorabilia and spied a Rocky poster. I pointed at it for Jonah's benefit.

"I like this place already." He slung his arm across my chair. "What would you like to talk about?"

"Well—"

"Ariana, is that you?" A heavy Southern drawl interrupted me.

I turned around to see Shelby Prescott and her husband walking toward us. They could win a pageant for most gorgeous couple. I swore it was like an invisible spotlight shone directly on them. And Shelby, with her locks of gold, looked like a fan was blowing on her, strategically making her hair bounce perfectly. They were dressed to kill in clothes that showed off their amazing figures. I supposed I could thank her for helping me look presentable tonight in my skinny jeans and mint duster cardigan, seeing as the clothes came from her store.

Shelby, in all her Southerness, was to me in no time, taking the seat next to me and hugging me. "Darlin', you look absolutely fabulous." She kissed my cheek. "I told your grandma that this outfit would be perfect on you." She stood and grabbed her husband's hand. "I don't know if you've met my husband, Ryder."

"I think maybe once." I stood and shook his hand. "I'm Ariana."

Jonah stood too.

"And this is Jonah."

Jonah shook both Shelby's and Ryder's hands. "It's a pleasure to meet you."

Shelby's lit-up eyes looked between Jonah and me. "Your grandma said when she was in the boutique that your beau had moved back to town. How nice."

I was going to have words with my grandma later.

Jonah put his arm around me. "Best decision I ever made."

Ryder, who seemed to read the vibe Jonah was putting off, started pulling his wife away. "It was nice to meet y'all. Shelby, darlin', let's get our seats up front."

I felt Jonah relax next to me. We were just about to take our seats when another group of people walked in.

"Is that Taron Taylor?" Jonah gazed at Miles Wickham like he was a large bag of lime-flavored Skittles.

"Yes," Shelby answered happily, "but we just call him Miles."

"I've read all his books." I was pretty sure Jonah was about to fanboy.

"Then we better introduce y'all." Shelby went into Southern hospitality mode. She waved over the two couples, both of whom I knew. Emma and Sawyer King and Miles and Aspen Wickham. I didn't know Jonah was such a fan of Taron Taylor. If I'd known, I would have mentioned he and his wife had taken a class at the studio before.

Shelby introduced everyone to Jonah, but Jonah only had eyes for the British author. "I'm a huge fan of your work." Jonah vigorously shook Miles's hand. "I finished *Ascending Stones* last month and it was brilliant."

"Thanks, mate," Miles responded. "I always love to meet fans."

"I'm your biggest one," Jonah bragged.

Aspen, Miles's wife, leaned on her husband, patting his chest. "I think I might disagree with you on that account."

Everyone around us laughed, including Jonah.

"I'll take second biggest." Jonah wasn't deterred.

"Sold," Miles teased. "So, tell me what you do, Jonah." The famous author was awfully generous.

"I'm a doctor of internal medicine for a clinic in Pine Falls," Jonah replied.

"Really?" Miles seemed interested. "I'm actually working on a medical thriller, and I would love to pick your brain sometime, if you're amenable."

Jonah's face lit up like Whitney had just used three contractions in a row and called him Daddy. "Absolutely. Let me get you my card." Jonah reached into his pocket.

Meanwhile, Emma King got my attention. "It's so nice to see you again, Ariana. How's business going for you?"

I scooted out of the row so I could better converse with Emma while Jonah and Miles struck up a friendship. "It's been really busy, but good. How is your dad and your little ones?" She'd had twins earlier in the year.

"Our babies are perfect. Still keeping us up all hours of the night, but we couldn't be happier. My dad is in grandpa heaven. He bought my children actual ponies for Christmas this year. It's all downhill for them now. Sawyer and I can't top that."

Sawyer turned from talking to Ryder. "Did you say my name, babe?"

"I was just telling Ariana that we are doomed to be second best in the eyes of our children."

Sawyer wrapped his arm around his wife. "You'll always be number one in my book. We better go get our seats. Jenna and Brad are waving us to come up." They were the cutest couple.

"It was nice to see you both," I commented before they moved to the front with the Prescotts.

That left me standing and smiling at Jonah, who was animatedly using his hands while talking to Miles and Aspen. I was happy to see him so happy. When he took a breath, he noticed I had moved from his side. I loved that he paused and reached out his hand to me. I returned to his side and took his hand.

"I'm sorry," Jonah apologized to Miles and Aspen. "I'm keeping you from your friends."

Miles held out his hand to shake Jonah's. "It's been a pleasure, mate, I'll be in touch after the holidays."

Jonah gave Miles's hand a good shake. "I look forward to it."

The couple waved goodbye to us and we took our seats once again. The club was starting to fill up.

Jonah was buzzing next to me. "I can't believe I met Taron Taylor tonight. He's a top five author for me."

"It's a big night for you. I'm happy for you."

"You're teasing me." Jonah slid his arm across my shoulders.

"I really am happy for you. I just didn't know you had a man crush on Taron Taylor. Though he is very attractive." That accent would do anyone in.

Jonah's lips pursed. "Better looking than me?"

"Not to me." I leaned in and kissed his cheek.

Satisfied with my answer, Jonah pulled me closer to him. "What did you want to tell me?"

I looked around and not only was the club getting more crowded, but music began thumping in the background. It was getting to the point where we would have to raise our voices just to hear each other.

"It can wait." I spoke close to his ear so he would hear me.

His face pinched while he thought for a moment before unceremoniously standing.

"What are you doing?"

He held his hand out to me. "We're too important. We aren't waiting."

"Don't you want to watch the show?"

He shook his head, slow and careful, before reaching his hand farther out to me. I took it and he helped me stand and get into my coat, always the gentleman.

We ended up nearby at Sage Café. Jonah wrangled us a corner table near the hearth. It was quiet and cozy. We made small talk before our hot chocolate and brownie sundaes arrived. I figured what I had to say would sound better with chocolate. Wasn't everything made better by chocolate?

One of the things I loved about Jonah was that he didn't push. He let me sip my hot chocolate while I contemplated, or more like worked up my courage, to say what I needed to say. This wasn't exactly my strong suit. I barely admitted my feelings to myself and my goldfish. Goldie honestly was a little put out I didn't talk to her as much now that Jonah was back in town. I supposed I should quit stalling. But the hot chocolate was amazing. It was dark chocolate with a hint of peppermint and the yummiest whipped cream. I kept telling myself after each sip it would be my last one before I just let it out.

With my last sip, I'd finished the entire cup. I swallowed hard over and over. This was ridiculous. I set my cup down.

Jonah set his spoon in his empty dessert dish. He had polished off his brownie sundae and half of mine. He reached across the table and took my hand.

I looked down at our hands. The way his strong hand enveloped my slender fingers felt indicative of our relationship. I drew some courage from that.

"Today in therapy," I started, "Dr. Morales said it was important for me to be as honest as possible with you about how I feel."

"I hope you will be."

"You say that now." I gave him a small smile.

He held unnaturally still. I knew I had worried him. I just needed to get this over with and put us both out of our misery. "So, here's the thing. I'm uncomfortable with Eliza staying with you over Christmas," I rushed to say.

Immediately Jonah's tense shoulders relaxed, but in the next second he squinted. "I told you there's nothing going on between us."

"That's not exactly true. You were married, and you share a child. There's a lot going on between you."

"Ariana," he brushed his thumb across my hand, "she stays with us for Whitney's sake. There's nothing romantic going on between us."

"Now. But there was, and feelings like that just don't go away. She's admitted to still being in love with you. And look how quickly we rekindled our romance after so many years."

"That's different."

"How?" I used my free hand to pick up my spoon and indulge in what was left of my brownie sundae. Like I said, chocolate made everything better. At least I hoped it would. I shoved a large spoonful of brownie and fudge in my mouth and let it settle my nerves.

Jonah reached across the table and swiped some lingering chocolate off my lips with his finger. I would have been embarrassed except it was him, and when he licked the chocolate off his finger, I had to catch my breath. Dang, that was hot.

"You want to know how it's different?" he whispered. "What I just did there would have had Eliza scowling at me. You look like you want to crawl over the table and onto my lap." He was spot on.

"Would you mind?"

He pulled my hand up and kissed my palm, letting his lips linger as if to say he wouldn't mind at all. He made me wish we were alone so I could curl up on his lap.

He set my hand down but kept ahold of it. "Ariana, the romance between Eliza and me died a long time ago. You and I just paused ours."

"What if we kill what we have?"

"I knew you were going to say that. But I'm not worried because you've never treated me like a business associate, or worse, an employee. You don't flinch when I touch you because it's outside of the intimacy schedule you created for us."

I tilted my head. "Intimacy schedule?"

"She had a schedule for everything," Jonah lamented.

"Everything?"

"Everything." He enunciated every syllable.

Yikes.

"You don't know how wonderful it is when I touch you and you reciprocate, not out of obligation, but because you want me."

"I do want you," I easily admitted.

"And you are the only woman I want."

"Jonah, I understand that, but what if the roles were reversed? How would you like it if my ex was staying with me? Regardless of the circumstances."

He paused and pressed his lips together like he had never considered it. "I wouldn't like it." Dawning washed over his face. "I'll ask her to get a hotel."

I almost said I didn't want to cause any problems because I felt guilty for getting my way and causing Jonah angst, but then I checked the guilt thermometer and it said my feelings were one hundred degrees of valid. "Thank you," I said instead, even though it was difficult for me.

"Thank you for being honest with me." He leaned over the table and motioned with his finger that I should do the same. "I think you missed some chocolate on your lips. I better help you with that."

I leaned in too, not quite meeting him. "Make sure you get it all."

"I've got you covered." He closed the gap and pressed his lips against mine for a few soul-stirring seconds. He still had the gift of making butterflies take flight in my stomach. He rested his hand on my cheek when his lips glided off mine. He peered into my eyes. "Will you be my girlfriend?"

Wow. It was getting real. We'd never had a title before. But he did just kick his ex-wife out for me. And was he ever charming. Dr. Morales's voice rang in my head, telling me to be honest about my feelings. The truth was I did want to be Jonah's girlfriend. Did it scare me? To death. But . . . "I guess it's a start."

His eyes widened. "I thought you were going to say no."

"I didn't say yes," I teased.

"Please say yes."

"Yes."

chapter twenty-two

"I can't believe you're Facebook official." Grandma dipped her brush into the pink paint.

"I can't believe you're on Facebook." I admired Grandma's handiwork from across her kitchen table. She was helping me fulfill the secret Christmas wish I'd overheard Whitney tell Tabitha two weeks ago.

Whitney was determined not to believe in Santa Claus. She had done the research, googled a thousand articles that told her all that she needed to know. Santa Claus was a big fat fake that parents used as a tool to make their children behave during the holidays. But on the off chance the jolly man was real, she wished for a doll that looked like her and was dressed in a pink frilly dress complete with petticoats.

Surprise, surprise, she'd never had a doll before. When I'd asked Jonah why, he said Eliza felt that it bred unhealthy stereotypes. Whitney wasn't even allowed to have a career girl Barbie. Well, that was about to change. Jonah and I had searched high and low the last couple of weeks for a doll meeting Whitney's requirements. We came up emptyhanded, which was why Grandma and I were furiously working late into the night on the twenty-third of December.

Grandma filled in the doll's rosy cheeks with the pink. "I have to keep up with the times, and apparently you. Kinsley helped me create an account after she told me Jonah had announced to the world you were in a relationship. Something you failed to mention." She flashed me a wry grin.

I rolled my eyes before focusing back on sewing the tiny pearl buttons on the back of the doll's dress I had sewn with Grandma's help. "I wasn't trying to keep anything from anybody. I figured it was obvious."

Jonah, Whitney, and I were pretty much inseparable. Unless I was working on secret Christmas projects, working, or going to therapy, we were together. But Jonah had thrown me for a loop when, a couple days ago, he made us Facebook official. That was so nine years ago. I didn't know people even did that anymore. But I didn't begrudge him the opportunity to announce it to the world. After all, I had made the man wait over nine years to say we were a couple. It was quite the shock, though, when I started getting dozens of notifications from people I had forgotten I was even "friends" with, all congratulating me. I wasn't a huge social media person unless I was posting on the studio's page. I mean, my personal profile picture was of Goldie. Maybe now that I wasn't wearing holey sweaters or baggy jeans every day, I should update that.

"I'm happy to see things are going so well for you," Grandma commented. "How are you feeling about his parents and his ex-wife coming in tomorrow?"

Ugh. I had been dreading it since Jonah and I had talked a couple of weeks ago about my feelings regarding Eliza staying with him. When he'd dropped me off that night, he threw in that his parents had decided to come for Christmas too. The same parents who didn't like me but loved their ex-daughter-in-law. They loved her so much, they'd decided to stay at the same hotel as her and not with Jonah. That seemed wrong somehow. I had asked Jonah how Eliza felt about getting a hotel and he said she understood. I asked if that meant she was okay with it, and all he would say was she understood.

So basically, I was hoping for some bad weather and flight delays so I could enjoy my holidays in peace—you know, after I opened the letter from Roger Stanton. This Christmas was fraught with peril. Which was too bad because it was putting a damper on my excitement to give Jonah his gift and to see him and Whitney in the matching pajamas I had bought the three of us. They had dinosaurs in Christmas hats on them and I had planned on us wearing them tomorrow night while living out my tradition of watching every Christmas movie known to man and eating as many sugar cookies as we possibly could. That was, after Jonah's parents and Eliza left to hang out at the chalet in Carrington Cove.

"I feel sick to my stomach," I responded to Grandma.

Grandma looked up from the beautiful doll's head. We had found the perfect sandy brown wig and Grandma had painted the eyes to look just like Whitney's. "You go over there tomorrow night and show them what you're made of. You should be proud of your life. You run a business and are a talented, respected artist in this community. And who is the one there for Whitney day in and day out? It's certainly not her mother," she was getting fired up. "I'm all for women living their dreams and having careers, but the way she stays away from her child like that, I have no respect for it." She clutched her paint brush so hard I thought it might snap. "The poor girl didn't even have any friends until you intervened. Honestly, Jonah bears some of the blame too, but at least he's trying and is present in her life."

Jonah wore that blame like a lead cloak. But Whitney was making progress. Her use of contractions was getting better, and she had made a friend at school. A new girl named Persephone who was behind in math and, unfortunately, teased because of her name. Whitney stuck up for her and helped her with math. They were now bosom buddies. And she and

Tabitha were still two peas in a pod, especially now since it was Christmas break and Whitney spent entire days at Tabitha's house, probably planning to rule the world or create a real-life Jurassic Park.

"I'm just hoping I can graciously swallow down the vegan meal his mother and Eliza are preparing and keep my foot out of my mouth." I cut a piece of thread with my tiny scissors.

Grandma dabbed her brush into the paint with a scowl on her face. "And why are they making dinner and not you and Jonah? You're the hosts."

"It's not my house and it's not like we're you know . . ." I mumbled. I was staying away from the M word and all the words associated with it. I was still getting used to *girlfriend.*

"But you're his better half."

That sounded weird, but I guess since it was Facebook official, it was true. "It's fine. Besides, I have to, you know, wait for a certain letter tomorrow and I never know when it's going to show up." Typically, it was always by early afternoon.

Grandma dropped the brush, splattering paint on her smock. She didn't bother to pick it up. "You're really opening it?"

Grandpa, walking down the stairs from the loft wearing plaid thermal underwear and a tweed trapper hat, prevented me from answering. He was quite the sight. "It's about time," he growled. "I should have tried to find the SOB myself, or insisted your mother show me those damn letters." Grandpa landed next to Grandma and stood behind her chair, putting a comforting hand on her shoulder.

Grandma's eyes welled up with tears.

I set the dress down. "Why are you crying?"

Grandma waved her hand in front of her face. "I keep beating myself up that we let this nonsense go on for so long. And . . . I'm worried that tomorrow will change things," she reluctantly admitted.

I tilted my head. "Change things how?"

Grandpa went and got Grandma a tissue from the kitchen counter before handing it to her. Grandma dabbed her eyes. "I know it's silly, but I've always wondered who you looked like with your strawberry blonde hair and your willowy figure."

It was true my mom and grandma were shorter and stockier than me. And no one had my hair color. Honestly, I had been staring at Roger's picture as of late and really looking at his eyes, wondering if mine truly were like his or if I had talked myself into it just because my mom had said he was my dad.

"Tomorrow," Grandma sniffled, "you may get the answer to that question and very well find out about your other family. You may love them more than us," she blubbered.

"Grandma." I stood, walked over to her, and knelt in front of her. Both her and Grandpa stared down at me. "How could I ever love them more than you? They've ignored me my entire life. For all we know, Roger Stanton isn't even my father."

"Then why has he been sending you letters all these years?"

I shrugged. "Are you sure Mom never said anything else about him?"

They both thought for a moment before shaking their heads.

I sunk to the floor.

Grandma patted my head. "Do you want us to wait with you tomorrow?"

"No," I sighed. I wanted to do this alone, and I would have the loft to myself. Dani was always busy delivering toys to foster kids on Christmas Eve, and Kinsley would be working late. A lot of people ate out on Christmas Eve. Jonah had, of course, offered to wait with me, but he needed to be with his parents and Whitney. I knew his parents wouldn't take kindly to him being gone, and I already felt like I would be walking on landmines around them. "This is something I need to face by myself. I want to do like my therapist said and internalize the truth before I share it," I explained to my grandparents.

I was hoping Dr. Morales was right, that the truth would set me free. She and I had talked extensively about it today during my appointment. And while she thought I was making good progress and was even proud of me when I'd admitted to hating my mother without making excuses, she knew I was holding back with Jonah, even if we were official. I still hadn't told him how I really felt about him after all these years. Dr. Morales said I needed to make peace with all the men of my past, including all my mom's loser husbands, but especially the mystery man, before I could move forward with the man in my present.

I rested my head in Grandma's lap and let her stroke my hair.

"We love you so much," she said. "We're here for you if you need us. Just say the word."

"I appreciate that, but hopefully after tomorrow I can put Roger Stanton in my past and move on."

chapter twenty-three

Has the letter arrived yet? Jonah texted for the tenth time in the last two hours.

Not yet. I looked at the kitchen clock, which said 1:00 p.m. Any minute now it could be here. I paced the apartment, wringing my hands, stopping to straighten the pillows on the couch for the hundredth time. I headed into my room. Maybe Goldie was hungry again. I approached her fishbowl and her bulging eyes begged me not to sprinkle any more food into her bowl. Fine. I sat on my bed and tapped my foot.

"What's taking so long?" I lamented to Goldie.

I popped off the bed and headed for my standing mirror. I looked at myself and smoothed out the cream cami under the blush blazer I was wearing. I stood to the side and checked out my profile. I pulled my hair back to see what it would look like up versus down in the current waterfall curls. I hated being this nervous about my appearance, especially for people I had little chance of impressing. I wasn't sure what I was more nervous about today, facing my past or my future.

Unfortunately, the parents and the ex-wife had arrived this morning. Where was a good blizzard when you needed one?

Let me know as soon as it gets there.

I'll let you know. I promise.

Hurry. I miss you.

I'll be there as soon as I can.

Apparently, his parents liked to have an early dinner on Christmas Eve.

You didn't say you missed me, Jonah responded, making me smile.

I'll prove it to you when I get there. I'm bringing mistletoe.

A woman of action. I like it.

I tossed my phone on my bed and rearranged Jonah's and Whitney's gifts I had stacked there. I had even made gifts for Jonah's parents and Eliza—little mosaics that could be hung on a kitchen window.

I had a feeling Jonah was going to lose his mind when he opened an entire box filled with bags of strawberry and lime Skittles. They made a special holiday edition with only the two flavors, and I bought out practically every bag from the nearby grocery stores.

I was even more excited for Whitney to get her doll tomorrow from Santa Claus. From me, she was getting illustrated classic books like *Little Women* and *Pride and Prejudice,* so either Jonah or I could read them to her at night. They were better than what Jonah was reading to her now. *How to Become a CEO Before You Turn 20.* That was Eliza's idea of a good bedtime story. Say what you wanted to about fairytales and coming-of-age stories, children needed to dream. And I don't mean dreaming about owning your own Fortune 500 company. They needed to imagine and play. As silly as fairytales may be, they gave children that opportunity.

Speaking of Eliza, I wondered how understanding she was still being about all this. Jonah told me not to worry, as Eliza prided herself on always being reasonable and in control. Oddly, Jonah didn't like that about her. He wanted her to be more emotional. I could be plenty emotional. Like right now. Where was that stupid courier with my letter? While I feared the letter for whatever reason I still couldn't put my finger on, I also wanted to get it over with.

After I rearranged the gifts for the tenth time, I headed for the kitchen where I received texts from Kinsley, Dani, and even Brock and Brant, all asking if I'd gotten the letter. I replied to each person before eating one of the sugar cookies I was taking to Jonah's. I bit the head off the red sprinkled snowman with a vengeance. Where was the freaking courier? Didn't he know I had other mountains to tackle today? Not to mention lips to kiss and the cutest girl to hug.

It was weird how I found myself missing Whitney as much as Jonah. That little girl had worked herself right into my heart and was planting deep roots. The kind that, if uprooted, would cause a hole that might never heal. The same kind her dad dug all those years ago, which were burrowing in deeper and deeper every day. I rubbed my chest. It hurt just thinking about us all not being together.

Positive thoughts, positive thoughts, positive thoughts. Dr. Morales's soothing voice came to me. She said I needed to rewire my brain to think positively. I was positive I was going to go mad if that stupid letter didn't show up soon.

Three hours later, I was beyond mad. The letter had never come this late. And I was late. Jonah's parents wanted to eat at four. I called Jonah again. "Maybe you should start without me. I'm sorry."

"Don't apologize. We can wait. Are you okay?"

I laid my head back on the couch. "I don't know. Why, out of all the years, is it late?"

"Who knows. Maybe the courier has had a busy day."

"Or maybe this is a sign."

"What kind of a sign?"

"Never mind."

"Ariana, you can talk to me."

"I know. I'll call you later."

"Hey," he got in before I could hang up, "even if the letter doesn't come, it's not the end of the world. Maybe you should just come over."

Tears stung my eyes. For whatever reason, it did kind of feel like the end of the world. I knew it was completely melodramatic, but I thought I might find out who my father was and why he never came for me. I was hoping this was going to be a new beginning for me.

"You don't know what this means to me," I said more testily than I meant to.

Jonah didn't respond right away. "Ariana, maybe you're right, but because it's important to you it's important to me."

"I'm sorry I snapped at you," I choked out.

"You're stressed. I get it."

"What am I going to do if it doesn't come?"

"We'll figure it out together."

"Okay. I'm going to give it until five. Will that be all right with your parents and Eliza?"

"It will have to be." I heard the strain in his voice, which wasn't helping my mental state.

"I'm sorry."

"Don't apologize. I'll see you soon."

I spent the next hour pacing in front of the door, even opening it several times to see if someone was coming down the hall or up the stairs. Each time it was desolate, like my heart was beginning to feel. At five I wrote a note and plastered it to the door directing any courier or delivery person to call. It took everything I had not to cry on the drive over to Jonah's. Why was this happening? Maybe it was a sign. A sign I wasn't meant to move on.

I arrived at Jonah's laden down with gifts, so much so, I could hardly see where I was walking as I approached his handsome brick house with white lights, courtesy of me, strung across his front porch. It brought me some peace and warmth just thinking about the day we put them up together. Whitney's face had split into a huge smile when she flipped the switch and the twinkle lights reflected in her beautiful eyes. Maybe I didn't need to know the man of my past to move forward with the man who opened his door half grinning and half harried.

"You're here," he said, relieved, while taking boxes and bags out of my hands.

"I'm sorry, I'm late." I didn't mention the letter. I had already texted him that it hadn't come. I texted everyone else too, though I had received phone calls from my friends and grandparents. I let them all go to voice-mail. I knew if I talked to anyone about it, the tears would flow and maybe never stop.

Jonah gave me a quick peck and headed for the tree to deposit every gift except for Whitney's doll. I was keeping that in my car until after she went to bed tonight. I followed Jonah but was stopped right outside his kitchen, while he went straight to the tree.

Whitney ran to me and hugged my legs. "You're here," she said excitedly. She had no idea what that meant to me in the moment.

I knelt and hugged her. "Hi, sweet girl. Don't you look gorgeous." She was wearing the cute denim dress I'd bought for her last week when I happened to run across it. And for some fun, I'd gotten her tights with reindeer on them.

"It's a lot of denim," a disapproving voice I hadn't heard in a long time said.

It was then I looked up and realized I was being stared down by three people who didn't seem to approve of the moment I was having with Whitney. I stood slowly and took Whitney's hand. I needed her to ground me while I faced her grandparents and mom.

Jonah's mother, Carol Adkinson, was the one who had lobbed the offending comment my way. She stood with her arms folded and her brow so furrowed she resembled a Pug, but her attitude was all Pit Bull. I would have said she was an attractive woman with her long silver hair and trim figure, but the angry waves coming off her made her ugly to me. But I would be cordial for Whitney's and Jonah's sake.

"It's nice to see you again, Mr. and Mrs. Adkinson." I turned to Eliza, who I could tell was trying to put on a reasonable face, but by the way her jaw was pulsing, I knew she wasn't the same woman from Thanksgiving who wanted to be my friend. The way she was staring at Whitney's hand in mine said she'd like to chop off my hand and throw it in the garbage disposal. "And it's nice to see you as well, Eliza. I hope you had a good flight." I hoped she'd have an even better one to wherever she was going next, but I kept that to myself.

She flexed her fingers like she was counting in her head, trying to compose herself. She looked stunning while doing it. She'd pulled out all the stops and looked amazing in a sleek cream pant suit that fit her like a glove. I felt drab compared to her.

"My flight was excellent. Thank you for asking," she stiffly replied, not bothering with any other pleasantries.

When Jonah finally joined us outside his kitchen, he wrapped his arm around me. "Mom, Dad, you remember Ariana, right?" He tried to ease the tension that was strung tight now between what looked like two camps. One for me, and one that would like to see me lose everything.

Jonah's dad, Paul, at least, had some manners. He buttoned his charcoal corduroy jacket and ran a hand over his balding head before walking my way. He stuck out his hand. "I'm glad you could *finally* join us." He had to add a jab in there.

I took his soft looking, age-spotted hand and shook it anyway. "I'm sorry I'm late," I apologized again and for the last time.

Carol began untying her apron. "I don't understand why we had to wait on a package. It couldn't have been that important." She threw her apron on the counter and grabbed a serving dish.

I wanted to yell that she had no idea what she was talking about, but Jonah beat me to the punch. "Mom, it wasn't just any package, and we aren't going to discuss it further."

He had no idea how much I appreciated his candor and the fact that it sounded like he hadn't mentioned what I was waiting for. I could only imagine what his dentist parents would think of that.

Carol tsked.

Eliza spun on her heels. "We should eat."

"Excellent idea," Paul agreed.

Paul, Carol, and Eliza each grabbed a dish from the kitchen counter and headed toward the table in the kitchen nook, which was decorated to look like a fancy five-star restaurant in white table linens and crystal candlesticks. I knew those weren't Jonah's. Did his parents pack that kind of stuff in their luggage? Weird.

"I want to sit by Arianna," Whitney announced, which I loved, but I knew it wasn't helping my cause.

Eliza slammed a silver platter onto the table. It was full of unrecognizable green leafy things that looked less like food and more like she had gone out to the forest near Jonah's home and foraged.

"As long as I can sit on the other side of you," Eliza tried to sound lighthearted, but she sounded more like a razor blade.

I looked up at Jonah and his eyes said, *hang in there with me*. What my grandma said about showing them who I was sounded in my head. And in a couple of hours, it would only be Whitney, Jonah, and me in Christmas dinosaur pajamas, binging on cookies and movies. I could do this. Maybe? The helpless little girl in me kept wanting to come out. I held her back, took Jonah's hand, and let him lead us to the firing squad, I mean table.

Whitney did, indeed, sit next to me. Thankfully, Jonah took my other side. Unfortunately, that meant I was staring straight at his parents across the round table. They looked between me and Jonah like I was their worst nightmare come to life. Then they looked at Eliza with pity. Did they even care that it was Eliza who'd left Jonah? Or that she hardly saw her daughter and couldn't even find the time to call her regularly?

Jonah cleared his throat once everyone was seated. "I'm glad you could all be here. And thank you to everyone who," he looked at the spread in front of him, "helped with the, uh, food."

I had a feeling he would be eating a lot of cookies later.

"I hope it isn't cold," his mother spewed.

"It will be fine," Jonah's tone said to knock it off. That made his mom glare at me.

For a small moment, I thought I might survive. While everyone was filling their plates, Eliza, Carol, and Paul seemed content to talk amongst themselves about world news and politics, which I wasn't touching with a ten-foot pole. But once everyone started eating, Carol and Paul wanted to show Jonah what he was missing out on with Eliza, while also showcasing the differences between Eliza and me.

"Eliza, I heard from your mother that there was a write-up about you in *Forbes Magazine*. I'm going to need a copy of that," Carol gushed.

Eliza flashed me a grin before she responded. "Yes. I was asked to take part in an exposé about unstoppable women. It will be out next quarter."

"I'm going to get ten copies. We always said you were a *winner*." Carol gave Jonah a meaningful look.

I got it. She meant I was a loser. Well, this loser was going to focus on what was important in her life—the people she loved. And swallowing down the roasted broccoli that hadn't been seasoned at all. Hadn't these people ever heard of salt?

"Did you have fun with Tabitha yesterday at the children's museum?" I asked Whitney.

Whitney's eyes lit up. "We played chess with pieces as tall as me. And I won."

"That's amazing. I'm proud of you."

My praise for Whitney got Eliza's attention. "Whitney, tell me what you learned there." Eliza gave me a condescending look as if I had no idea how to deal with a child.

Whitney thought for a moment. Her lips began to quiver. "Well, I . . ."

"It's okay, honey," Jonah entered the fray. "Sometimes it's good just to have fun."

Whitney's tiny shoulders sagged. "I did paint." Poor thing didn't want to disappoint her mother.

Jonah scowled at Eliza.

Eliza squared her shoulders and gave Jonah a pointed look. I, on the other hand, put my arm around Whitney. "I can't wait to see your painting."

Whitney looked up at me with her big green eyes. "It's a picture of you and me decorating the Christmas tree. I painted the clothespin dolls we made."

I tapped her nose and almost cried. That was the sweetest thing. "I bet it's the best picture ever."

Controlled Eliza dropped her fork and it clanged against the fine china—which was also not Jonah's. I'm not sure how all this froufrou stuff got here, but it was of little consequence now that the holy war had begun.

"I did not realize how crafty you are," Eliza said curtly.

"Jonah said you were still making stained glass for a living. I didn't even know that was a viable profession anymore." Carol turned up her nose at me. I guess that meant they were going to hate their presents from me. Why I ever thought I should bother, I didn't know. I would keep the mosaics for myself.

I squeezed Jonah's thigh under the table. "It pays the bills, but thank you for your concern." My sarcasm lit an unquenchable fire making Carol's gloves come off.

Carol wiped her mouth with a white linen napkin. "Where do you learn to do something like that?"

"At the hand of my grandma." I was proud to admit.

"Oh, that's right, I forgot you didn't go to school." She smiled in that condescending sort of way.

"Mom," Jonah's tone warned her, "don't go down this road."

"What road is that? The one where you're throwing your life away? Look at you, with an earring and making a third of the money you were back in Connecticut. All for what?" Carol glowered at me.

In that moment, I felt smaller than I had in a long time, but then I remembered that I wasn't a child anymore. I wasn't helpless. I did like Dr. Morales said and listed in my head all the things I had in my power. On top of my list was the ability to walk, and transportation. I pushed my chair back, making it screech against the tile floor, and stood. "I'll be going now."

Jonah grabbed my hand. "Please don't go," he pled. He whipped his head toward his parents and Eliza and addressed them. "Don't make me choose. You won't like the outcome."

I hated this. I would never make Jonah choose. "Merry Christmas, everyone." I leaned down and kissed Whitney's head. "I love you." The words fell out of my mouth so naturally. But it was true, I did love her, and it was why I was going to leave. I refused to cause any rifts in her family. "I hope Santa Claus is good to you tonight."

"She knows there is no such person," Eliza scolded me. "Only uneducated people believe in such nonsense."

"I guess it's a good thing I'm not as smart as you then." I walked out of the kitchen with my head held high, but inside I felt small. I felt like that girl back in second grade who wore the same dirty clothes to school every day.

Jonah was hot on my heels. I made it to the front door before he grabbed my hand. "Ariana, don't go. You belong here."

I looked around his beautiful home. The pit in my stomach deepened. The little girl inside of me with greasy hair wanted to shrivel inside herself. "You know, I don't think I do. I think today was a sign. I'm not meant to move on, and I don't belong in your world. I never did."

"That's not true."

He was wrong. I grabbed my bag and threw open his door. He followed me out into the thirty-degree weather in his bare feet. I marched toward my car and popped the trunk with my key fob. I retrieved Whitney's doll, carefully wrapped in a silver box with a big red bow. I handed it to Jonah.

"This is Whitney's doll."

Jonah refused to take it. "You can put it under the tree with me tonight."

"I won't be here," my voice was as unsteady as I felt. "Take it." I held it out farther.

He still refused. "I'll go kick my parents and Eliza out right now."

"No, you won't. Not in front of Whitney, and not on my account."

"What do you mean on your account? It's on my account. I want to spend the rest of my life with you. You and Whitney mean more to me than anyone."

I looked up at the clear night sky. I swear the bright stars were blinking out a message that said the universe was against me. Hadn't it always been, since my birth? "We aren't meant to last. We never were," I choked out.

"Dammit, Ariana, why are you always looking for an excuse to push me away?"

I met his furious eyes. The heavy breaths he was forcing out swirled in the cold air, making him look even angrier.

"I don't need to look for them. It's just our reality."

He threw his hands up. "Fine. I'm done trying to convince you. If you want me, I'll be here. But you're going to have to decide once and for all."

I felt like the world already had. I shoved the box at him. "Goodbye, Jonah."

His wide eyes said he couldn't believe I was leaving, but he determinedly took the box. "Goodbye, Ariana." He said it with such soul crushing finality I could hardly catch my breath.

Hot tears stung my cold cheeks while the universe laughed. It got what it wanted. It made sure I got my *return* in for the day. Never, though, had it felt like I'd returned my heart along with the letter.

chapter twenty-four

The stupid note I'd left the courier was on the door when I returned home. I ripped it off and crumpled it before tossing it down the hall. I walked into the loft to find it eerily quiet. I'd never felt so alone. I kept telling myself it was better this way. Better to return Jonah before it went any further, but I didn't feel better at all. I failed therapy. Or maybe therapy failed me.

I thought today was the day I would get my Christmas wish. That I would be free to love and be loved. That's what I always really wanted for Christmas every year. Maybe I asked for it in presents I never got, but those gifts represented the ache I had in my life to be truly loved. Once again, I would be going to bed on Christmas Eve knowing there would be no Christmas magic come morning. The tree would be metaphorically empty.

I didn't even bother putting on pajamas. All I did was turn off my phone, crawl into bed, snuggle in deep under my covers, and curl into a ball. One good thing my childhood had taught me how to do was fall asleep under any circumstance. It was like I had selective narcolepsy; it was my body's defense mechanism. While things weren't always better in the morning, it at least meant I got at least eight hours of not having to live whatever pain I was experiencing. When I was little it meant I was free of the fighting and drinking. If I was lucky enough, it meant waking up to my mom's husband or boyfriend being gone for the day, or gone for good, in some instances.

Tonight it would mean not feeling small and inferior, not feeling at all. I didn't think I could take the gnawing pain in my chest where my heart once beat. All that was there now was a desolate abyss. I closed my eyes and let sleep overtake me. Tomorrow I would feel the full loss of Jonah.

I didn't know how long I slept, but when I woke, it didn't feel like I had gotten in a full night of reprieve. My room was too dark, and I was groggy. But maybe I was dreaming because I could feel Jonah. He was stroking my brow and brushing back my hair. He sounded unwell; his voice was hoarse.

"Ariana," he whispered over and over again. I squeezed my eyes shut, willing this tortuous dream to go away. I couldn't afford to love him even in my dreams.

"Ariana," his voice came again, but this time it was accompanied by a kiss.

My eyes flew open. I could make out a man's shape kneeling near my bed, outlined in darkness. "Jonah," I squeaked, "who let you in here?"

"I called Dani and told her what happened tonight, and she let me in. I'm sorry to wake you, but it couldn't wait until morning."

Panic overtook me, and I pushed myself up, propping half my body up on my pillows. "Is someone hurt? Whitney?"

He raised himself, but still remained on his knees. He ran the back of his hand down my damp cheek. I must have cried myself to sleep. "Shh. Everyone is fine."

I pulled my knees up to my chest. "Then why are you here?" His words rang loud in my head that he was tired of the chase. I could hardly blame him, even though I never meant for him to feel like I had him on the run.

He sat on the edge of my bed. It was then in the dim light from under the door I noticed his eyes were brighter than normal because they were bloodshot.

"Have you been crying?" I asked.

"Would you think me less of a man if I said yes?"

"Of course not." I rested my head on my knees. "Why have you been crying?"

"Because," he scooted closer, waves of heat rolling off him, "I promised you I would fight for you, and tonight I didn't. I broke my promise to you."

"I'm the one who left." I paused. "Just go home," I begged. I couldn't take the hope his presence brought.

His strong hand rested on my cheek. "I'm not going anywhere."

"Where's Whitney?" emotion crept into my voice.

"She's home, sound asleep with my parents and her mother," he growled.

I stiffened at the mention of his parents and ex.

His thumb brushed across my cheek. "I'm so sorry for the way they treated you. For the way I treated you."

"You? What did you do?"

"I knew you were upset about the letter not coming. I was stressed because of my parents and Eliza. I should have told them to all go to hell and brought Whitney over here."

I closed my eyes. "Tonight was a good reminder. I don't fit into your world. Your parents are never going to like me, and I've had enough of people who don't want me or like me. I have a father and five stepfathers who never wanted me. I don't need a future mother-in-law and father-in-law who despise me. Or an ex-wife who thinks I'm below her."

"Ariana, please stop saying you don't belong in my world. You are my world. After you left tonight, I made it very clear to my parents and Eliza that it is they who don't belong. And if they want to be part of my life, and Whitney's, they need to change their behavior, whether or not you're part of the picture. But I can't imagine my life without you. I don't want to," he pled.

I opened my eyes and lifted my head. "How did they take that?"

"Not well at first, but then Whitney said, 'Ariana is my best friend. She always helps me when I'm afraid and she does nice things for me. I love her.'"

Tears rolled down my cheeks. "She really said that?"

"She did." He beamed.

"I love her too."

"I know you do. Eliza knows it too, and that's harder for her than she thought it would be, but I'm not making excuses for her or my parents. Whitney gave them a lot to think about."

"I have no doubt." I smiled thinking about that sweet girl.

Jonah moved in closer and placed his arm across me. "Ariana, please forgive me. I was a jerk tonight. I didn't mean what I said. I will spend my last breath trying to convince you we belong together if that's what it takes."

"That's not fair to you."

"Then make it easy on me and believe me when I say there is no other woman I want to share my life with." He rested his head against mine, making our noses touch. He nuzzled mine with his own.

A small giggle escaped me.

"I love that sound. I know it scares you to hear this, but I love you even more."

I knew he did. And I wanted to tell him how much I loved him, but the words wouldn't come. That scared little girl inside of me still lived. I needed to make her whole before I could say such things to him.

"Do you forgive me?"

"You don't have anything to apologize for."

"I'm going to take that as a yes." He brushed his lips against mine without actually kissing me before gently stroking my lower lip with his thumb. The tease made the anticipation grow between us. He leaned in with his lips slightly parted, allowing us to breathe in and out together. Then he did something he had never done before—his tongue outlined my lips, making me gasp and sending shivers of delight through my body.

"You like that," he whispered.

I nodded.

"How about this?" He trailed soft kisses down my neck.

I wove my hands into his hair.

He moved down, pressing kisses against my collar bone. "Mmm," he groaned against my skin before his lips found mine again. He pressed his body against mine, pushing me against my pillows. The tip of his tongue parted my lips. We fell into a gentle rhythm until he abruptly pulled away, breathing hard.

"We shouldn't do this in your bed."

I sat up and ran my fingers through my hair. "That's probably a good idea."

He gave me a sly smile. "This calls for bundling."

"Bundling?"

"It's a colonial courting tradition where a girl's parents would wrap a boy and girl together in bed, fully clothed, so they could spend the night being intimate without sex."

"Is this a real thing? I feel like taking a page out of Whitney's book and googling it."

He held up his hand. "I swear on my honor as a gentleman it's true."

"What time is it? Don't you need to go home?"

He looked at his watch. "It's almost midnight and as long as I'm home before Whitney wakes up it's fine. In fact, I was hoping you would come home with me. I want us to be together on Christmas morning."

I bit my lip and contemplated his offer.

"Don't you want to see Whitney's reaction to the doll?"

He got me there. "I do."

"It's a plan. Now scoot over. We have some bundling to do."

I inched over to give him some room on my full-size bed. He kicked off his shoes and crawled under the covers with me. He opened his arms and I accepted his invitation to snuggle against him. My head landed on his chest. My favorite place to rest.

"Merry Christmas," he whispered.

"Merry Christmas, Jonah."

"This is nice," Jonah stroked my hair. "We should bundle more often."

I kissed his chest. "I'm still fact-checking you in the morning."

A laugh rumbled in his chest.

We lay still and quiet for a moment. Only the sounds of our beating hearts and breaths could be heard. After several minutes I sighed. "Why do you think the letter didn't come today?"

"Hmm." His fingers glided down my arm. "I don't know. Maybe it got lost or . . . maybe he died," he hesitated to say.

I hadn't thought of that as a possibility. I wasn't sure how to feel about it. Did I even have any emotion for a dead father who'd ignored me my entire life?

"If that's true, how will I ever know who my father is and why he sent me a letter every year? How will I put my past to rest when it's still a mystery to me?"

"I'll hire a private investigator and you can take one of those DNA tests to see if it gives us any clues. Hell, we'll post about it on Facebook. We'll figure it out. I promise you, we'll find out who he is. And when you're ready to close the door on that chapter in your life, I'll be there on the other side, pen in hand, waiting to write out the pages of our life together."

That was the most beautiful thing anyone had ever said to me. I snuggled closer against him. "Please be patient."

"I'm not going anywhere."

For once, I allowed myself to believe him. I closed my eyes, but this time I knew things would be better in the morning because I knew whose arms I would find myself in. And for once, on Christmas morning, I wouldn't feel alone.

chapter twenty-five

Jonah and I waited—snuggled up on his couch in the light of the Christmas tree—for my *best friend* to get up and see the wonders that awaited her. It really was a wonderous sight. The tree overflowed with presents. Jonah had gone overboard in light of this being the first Christmas where he'd actually purchased gifts instead of an experience for his daughter. A fire crackled in the low lighting, making it extra cozy even though his great room was, well, great in size. And we had the cookies that hadn't been eaten from the night before. I was starving since I had basically eaten the equivalent of a handful of leaves last night at the disastrous dinner.

I still couldn't believe Jonah had convinced me to come home with him, seeing as those who ruined Christmas Eve dinner were asleep upstairs. I didn't begrudge Jonah letting Eliza spend the night on account of he'd spent the night with me, bundling. Which really was a thing. I had verified it this morning on the drive over before the crack of dawn.

It was a lovely courtship ritual in my book. There was something wonderful about sharing your bed with someone whose only intentions were to intimately get to know you. There were so many deeper ways to know someone other than sex.

I thought our society had somehow forgotten that. It made sense, since we were a society of quick fixes and no patience. We tended to think lots of sex led to better relationships, instead of working on the relationship part first. My grandma once told me that the best sex happens when you and your partner have been together for so long that sex is always an exclamation mark in your relationship, never a question mark. I liked that. It's what I wanted with Jonah when the time came. Lots and lots of exclamation marks. If only we could get there.

I untangled myself from Jonah long enough to reach for a sugar cookie, and then I was right back in his arms, enjoying another sugar rush at six in the morning.

"We should probably hide the cookies. I don't think Whitney would approve of our breakfast choice."

Jonah chuckled. "Maybe someday we can convince her to come over to the dark side."

I broke off a piece of cookie and shoved it in his mouth. "Are you sure me being here isn't going to cause an uproar? I don't want to ruin Whitney's Christmas."

He chewed and swallowed before answering, "You not being here would ruin it for her. And I promise my parents and Eliza will be on their best behavior. If not, I'll show them the door."

"Okay," I said uneasily.

"Trust me." He sat up. "I want you to open one of your gifts before everyone wakes up."

I tugged on his shirt. "How about you stay here on the couch with me?" I wanted to enjoy our alone time before the firing squad was awake and aiming their sights on me.

"I promise I'll be right back." He winked.

I watched him carefully search through the plethora of gifts until he found a slender white box with a gold bow on it. If I didn't know better, I would think it contained long-stemmed roses. But Jonah knew I was more of a wildflower or sunflower kind of woman.

"Those dinosaur PJs look sexy on you, by the way," I let him know. I had insisted that we change into our Christmas pajamas when we arrived at his house. I had also pulled my hair up and washed my face. The mascara-stained eyes were frightful this morning.

He was back to me in no time, smiling, with gift in hand. "I was thinking I would wear these in the office. I think they work well with the earring," he teased.

I laughed. "Make sure you wear your shirt unbuttoned so they can see your henna tattoo. Or has it faded away yet?"

"I think you just want me to unbutton my shirt."

I leaned toward him. "If you really want to, I wouldn't be opposed to it," I playfully replied, though I was serious.

"How about you open your present first and then I'll show you your handiwork?"

"You drive a hard bargain, but okay."

He handed me my gift.

I set it on my lap, curious about the contents, and lifted the lid. He had asked me what I wanted for Christmas, like, ten times, and my response was always, "Something from your heart." But I wasn't at all expecting what was beneath the glittery tissue.

I picked up the embroidered lace umbrella and admired it, but it was what was under it that brought me to tears. A simple, hand-written note from Jonah that read, *To my Jo, I offer you my love and protection. From your Professor Bhaer.*

I placed the umbrella back in the box and threw my arms around Jonah. "Thank you. This is the most thoughtful gift I've ever been given. You are—"

"Good morning," Eliza interrupted us.

With my arms still around Jonah, I whipped my head toward the staircase Eliza seemed to be gliding down, looking way too good for this early in the morning. She was wearing red silk pajamas that, while they didn't show any skin, showed exactly how perfectly curvy her body was. And she was wearing makeup, whereas I was fresh-faced with only some moisturizer on.

I released Jonah and settled next to him while he put a protective arm around me. "Good morning," he replied stiffly.

I put the lid back on the box, not wanting to share it with anyone. Especially her, since she was, you know, married to my boyfriend not all that long ago, and she wasn't exactly my favorite person.

"I am sorry to interrupt you." She finished descending the stairs and made her way to us. "I heard voices and I was hoping you were here, Ariana."

Why? So she could humiliate me some more? Or maybe she had some sixth sense and knew Jonah was going to take his shirt off for me and she wanted to prevent me from enjoying myself.

She took the wingback chair near the fireplace and sat with perfect posture, her eyes still zeroed in on us. "I realize I am not a favorite person for either of you at the moment, and that I owe both of you an apology."

Jonah's shoulders relaxed and we both leaned against the couch, waiting to hear what Eliza had to say.

She cleared her throat. "Last night I behaved horribly. I spent the night taking inventory of myself and my actions. I did not account for how difficult it would be to see my daughter and Jonah move on so quickly and so well from me."

Jonah's eyes narrowed. "We didn't move on from you, you moved on from us a long time ago. We just adjusted. But you're right, we've done well without you, thanks to Ariana," he snapped.

Eliza gripped the chair. "I did not come down here for a confrontation." She squirmed as if she was begging him not to make her show any emotion other than her calm, cool exterior.

"That's the problem. We should have had more of that when we were together." Jonah wasn't letting up on her even though there were hints of regret in his tone.

I wasn't going to lie, it panged my heart that he still had enough feelings for her that he regretted the end of their marriage, but I suppose that's what made him a good person. And did I want to be with someone who could walk away from something that was supposed to be permanent without any thought or feelings at all? Of course not, but looking at the beautiful, well-put-together Eliza made it difficult for me.

Jonah must have known I was feeling uncertain. His arm around me tightened and he took my hand. He shifted his gaze from Eliza to me and the tender look he gave me said I had nothing to fear in regard to his feelings for me. I wanted to believe that. So much.

"I did not come down here to revisit past choices," she reiterated, her voice desperately trying to remain steady. "I did what was best for all of us."

"I'll agree with you there," Jonah zinged back.

Eliza blinked several times as if Jonah slapped her, but she took a deep breath and, while letting it out, rested her neatly folded hands in her lap. "We are on different paths now, and I have to come to terms with that. I thought I had. But obviously I have not worked through it as I should, but I will." She sounded unnaturally determined, like she could will herself to do anything. Maybe she could.

"You do that," Jonah sighed in frustration.

I was beginning to see why their marriage had ended. She had no fight in her, at least not for the things that mattered most. Once she decided something, that was it, even if it meant breaking up her family. I wondered if Jonah saw that I was trying to fight for us, even if I wasn't all that great at it and gave up from time to time. Case in point, last night. But I was trying. I was no longer seeking therapy from Goldie and had moved on to Dr. Morales. And the fact I was here with him now was an incredible feat for me.

Eliza steeled herself and zeroed in on me. "I truly am sorry for my behavior last night, Ariana. You are doing what I asked at Thanksgiving, allowing Whitney to be part of your life. We may disagree with how she should be raised, but that does not make you wrong. And I am pleased she loves you," she stuttered, not sounding pleased at all. "I will not interfere with your relationship with her."

I tilted my head, not sure how to take this woman. It was as if she was relinquishing her rights to me. "Eliza, I'm not trying to take your place. There's room for all of us in Whitney's life."

"That may be," she choked out some real emotion, "but I know it is you who will make room for her."

I rubbed my heart, aching for Whitney and in shock that Eliza would admit so freely that she was going to neglect her daughter. I wanted to yell at her that she was making the wrong choice, that she had no idea what repercussions she was setting in motion. But I didn't, because the wonderful girl I would make all the time in the world for had woken up.

She appeared at the top of the stairs with her grandparents, who were already dressed for the day in business casual clothing. This was a weird family. I tried to ignore that Carol and Paul were with her and focus in on how cute she looked in her dinosaur PJs. Jonah hadn't told me he had given them to her. She looked absolutely perfect with her bedhead.

Jonah stood, bringing me along with him. "Merry Christmas, honey," he beamed up at his baby. She looked down at the tree and all the presents, even the full stockings hanging on the mantle. I could tell she didn't know what she should do. At first it made me sad because at her age, honestly, I wouldn't have known either except for what I had seen on TV and movies. But Whitney didn't even have that going for her. Then it hit me: she had me and Jonah going for her.

"Merry Christmas, sweet girl. Come see what Santa brought you," I called out.

Eliza winced in her chair but didn't say anything.

Whitney's eyes drifted toward me, just now realizing I was there. "Ariana!" She ran down the stairs to me.

I knelt, ready to receive her. She flew into my arms and I held her tighter than I ever had. I vowed then to always make room for her. To never let her be a distraction, but my purpose, regardless of how things worked out with Jonah and me. Whitney would always know I loved her.

"You came back." She put her tiny arms around my neck.

I kissed her cheek. "Always, for you."

She leaned away and put her small hands on my cheeks. "But, Ariana, I do not believe in Santa Claus."

"Are you sure?"

She nodded, not so sure.

"Well, I did see a package from him with your name on it." I pointed at the tree and the silver box that was front and center with Whitney's name on it.

She turned her head and spied the gift. Her nose crinkled, unsure.

"Why don't you go see what's in it?" I stood while she debated.

Eventually, she tiptoed over.

Jonah came and wrapped his arms around me from behind. He kissed my head while we watched our favorite girl discover what I hoped was the magic of Christmas.

Jonah's parents stood to the side, but closer to Eliza than me and Jonah. They gave me an appraising glance before we all watched to see what Whitney would do.

She sat in front of the tree and stared at the box for a moment, while touching the tag and brushing her finger over the bow. "I don't recognize the handwriting on the card," she declared, half disappointed, half intrigued.

I smiled to myself. Kinsley had written it in her fancy script she was so good at.

Whitney nibbled on her lower lip and carefully slipped off the bow. Gently, she inched the lid of the box up, trying to peek inside, but afraid to. I was so anxious for her to see the doll I almost told her to throw it off, but I waited patiently in Jonah's arms. It wasn't a bad place to be.

Finally, she braved taking the lid off. When she did, her big green eyes widened. "It's the doll I wished for. She looks just like me." She put her hands to her mouth.

"Let's see," Jonah encouraged her to show us.

Whitney carefully lifted the doll out of the box and admired it. "She has hair just like me and a pink dress with a petticoat," Whitney said in awe before turning toward her dad and me. "Did you buy this?"

"No," we said at the same time. Thankfully, that was true—we didn't *buy* the doll.

Whitney stood, not sure what to make of it, but hugged the doll to her. She looked between her mom and grandparents. "Did you buy the doll?"

They each shook their head no, but I could tell there was something on the tip of Eliza's tongue. I swore if she ruined this, I was going to have words with her, and not the controlled, carefully crafted kind. Thankfully Eliza pressed her lips together and let it be.

Whitney walked over to Jonah and me. She was smart enough to assume we were the culprits. She stood with one arm cradling the doll, the other with her hand on her hip. "I know it has to be you. I read on Google that Santa isn't real. That magic doesn't exist."

I knelt and got eye level with Whitney. I ran my hand down her silky hair. "Honey, even if your doll wasn't delivered by a magical being, it doesn't mean that magic doesn't exists. Magic happens when someone, no matter who they are, cares enough about you to make your dreams come true. That's the best kind of magic."

"Really?" she responded so innocently.

Jonah knelt next to me. "Really."

"Do you want to make my dreams come true?" she asked me.

"Yes." I cried some happy tears. "All of them."

chapter twenty-six

It was the most magical Christmas I'd had, and it wasn't over yet. I was happy, though, that the remainder of the day would be spent with my family at my grandparents' place. I knew we were a weird family, but at least I could be casual and comfortable while being weird.

And I could eat pie and ham instead of vegan shrimp made of soy, and caviar made from black seaweed. I didn't even want to know how that was done. Most importantly, I wouldn't have to put up with the strange stares from Jonah's parents and ex-wife. I swore their eyes were like microscopes, and I was their petri dish. They were waiting to see what I grew into. I had a feeling they were betting it wasn't going to be anything good, but they were keeping a tiny door open that it might all turn out okay.

They could think what they wanted. I needed to shower and get ready for the day before I did start growing weird microorganisms. Jonah had dropped me off at the loft after we'd opened our gifts at his place. The man was completely smitten with me now that he had a box full of his beloved lime Skittles. And maybe because he thought I was pretty magical. I was beginning to think he and Whitney were too. I realized today that creating magic for someone else was the best healing magic in the world. It almost made me forget that the courier hadn't come. Almost.

I still wondered why. Maybe Jonah was right, Roger Stanton had died, or maybe he just got bored of the same old routine. Jonah said we should google obituaries tomorrow. I supposed it was too morbid to do it on Christmas. It didn't scream holly jolly activity.

Dani and Kinsley sat on the bathroom counter while I showered. When you lived with two other women and those women were your closest friends, privacy went out the window.

"So, Jonah spent the night last night. Is everything okay with the two of you?" Dani asked.

"Yeah, it was just a rough night with his parents and Eliza."

"But you're not breaking up, right?" Kinsley asked, worried.

"Not today." I was ever noncommittal.

"You love him." Dani called me out.

I peeked out of the shower curtain with my hair full of suds. "Yeah, I do."

"So why are you holding back?" Kinsley asked while applying a thin layer of lip gloss.

"How do you know I am?"

"Oh, please, Jonah was in a panic last night when he called. He's afraid of losing you," Dani half scolded me.

I gripped our ruffled shower curtain. "I'm not purposely trying to worry him, it's just . . ." I closed my eyes. "I need to know who my father is and why he didn't want me."

"Why is that so important to you?" Dani sincerely asked in a way no one but her could. She herself never knew who her father was.

I opened my eyes. "Don't you ever wonder who your father is? Doesn't it bother you that he abandoned you?"

Dani tapped her heels against the cupboards. "I used to wonder, and of course it bothered me, but then I realized he's not worthy of my thoughts. Besides, I consider Grandpa my father; he showed me what a real man was. He and Grandma saved me from myself. Oh," she paused.

I darted back into the shower and started rinsing the shampoo out of my hair.

Dani sounded like she'd moved right next to the shower. "I'm sorry, Ariana, I know it hurts you that they didn't do the same for you."

I wasn't angry with them. But deep down I had always felt like they took in Dani and Kinsley because it was somehow their penance. They wanted to make up for what they couldn't do for me.

"I understand why you would want to know why your father wasn't there for you," she spoke loudly so I could hear her over the water. "But don't let him take Jonah from you. He doesn't deserve the honor."

I let the water wash over me one more time before wiping the excess off my face. I popped my head out again to find Dani right in my face. "I just want to be able to bury the past so it won't keep rearing its ugly head in my future. It's loomed over me my entire life. That's not fair to Jonah."

"Why don't you let Jonah decide what's fair to him? I would say he's getting the deal of a lifetime with you."

She had me tearing up. "I just don't want to return him."

"Not all men leave, and some even come back after you've pushed them away." She grinned. "You're going to figure this out."

"Promise?"

She held up her pinky. "Pinky swear."

After I showered and dressed in my *Naughty but Nice, I'm a Multitasker* sweatshirt, I threw on some makeup and blew out my hair. I thought it might be nice if I curled it instead of throwing it in a bun, but there was a knock on our door. I smiled, thinking Jonah couldn't wait to see me so he'd come early to pick me up.

"I'll get it," I yelled. Dani and Kinsley were wrapping some last-minute gifts in their room.

I pranced over to the door on my tiptoes, anxious to see Jonah and Whitney. I threw open the door, "You just couldn't wa—"

I stared at the middle-aged distinguished man who was not Jonah. He held a leather satchel across his chest like body armor. I didn't recognize him at first, but then something struck me. His eyes. Not just blue, but sapphire, like mine. They may have been more crinkled around the edges, but I would know them anywhere.

"You look just like her," the man choked out like he had a serious case of dry mouth.

I slammed the door in his face and leaned against it, hyperventilating.

Kinsley walked out of her room wearing ribbons around her neck and in her hair as if Dani had wrapped her. She was smiling until she saw me and heard another knock. "Are you okay? Who's at the door?"

I had no words. I tried to say something, but my brain and my mouth were having a major disconnect. I tried pointing, but my fingers wouldn't work either.

Concerned, Kinsley approached me. "Is it Jonah?"

Somehow my head was functioning, and I shook it no.

She started to reach for the door handle. "Who is it?"

I grabbed her hand. "Don't."

"Ariana," the man shouted through the door. "I didn't think you would recognize me, so this must be quite a shock to you. I'm assuming you must have some questions. I promise you, if you open the door, I'll answer them."

Dani walked out wearing ribbons too. "Who in the world is at the door?"

"It's him," I croaked.

Dani and Kinsley looked at each other, confused.

"Roger Stanton," I squeaked out.

"No!" they said in unison.

"Please," Roger begged. "I've come a long way."

"Are you going to open it?" Kinsley asked.

"I don't know," I stuttered. Was this even real?

"Ariana," he said through the door. "I didn't know about the letters. I just found out about them. This must be very confusing for you—"

What? I threw open the door. "What do you mean, you just found out about them? You've been sending them to me for years!"

Roger swallowed hard and let out a deep breath. "I know that's what you think, but please let me explain." He held up the satchel. "If I could please come in, I'll tell you everything."

I looked at Dani and Kinsley to tell me what to do. I knew this was what I had wanted forever, but now that the mystery was about to be solved, I wasn't sure how to handle it. What if I couldn't handle what he told me? And where the hell had he been all my life? How could he not know about the letters?

Dani took my hand and patted it. "Maybe we should let him in to hear what he has to say?"

I nodded like I was in a trance.

"Come in," Kinsley invited.

Once he'd walked in and Kinsley had shut the door, I stared intensely at him trying to process this very unexpected event. His hair was almost completely gray, and his hairline was a lot farther back, but he was still in good shape. He wasn't as tall as I thought he would be, but he probably looked taller in the picture because my mom was short. Thankfully, he wasn't wearing sky-high shorts. Instead, he was dressed neatly in dark jeans and a sports coat.

He stared at me with the same intensity, but it was as if he recognized me. He had said, "You look just like her." Who did he mean? Surely not my mother. No one ever said I looked like her. Admittedly, I found comfort in that. Not that my mom wasn't pretty—once upon a time she had been, she was beautiful in fact—but she had become hardened by life, by this man in front of me, I believed, and it had manifested itself physically.

"Who do I look like?" I blurted.

A soft smile appeared on Roger's face. "I have a picture I'd liked to show you. Maybe we can sit down?" He held out his hand. "I'm Dean by the way, your—"

"Dean? No. You're Roger," I corrected the man like I knew better than him.

He extended his hand farther. "Ah. I think I know why you know me by that name. There is a story there I will share with you as well."

This was getting more and more bizarre. I reluctantly took his hand anyway. When I did, something odd happened. It was almost as if I could physically feel a piece of my life's puzzle click into place. Like I was supposed to know his hand. It freaked me out because I was supposed to hate him, so I pulled away, but Roger or Dean or whoever he was wouldn't let go.

"I can't believe I have a daughter and here you are." He choked up. He squeezed my hand before letting it go.

"Would you like some coffee?" Kinsley offered.

I almost forgot Dani and Kinsley were there.

Dean smiled at Kinsley. "That would be most welcome. It's been a long few days and a very early morning."

"I'll come with you," Dani sang. I knew that was translation for, *let's go to the kitchen and text everyone we know about what's going down over here.*

"Would you like to sit down?" I waved toward our living area.

"Thank you." He followed me.

I sat on the burnt orange couch and waved him toward the floral chair next to the couch.

"Would you mind if I sat on the coffee table?" he asked. "I want to get a good look at you."

I didn't say anything. I wasn't sure if that creeped me out or if it was sweet.

"You're unsure of me. Of course you are," he said more to himself than me. "I'm sorry. I'll take the chair and we'll talk."

We both sat and faced each other. There were whisperings in the kitchen. I was sure Dani and Kinsley were on the phone, but my focus was on my father. Wow, that was weird to think.

"First of all, I should probably give you some proof that we're related."

He reached into his satchel and pulled out a picture. I knew it was old even before he handed it to me. Not only was it faded, but it was small and square, unlike printed photos today. He handed it to me, and I took it, anxious to see his proof. When I flipped it over I was shocked. It was like looking in a mirror, except the woman in the photo had that 70s long hair parted down the middle with disco curls. She was wearing bell bottoms and a big flowy shirt that I honestly kind of dug. She had her arm around a teenage version of Dean. It looked like they were at the Grand Canyon.

"That's my mother," he said, "shortly before she died. She wasn't much older than you are now."

I brushed my fingers across the picture. This woman was my grandmother. It all seemed so surreal. "I'm so sorry. What happened to her?" I kept staring at the picture.

"My mother, Ariana—"

"Her name was Ariana too?"

He nodded with a smile. "I was as surprised as you when I found out."

I lay the picture in my lap. "I need to know the truth. Where have you been my entire life and what about the letters? And your name? And my name?" I cried.

He scooted closer, so he was sitting on the edge of his seat. "I know this seems farfetched, at least it does for me, but I swear to you until three days ago, I didn't know you existed. You see," he swallowed, "my legal name is Roger Dean Stanton, but for a very brief period of time I went by Roger. It was a summer many years ago when I met a young woman named Joanie," he said fondly. "We were both at Camp Alpine that summer as camp counselors. It seems silly now, but during orientation, the nametag they created for me had my legal first name on it. I was going to have them correct it, but I met this beautiful girl who said she liked the name Roger. She said it was a strong name. So I went with it. I don't ever recall telling her that I went by Dean."

"Then why did the letters I received every year come from a Dr. R. Stanton?"

Dean grimaced before clearing his throat. "My father is Dr. Roger Stanton."

"He sent the letters?"

"He did," Dean cringed.

"Why? And how did he know about me if you didn't?" This really did seem farfetched and I wasn't sure if I was buying it.

Dean reached into his satchel again and pulled out several letters, all the letters that had been marked with *return to sender*. They were tied neatly with some string. "Ariana," he sighed, "my father is dying, and he had his attorney bring these to me. He wants to clear his conscience before he dies."

I sat back on the couch, my brain buzzing. I looked up to find Kinsley and Dani staring at me from the kitchen. They were as stunned as me. I could really use that coffee now.

"I know this is a lot to take in. It has been for me as well. I will try and explain the best I can, or at least what I know. My father goes in and out, so it's hard for him to speak for long periods of time. And though he is in the wrong here, very wrong, I don't want to distress him in his fragile state."

I folded my arms, waiting to hear what I had been wanting to know for my entire life.

Dean shoved the letters back into his satchel before moving to the coffee table so he could be closer to me. He patted my knee in a fatherly fashion. "Feel free to stop me or ask me anything. I will be as honest as I can with you," he started out. "From what I've been told, when your mother called to tell me she was pregnant, she asked for Roger. I was already back at school and my father took the call. When she admitted the reason for the call, my father didn't tell her who he was. And we do sound similar on the phone. She probably never even had any inkling it wasn't me."

"How did she get your number?" I interrupted him.

"We had exchanged numbers at the end of the summer before we parted."

"Did you ever call her?"

He hung his head. "No."

"But you had sex with her," I said bluntly.

He lifted his head slowly. "I know. It makes me sound like a cad. But I was young and we lived so far apart."

"Did you care for her at all?" Tears filled my eyes.

He scooted closer. "Yes. That summer was the most fun I'd had up to that point in my life. Your mother had a zest for life that I had needed at the time. I thought of it as a summer affair. I had no idea it was more than that."

"She fell in love with you. Did you know that?"

He reached into his pocket and handed me a handkerchief. I didn't even know men carried those around anymore. I took it and dabbed my eyes. It smelled like fresh brewed coffee and aftershave.

"Ariana, I'm not proud of my actions. She did tell me that she loved me, and in the heat of the moment I returned the sentiment. But honestly, I didn't know what love was back then."

I held my stomach. I don't know why, but I guessed I'd always hoped I was conceived in love.

"I was careless, I know," he shamefully admitted.

"She thought you were going to get married."

He leaned back, surprised. "I don't know how she got that impression. I never mentioned marriage. I was only twenty-one with a lot of years of school ahead of me."

I started questioning everything my mother had ever told me about him. "Were you a premed student?"

He gave me a closed lip smile. "I was. I ended up going to medical school and practicing for a while, but to my father's chagrin, it didn't make me happy. I decided business was more my style. I currently own a company that makes state-of-the-art ultrasound equipment."

Of course he did. Was everyone in my life going to be a freaking genius? "Where's this business?"

"I still live in Chicago, with my wife and two sons."

I grabbed one of the throw pillows and hugged it to me while glass crashed onto the floor in the kitchen. I could hear Kinsley and Dani scrambling to clean it up. I was sure they were as shocked as me.

When the commotion died down, Dean continued. "You have two brothers, Maxwell and Sebastian. They are eighteen and twenty, respectively," he beamed with pride.

"Oh," was all I could manage. Why hadn't I ever thought of having siblings I didn't know about?

He patted my knee. "I know this is a lot to take in, but why don't we get back to the crux of the story. Shall we?"

I nodded.

Dani and Kinsley had apparently all but forgotten about the coffee. They came closer and stood, holding hands, eager to hear what Dean had to say.

Dean clapped his hands together nervously. "When my father heard the news that your mother was pregnant, he pretended to be me, dismissed her claims, and told her I wanted nothing to do with her."

My hand flew to my mouth.

"It was an awful thing to do."

"Do you know what my mother said?" I asked.

Dean shook his head. "All I know is that she didn't contact him until the next year, on Christmas Eve. I believe you were about seven months old, if I'm correct. Your birthday is in May, right?"

"It is. How do you know that?"

"I'm getting there, I promise," he responded uncomfortably. "The second time your mother called, she informed my father, who she thought was me, that he had a daughter named Ariana," he said my name, his mother's name, with such emotion. "It took my father by surprise."

"Do you know why she gave me that name?"

"I think so. I'd talked of my mother often that summer. She was a wonderful woman and I missed her dearly. Your mother was a good listener, and I believe I told her that if I ever had a daughter, I wanted to name her after my mother. I'm not sure why your mother honored my desire. I thought maybe you would know."

"My mother rarely spoke of you. I believe she grew to hate you." I had too, but I didn't mention it, yet.

Dean's face flushed. "I don't blame her."

"Is that the only reason my mother called?"

"No," Dean gave me an uneasy smile. "She begged for money. She was in poor circumstances, I believe."

"We always were."

Dean cringed. "You don't know how much it hurts me to hear that, especially since you didn't have to be."

"What do you mean I didn't have to be? I had no other option, thanks to you and your father," I spewed angrily.

"Ariana, I don't blame you for being upset, but please hear me out. I meant that my father did send her money."

Kinsley, Dani, and I all gasped at the same time.

He reached over and retrieved not only the letters, but a large manila envelope. He held them in his lap and stared down at them regretfully. "The money came with a price. If she accepted the money, she had to admit that you weren't mine and agree to never pursue the claim any further, relinquishing me of any responsibility toward you." He pulled out one of the letters. It had been discolored by time. "This first letter was returned, with your mother's response." He cautiously handed it to me.

I set the pillow aside and took the letter while Dani and Kinsley each took a seat next to me. They instinctively knew I would need their moral support for this. I looked at each of them and Dean, who gave me an encouraging nod. I inhaled and exhaled loudly while I carefully opened the envelope and pulled out the letter. It was a lot of legal jargon, but the gist was what Dean had said. Roger Stanton was willing to wire my mother ten thousand dollars in return for her silence, as long as she admitted that I wasn't his daughter. That wasn't the heart wrenching part. It was the scribbled note on the bottom from my mom.

I've given your offer a lot of thought. I've lied about a lot of things in my life and done too many things I'm ashamed of, but I won't let Ariana be one of them. She is your daughter and no one, not even you, can take that away from me or her. So you can take your money and shove it up your snooty, high-class sphincter."

Between wiping the tears away, I had to smile. That last line was so her. I could even hear her saying it. Dani and Kinsley chuckled too. They both knew how feisty my mother could be. But more than that, she didn't want to make my life a lie. I honestly didn't know she had that in her. It was the most decent thing she had ever done for me and I never knew about it.

I set the letter in my lap and faced Dean. "If she didn't take it, why did he keep sending the letters?"

He handed me the manila envelope. "You can look through this later. My father hired a private investigator, who checked in on you every year."

"What?" I squirmed. That made me feel so violated, but I supposed it explained how the letter always knew where to find me.

"I know it's disconcerting, but I think he had a feeling you were his granddaughter, and while he wanted to protect me, he also felt guilty. And he didn't want to admit he had lied and kept you from me. He kept sending letters on Christmas Eve hoping the desperate circumstances you were in would entice your mother to take the money and relinquish him from the secret he had kept, and his responsibility. My responsibility," he sighed remorsefully. "Every year the amount grew, but she never would take it."

I wasn't sure if I should be happy or disgusted knowing how much that money would have helped us. "If your father knew so much about my life, why did he keep sending the letters once I became an adult or after my mother died? It makes no sense."

"Ariana," he took my hand as if he had been wanting to forever. He lovingly held it. It felt different, but not in a bad way. Not bad at all. "Once you became a young woman there was no denying you were his granddaughter. You looked like his beloved. She would have never allowed him to treat you so horribly. He knows that. He wanted you to have the money to assuage his guilt. And most recently, because he could no longer live with the lie and . . . he wanted to meet you."

"What?" My mouth fell open. "Because he's dying?"

Dean tossed his head from side to side. "I think that's part of it."

I sat dazed for several minutes, trying to comprehend what I had just been told. It was a lot to take in. All I could say was, "Where do we go from here?"

He enveloped my hand in his own. "That is entirely up to you."

chapter twenty-seven

Everyone was in a tizzy. Kinsley's and Dani's texts and calls had the masses storming our loft—and by masses, I meant Jonah, Whitney, my grandparents, and Brock and Brant. I'm not sure why the last two showed up, probably for the pie and coffee, and it was a good excuse to see Dani, perhaps Kinsley too, though I still worried about that situation.

But I had more pressing matters to be concerned with, like my father standing in the corner talking on the phone to his wife Sabine. Apparently, Dean had tried to make it here yesterday, on Christmas Eve, but his flight had been canceled due to weather, so he took a predawn flight this morning and would be leaving soon so he could return to spend at least Christmas night with his family. My family? That was just too weird to think about.

"How are you feeling?" Jonah whispered in my ear while we sat on the couch together and watched all the chaos around us. Brock and Dani were trying to entertain Whitney by playing chess with her. She was wiping the floor with them even though Brock and Dani had teamed up. Brant was helping Kinsley in the kitchen with the food, and Grandma and Grandpa were both pacing the apartment shooting daggers with their eyes at Dean. Introducing them was awkward. It was like saying, here's the man who knocked up your baby girl.

"Stunned. Almost like I'm in a dream." I kept staring at the letters and manila envelope on the coffee table, itching to go through each one while also wanting to put it off.

"It's quite the Christmas surprise," Jonah replied.

"That's one way to put it."

"Hey," Jonah kissed my nose. "I'm here for you."

"I know. I'm just trying to process. It's hard not to think about the could have beens. How the balance of my life hinged on a name and a phone call."

"True, but," he took my hand and kissed it, "those all brought you to me. And as much as I hate what you've been through, I'm so happy we're together."

"Me too. Not for all the hell, but for you."

"Well," Dean interrupted us by taking the floral seat next to us, "Sabine promised to hold off roasting the goose." He grinned. "Her grandparents are from Germany and it's a traditional Christmas meal. Her hot spiced wine and apple tart aren't bad either."

"Sounds delicious," I responded, not sure what else to say. It was weird we were talking about normal things like food.

"It is. I hope, actually, that . . . what I mean to say is, Sabine, and of course Maxwell and Sebastian, would love for you to visit soon and try it for yourself."

Jonah and I looked to each other, both dumfounded.

"I know it's sudden," Dean stuttered, "but I just found out I have a daughter, and I would like to get to know her." There was this look of adoration and awe in his eyes when he looked at me. He turned to Jonah. "We would be happy to have you too. Just name the dates and I'll secure the travel arrangements. Maybe for New Year," he blurted nervously.

That was in less than a week.

"Uh . . ."

"Think about it," Dean pled. "The boys have to go back to school at the beginning of January and my father would like to meet you as well."

I squeezed Jonah's thigh with the mention of Roger Stanton.

Dean's eyes drifted toward my grip on Jonah. "I know you have every good reason not to meet him, but he isn't long for this world and perhaps meeting him would allow all of us to begin to heal from this ordeal."

I released Jonah from my clutches. "I'll think about it."

Dean stood. "I hate that I need to leave already, but I feel like I've intruded long enough."

I stood as well, which meant Jonah did too. He was ever protective, and I loved him for it.

Dean gave me a good once over. "Your pictures didn't do you justice. You are more beautiful than I imagined. I hope this will be the first of many *get-togethers*," he laughed, "for lack of a better word. Do you mind if I hug you?"

Did I? I supposed not. He was a victim too.

That alerted my grandparents, who stopped their pacing and darted toward us. Their eyes were keenly on us. It made it all the more awkward, like I was betraying them somehow. My head bounced between my father and my grandparents. Thankfully, Grandpa flicked his head as if he was giving me the green light. I edged closer to Dean. He gave me one more good look before he wrapped his arms around me. At first I was stiff, but it was like shaking his hand—another piece clicked into place, and I relaxed and put my arms around him.

"Ariana," he whispered, "I'm sorry for all the time we've lost. I know nothing I can say will make up for what my father has stolen from us, but I will do whatever I can to see that we forge a good father-daughter relationship, if you are amenable. If not, I will take friendship."

I rested my head on his shoulder and soaked in his scent. He smelled fatherly, like old aftershave and coffee, just like his handkerchief. It was so different than smelling Jonah or even my grandfather. While my senses memorized him, my heart reminded me I had wished for this day. I had wished for him, even if he wasn't a prince.

"I think I would like that," I eked out. Dr. Morales would be so proud.

He patted my back. "Good. Good. Please think about visiting. Sabine loves to play hostess."

I nodded against his shoulder before pulling away and back to Jonah, my safe person.

Dean turned toward my grandparents, reached into his sports coat pocket, pulled out a business card, and handed it to them. "I feel like we should talk. Here's my card. My personal cell is on there. I'll make myself available to you anytime."

Grandpa took the card and shrewdly glanced at it. Yes, I wanted to say, he was very successful. Dean had already given me a card. Mr. CEO-/President/MD/MBA. Apparently, the entire family was a bunch of overachievers. Roger Stanton was an orthopedic surgeon. Sabine Stanton was a concert pianist, and my brothers were both honor students at some private college I didn't recognize the name of. It made me not want to visit. At least I could claim I was in love with a doctor.

"We'll be in touch," Grandma huffed.

"I look forward to it," Dean replied, and he sounded like he meant it, even though he had to have known how unpleasant it would be. But as a businessman, he probably dealt with unpleasant situations all the time. And what could be worse than your father keeping your child from you for thirty-five years?

Dean waved to everyone in the room. "It was a pleasure to meet all of you. Merry Christmas."

"I'll see you to the door," I offered.

We slowly walked the short distance together. I wrung my hands the entire way. "So . . . this was weird," I laughed.

He chuckled. "So it was, but it was also wonderful. I'm thrilled I got the chance to meet you. Maybe next time it won't be so weird."

I shrugged. "I'm pretty good at attracting awkward situations, so don't count on it."

"You're funny, like your mom," he hesitated to say.

"Really?"

He tilted his head. "Don't you know?"

"There are a lot of things I never knew about her."

He pressed his lips together. "I will always regret that she died thinking I had abandoned you and her."

"Would you have believed her if she told you she was pregnant with your child?"

His face turned pale. "I would like to think yes. But we can discuss this more when you come to visit. I don't want to end on this note. Let me take you in one more time." He rested his warm hand on my cheek. "Please don't be a stranger. If you ever need anything, anything at all, I'm a phone call away. Of course, I'll call you too. And I'll have Sabine call to convince you to visit."

"Okay." I smiled.

"Goodbye, beautiful Ariana." His eyes misted, making mine do the same.

"Goodbye." I opened the door and watched him walk out. He stared back at me and waved until he came to the steps. I waved one last time and closed the door.

Jonah was waiting for me, and into the safety of his arms I went. There the floodgates opened. I bawled into his chest, like, racking sobs. The emotion and revelations of the day had overwhelmed me.

Jonah stroked my hair. “Let it out, my love, I’m here for you.”

“I know,” I managed to say between sobs.

I stayed wrapped up in Jonah for pretty much the rest of the day. We ended up doing Christmas dinner at the loft and exchanging gifts. It all passed in a haze. That evening everyone but Jonah and Whitney left. Dani and Kinsley went to the Hollands’ for some swanky Christmas mixer while my grandparents headed home, I’m sure to discuss the day’s events in detail.

Whitney had had an eventful day and fell asleep on the couch clutching her doll. There was nothing sweeter or more innocent than seeing her curled up asleep, probably dreaming of dinosaurs and chess moves. We ended up putting her in my bed so Jonah and I could have the couch. It was pretty much our favorite place to be. And it was a good place to go through the envelope and letters Dean had left me.

In the low lighting, sipping on Kinsley’s spiked wassail, we stared at the pictures and reports the private investigator had sent to Roger Stanton over the years. I was seriously disturbed. He had gone to great lengths to hide his identity. I noticed that for the first several years the letters came from R. Stanton, and it wasn’t until later, when I assumed my real father had graduated from medical school, that he started addressing the letters with Dr. R. Stanton. He was like an evil genius. I was even more disturbed by all the photos of me. I wasn’t sure which photos I hated more, the ones as a child where I looked homeless, or some of the more recent years where I looked homeless.

I thought for sure Jonah would break up with me right there when he flipped through my less than flattering state. However, all he said was, “You looked cute.”

“Right.” I snorted. “Cute as a rabid raccoon. It’s so creepy that someone was following me around, taking pictures of me and grading me, in a way.” I shivered, and not from the cold.

Jonah tossed a report on the table. "What's worse was he didn't help you," Jonah snarled.

"I still can't believe my mom didn't take the money. By the time I was eighteen, he offered her over $100,000. Do you know what she could have done with that kind of money?"

"Are you going to take it?" Jonah asked.

Dean had said Roger still wanted me to take the money. The last letter I'd returned had offered me $250,000. I didn't know what to do with that kind of cash "I don't know. It almost seems wrong. Like I've accepted a bribe or blood money."

Jonah downed the rest of his drink and set his glass on the side table. "You could look at it like child support back payments, which you are more than owed."

"True." I leaned my head on Jonah's arm. "I'll have to think about it."

"Have you thought more about visiting? The clinic is closed on New Year's Eve and New Year's Day, so I have the time off. We could fly out late on the 30th."

"What about Whitney?"

"We'll bring her with us. She's been begging to go to the Field Museum there. They have a huge dinosaur exhibit."

"We could just go do that," I teased, sort of.

Jonah pulled me onto his lap. "As much as I would love to get away anywhere with just my girls, you need to face this, for you and us. You need to deal with your past. You need to face Roger Stanton once and for all."

"I know." I lightly outlined his handsome face with my finger. I brushed my lips against his. "I will fight for us, Jonah."

"That's the best Christmas gift you could give to me."

"Better than lime Skittles?" I teased.

"Those are a close second." He pressed his lips to mine. "How would you like a taste of those Skittles?"

I parted his lips with the tip of my tongue. "Mmm."

He deepened the kiss and held me close, pouring all his feelings for me, for us, into my mouth. It was soul reaching and electrifying. The intensity had me gasping for air.

"Wow." I rested my forehead against his and caught my breath. "You're good at that."

He exhaled with me. "I want you, Ariana. All of you. You need to be whole for that."

"Let's go to Chicago."

chapter twenty-eight

"Are you scared, Ariana?"

I smiled at Whitney, who looked so small in the first class window seat holding her doll. *First class.* What a notion. I'd hardly ever flown, but I had never flown first class. Dean had purchased the tickets.

"Not of flying," I responded to my cute flight buddy.

"Do you want to hold Mary?" Mary was Whitney's doll, named after Mary Anning, the first woman paleontologist.

I ruffled Whitney's hair. "That's okay, but thank you."

"Hmm." Whitney was obviously still concerned that it must be a fear of flying that had me shifting in my seat and wringing my hands. She was such an observant girl. "Do you want to hold my hand?" she offered.

My heart melted. "I would love to hold your hand." I took her tiny hand in mine and smiled over at Jonah who sat directly across the aisle from us. That was the downside to first class, we couldn't all sit right next to each other.

Jonah was staring at the two of us adoringly. I thought he might have been hurt that Whitney insisted she sit by me on our flight to Chicago, but he said it was everything he had ever hoped for.

"Are you ready for this?" Jonah asked.

"Not even a little." But I knew it had to be done. According to Dean, Roger Stanton had less than a few months to live, if even that, so if I wanted to face him, it was now or never. Besides, Dean was thrilled we were all coming. He'd called me every day since Christmas to say hi and chat for a few minutes. We didn't talk about anything meaningful other than it meant a lot to me that he was trying and was interested in my life.

"You've got this. We've got this," Jonah assured me.

I hoped he was right. I'd snuck in an appointment to see Dr. Morales yesterday before we made this little trip. To say she was shocked at the turn of events was an understatement. She suggested I write a book about it all. Our appointment actually went long, there was so much to discuss regarding Eliza, Jonah, Dean, and Roger. She was proud that I was honest with Jonah about my feelings for Eliza, and even though I'd let Eliza get to me on Christmas Eve, she said walking away wasn't a bad thing. Now, pushing Jonah away was another thing, but according to her it was progress that Jonah and I had come back together so quickly. "That's how it works in healthy relationships," she had said.

Dr. Morales thought it was wise that I go to Chicago, but she cautioned me that Roger Stanton may not recognize his part in my childhood trauma and to be cautious that I don't allow him to retraumatize me. She said I needed to go in with zero expectations, but that I should be direct with him. She was honestly more concerned about my relationship with my father. She made me think about things I hadn't thought of, like while I might feel happy to be part of this new family, I might also feel a great sense of loneliness and loss when I see my father, his wife, and my half-brothers all together. She said there would be pain, but hopefully also joy, and I should embrace both. I was grateful for the mental preparation.

But . . . Dr. Morales was most concerned about me being completely honest with Jonah about my feelings for him. She wanted me to work on saying the L word. More than that, not being afraid of it. I knew he deserved to hear it and longed for it. I wanted to say it. Truly I did, but it always got stuck in my throat, more like my heart.

I knew if I said I loved him there was no going back. Jonah would never be satisfied with us staying boyfriend and girlfriend. He wanted to share his life and bed with me as his wife and the mother of his children. Yes, he would be patient, but after Eliza, he deserved someone who not only pursued him, but was in it for the long haul. Someone who made him and his child a priority. I only had to trust that he was in it forever too. That I wouldn't have to give him back.

Dr. Morales and Dani were quick to remind me that Jonah had returned to me, despite me pushing him away. And my father had never truly abandoned me. I really had to look at my life through a lens I didn't even know existed. Adjusting to the vision correction wasn't easy, but I was trying. Dr. Morales told me to keep on trying, and soon I would find I was doing.

I was doing something all right.

"Ladies and gentlemen this is your captain. We will be landing in Chicago at approximately 10:15 p.m. Central Standard Time. Enjoy your flight."

I looked between Whitney and Jonah and thought I would definitely enjoy myself. I was hoping the same would be true for Chicago. But as Dr. Morales reminded me, a lot of that depended on me.

I stared out of the car window at my father's house once we drove through the gated entrance protecting the property. I almost laughed when I noticed the turret gracing the large brick home still decked out in Christmas decorations. Bright white twinkle lights covered everything from the hedges to the large pine and deciduous trees that dotted the property.

What were the odds my father lived in a mini castle? Maybe he wasn't the European prince I'd always imagined him to be, but he lived pretty royally. Case in point, the Mercedes SUV he was chauffeuring us in. Dean had insisted on picking us up from the airport even though it was late and lightly snowing, which made it seem even colder here. The humidity made it biting. I was used to arid conditions in Colorado.

Dean stopped the car in front of the house in the middle of his circular driveway. He looked past me out the passenger side window. "Welcome home."

His words surprised me. Did he want me to think of this as my home?

"It's beautiful," I remarked.

"Wait until you see the inside. Sabine loves Christmas and she has a tree in almost every room. She didn't want to take them down until after you arrived."

That was thoughtful of her. "I'm excited to meet her," I replied, causing Dean to give me a toothy grin.

"I'll grab your luggage while you head in. Sabine is waiting for you."

I felt bad she had waited up so long. It was almost midnight. The drive from the airport to here was almost forty-five minutes in the winter driving conditions.

Jonah carried a sleepy Whitney while still managing to hold my hand as we walked up the stone steps of the house of my childhood dreams. It was freezing but the glow of the home and Jonah made me feel warm.

We didn't even make it to the large solid wood double doors before they flew open. There we were greeted by the cutest woman alive. Sabine was an Audrey Hepburn clone with her dark pixie cut and lithe body. She was even wearing a turtleneck and black slippers that looked like ballet flats.

"Welcome. Welcome." Sabine stretched out her arms. Her enthusiasm was impressive for the late hour. As soon as we crossed the threshold of the majestic home, I found myself torn away from Jonah and into those tiny arms of hers. For a little thing, she was strong. "Dear, dear, Ariana, it is so lovely to meet you. Dean was right, you are absolutely gorgeous."

"It's so nice to meet you." I hugged her back, but not too hard. There was hardly a thing to her.

She leaned away. "I hope your flight was good."

"It was. Thank you." I shifted my focus to Jonah and Whitney, who was all but asleep in her daddy's arms. "This is Jonah and Whitney."

Sabine left me briefly to give Jonah a side hug. "Yes, I've heard so much about you. Welcome."

I wondered what Sabine had heard about Jonah, seeing as Dean had only met him briefly.

Sabine patted Whitney's back. "We better get you all to bed. You've had a long day. Can I offer you anything first? A drink or a snack?"

Jonah and I both shook our heads.

Sabine came right back to me and looped her arm through mine. "If you need anything, you just ask or feel free to help yourself." She pointed down the large hall with marble floors and fine artwork. "The kitchen is down that hall and to the right. Hopefully your brothers haven't eaten everything. Those boys are empty tanks when they come home. You can meet them in the morning. They are off with friends tonight making mischief, I'm sure."

It was weird to hear the word brothers in relation to me.

Dean walked in from the cold with our luggage, which was only three carry-ons. "I see you met my better half." He flashed his wife a smile.

She blushed as if they were two kids dating. It was adorable, and couple goals. "I think we better get them up to their room." Sabine waved to the split staircase in front of us.

I felt like we were staying in a five-star hotel. All we needed was someone to be playing the sleek black grand piano in the open room to the right of us, complete with crystal chandelier and professionally decorated Christmas tree.

"I'll follow you," Dean said.

Sabine tugged on my arm and led us up the stairs. "I'm so sorry, only our small guestroom is available. We had to give Dad the large guest room and his private nurse uses the one next to him. And with the boys home, we are full up."

I knew Roger Stanton lived here. But it really hit home that I was just steps away from him. I couldn't believe I would be meeting him tomorrow, if he was well enough for visitors.

I had been racking my brain for days thinking of what I would say to him. Even now, I tried to come up with an opening line. That was, until it dawned on me what Sabine was saying about our accommodations.

"We're all staying in the same room?" I regrettably said out loud. I'd told Dean I would make our next visit awkward. It took me all of five minutes.

Sabine stopped on the step near the top. "Oh. I just assumed you would want to. I figured you . . . Well, that's not important. Oh goodness, let's see what we can do," she fretted.

Jonah gave me an amused smile.

I rolled my eyes at him. "Please don't make a fuss. One room will be great."

"We love bundling," Jonah teased me. "We'll use Whitney as our bundling sack." That was a great idea. Put the innocent child in the middle of the bed to prevent us from having sex. Huh. That actually was a good solution. But did he need to announce it? I thought I had already done a good enough job of embarrassing us. Or at least myself.

Both Dean and Sabine laughed while I turned ten shades of red.

"Bundling." Sabine giggled. "Your dad tried that tactic on me once too."

I was surprised anyone knew what that was, but I was surrounded by some of the most educated people on the planet.

"Tactic?" Dean acted faux offended. "I thought I was being romantic."

"You were very romantic, dear, but I saw right through you." Sabine winked at him.

I raised a brow at Jonah. Did he have ulterior motives?

He gave me a wicked grin that said all I needed to know.

With all that, we continued our trek to our room. On the way down the hall, I took note of all the family photos. My brothers were darker like their mother but built more like Dean. Sebastian shared his eyes. What really struck me, though, were the four happy, smiling faces in each picture. It didn't matter if they were formal photos, or whether they were at the beach or the Sydney Opera House; there were smiles for days. I knew pictures didn't tell the whole story—I'd thought Jonah was blissfully happy in all the family photos he sent every year. But looking at *my* family, I could see in their eyes they were truly happy. I could even feel it in the energy of this home.

Suddenly, that loss Dr. Morales warned me about hit. This is what I had missed out on. Part of me wished I never knew that's how deep the loss cut. I had to swallow down my emotions before I made everything even more awkward.

Before I knew it, we were to our room. Sabine opened the door and revealed the "small" guestroom. If this was small, what did she consider big? The room was more like a suite, with a four-poster king-size bed and a sitting area complete with a couch and chaise. It was light and airy, painted in a soft gray and accented with creams and hues of green.

It was like I had died and come back as Julia Roberts in *Pretty Woman*, complete with my own Richard Gere. Except Jonah wasn't paying me to be his escort, so there was that. But maybe Jonah would want to play out the grand piano scene later. Oh my gosh. I couldn't think like that. We had a child with us, and I was sure Sabine and Dean wouldn't appreciate us making out on the piano.

"I do hope this will do." Sabine sighed. "It's the only room that doesn't have its own bathroom, but the one across the hall is for your special use while you stay with us.

I took her delicate hands in mine. "It's perfect. Thank you."

She threw her arms around me. "I just want you to feel at home."

She was nicer to me than my own mother had been, which was wonderful and disconcerting all at once. "You don't know how much that means to me," I choked out.

She released me and tilted her head. "I look forward to a nice long chat tomorrow. I'll have breakfast ready by eight, but take your time. We are down the hall if you need anything."

Dean set our luggage near the bed and approached me. He kissed my cheek. "It's so good to have you here. Goodnight." He waved at Jonah and he and Sabine walked out together, closing the door behind them.

I bit my lip and looked at Jonah. "I guess we're roommates for the next couple of days."

He shifted Whitney in his arms. "This trip just got a whole lot better."

"Don't get too excited."

"Too late." He wagged his brows.

I ignored his sultry comment. "We better put Whitney in her PJs so she doesn't freak out in the morning that she didn't sleep in the proper attire."

"Good thinking. Do you mind getting them from her suitcase?"

"Not at all."

We got Whitney situated and in bed—the middle of the bed. Jonah and I each took a turn changing in the bathroom and brushing our teeth. Then we were crawling in bed together. He on one side, me on the other. We grinned at each other while settling in under the crisp cool sheets and feather down comforter. Whitney, still asleep, curled into me. I cuddled her against my chest. Such love for her filled me.

Jonah rested his head on his pillow and stroked his daughter's hair. "What I wouldn't do to switch places with her tonight." He scooted closer and rested his hand on my cheek. "You're so beautiful."

I closed my eyes and enjoyed his touch, enjoyed this quiet moment with him and Whitney. "I could get used to this."

"I'm happy to hear you say that."

I opened my eyes to find Jonah's face even closer. "Thank you for coming with me."

He inched over and pecked my lips. "I wouldn't want to be anywhere else."

Me either.

chapter twenty-nine

As we headed down the hall toward the stairs, my eyes were fixed on the doors on the other side of the staircase. In one of them, Roger Stanton lay dying. It made me feel guilty for all the hateful things I had thought about him for not only my entire life, but last night as I fell asleep.

I hated him for what he had deprived me of. I could have grown up in this house. Maybe. I didn't know how long Dean and Sabine had lived here. I didn't even know how long they had been married. I didn't know a lot of things. I didn't even know for sure if Dean would have believed my mother, had he answered the phone that fateful day that set in motion the circumstances of my childhood. The circumstances that made me so scared to admit my feelings to the man who I had woken up to smiling at me as if he wanted to do this for the rest of his life.

Dr. Morales's words spoke to me on a spiritual level about my guilty feelings and the underlying emotions associated with them. I could hear her say I needed to separate Roger's actions from his current state, and that there was room for compassion *and* hate.

With that thought, we followed the noise downstairs. I assumed my brothers were down there, as I heard two male voices I didn't recognize and a lot of commotion. Like the happy kind of a family glad to be together again for the holidays. I could hear the razzing, accentuated by the sweet tones of Sabine telling them all to act like they loved each other. But there was no doubt they did.

Whitney looked tentatively between Jonah and me before we arrived in the kitchen. "Do you think there will be healthy food? I don't want to eat cookies for breakfast, even if it is New Year's Eve." She apparently was still appalled that Jonah and I had eaten cookies for breakfast on Christmas morning.

I wasn't sure if the food would be healthy, but it smelled divine, whatever it was.

Jonah ruffled Whitney's hair. "If there isn't anything you like, we'll stop on the way to the museum to get you something." Jonah was taking Whitney to the museum after breakfast to give me time to speak to Roger. We thought it would be better if Whitney wasn't here. We weren't sure if Roger's state would frighten her or not. Or my state of mind after facing him.

Whitney let out a breath of relief. "We should hurry. I have lots of research to do today. I need to learn all I can about Máximo. He's the biggest dinosaur ever discovered and he's at the museum!"

Seriously, this girl owned my heart. Whitney's loud declaration drew attention to us. Sabine rushed to the hall to pull us into the kitchen. Oh my. Kinsley would be in heaven if she were here. The restaurant style range and cooktop along with the wall ovens had even me drooling. Not to mention the beautiful dark cabinetry.

"Come, come, we are all here," Sabine sang.

I nervously peeked in the direction of the breakfast nook. It was as light and beautiful as our room. The built-in booths, chairs, and country table fit perfectly in the naturally sunlit space. My father and brothers filled the chairs around the table. They turned and gazed our direction. And as if on some unknown cue to me, they all stood at the same time.

"Ariana, Jonah, Whitney." Dean walked our way. "I hope you all slept well."

I know I had—I always did—but poor Jonah said he'd had a hard time. Apparently, sleeping in the same bed as me had him tossing and turning, trying not to think about being in the same bed as me. He didn't mention that to Dean. A fact I appreciated. I already worried about what Sabine and Dean had said about me after they left last night. Little did they know I had much deeper issues than sleeping with my boyfriend.

"I slept well, thank you."

"Me too," Whitney chimed in, "but now I must get to the museum."

Everyone chuckled.

Dean took my hand and led me to the table. "Maxwell, Sebastian, this is your sister, Ariana, and," Dean turned, "this is her boyfriend, Jonah, and his adorable daughter, Whitney, who I hear loves dinosaurs."

"I do," she confirmed. "I'm going to be a paleontologist one day."

Jonah shook hands with Maxwell and Sebastian who both had serious cases of bed head and were still in flannel lounge pants and t-shirts. I stared at them, trying to judge if I looked like them. Sebastian and I shared the same eye color, but they both favored Sabine, with their dark hair and celestial noses. I had more of a button nose, like my grandmother I never knew.

After shaking hands with Jonah, Maxwell and Sebastian approached me cautiously.

I took a good look at them. "Wow. Brothers."

Without warning, they rushed to hug me, making a sandwich out of me.

"We always wanted a sister to torture." Sebastian laughed good naturedly.

Maxwell let go and turned toward Jonah. "We'll grill you later to see if you're good enough for our sister."

"He is good enough." Whitney stomped her foot, making everyone laugh.

"Yes, he is," I agreed.

"Boys, be good," Sabine chastised her sons. "Don't scare Ariana. Let her get used to us first. Everyone sit down. The food is getting cold."

Dean waved to one of the benches. "After you."

I slid in and Whitney and Jonah followed. Dean sat on the corner so he was next to me, and Sabine, Maxwell, and Sebastian sat across from us. Dean looked around the table, his face alight. "It's so good to have all my family together. Let's eat, shall we?" He admired the spread on the table. "You outdid yourself again, my love," he said to Sabine.

"I know." She patted Dean's arm.

I loved the dynamics between them.

"Don't be shy." Sabine reached for the coffee.

That gave my brothers the go ahead. They began reaching for everything, from the citrus almond brioche to the fruit platter, which Whitney was eyeing. I dished some fruit and scrambled eggs for her. All things she found appropriate for her morning meal. I took very little, even though everything looked delicious. I was nervous about meeting Roger. I still didn't know what I would say.

I was glad the table conversation was bout normal things, like Jonah's job and the studio. I was grateful I didn't have to give a history of my life. But I was very interested in my brothers lives and peppered them with questions. Everything from their favorite music and bands to what they were studying and if they liked school.

I was so pleased that Maxwell was a classic rock guy, and to my surprise, didn't love school even though he was an honor student. He wanted to have a gap year, but Dean and Sabine had "convinced" him to try out higher education. Sebastian, on the other hand, loved classical and alternative music. Like his mom, he was a music major and was a talented musician, if he did say so himself. He played in an alternative band in some of the local clubs near his school. He invited me to come listen to them sometime. I definitely would.

Whitney, though, was growing impatient with the grownup talk; she needed to get to the dinosaurs. "I think it is time to go, Dad," she declared after wiping her mouth like a little lady.

Jonah swallowed down his last bite of the to-die-for brioche. "I guess that's my cue."

I wanted to hold onto him and tell him not to leave me, but I knew I had to do this—and not with Jonah, but with my father.

Surprisingly, Sebastian asked Jonah, "Do you want some company? Max and I can drive you downtown. We know the city inside and out. This way we can grill you when Ariana isn't around," he teased.

By the look Sabine and Dean gave Sebastian, I had a feeling they'd orchestrated this unexpected turn of events.

"I was going to call an Uber, but that would be great," Jonah replied.

"Please hurry and get ready," Whitney implored, narrowing her eyes at my brothers, still in their pajamas.

They saluted Whitney and hopped to it, racing out of the kitchen.

"I bet they kept you on your toes," I said to Dean and Sabine.

"They still do." Sabine took a sip of her coffee. "Always on the go, always wanting money, and always a lot of fun. I bet you weren't a trouble-maker, were you?" she asked me.

"I admit I did sneak out once in a while."

"What?" I'd horrified Whitney.

I gave Jonah a strained smile.

"Honey, why don't we go brush our teeth," Jonah suggested.

Whitney gave me such a look—I felt like I was in trouble. I kissed her head. "Have a good time today. I can't wait to hear about your research."

"I'll let you read the notes I write."

"Even better." I tapped her nose.

Jonah leaned over Whitney and gave me a goodbye kiss. "I'll see you later. Call me if you need me."

"I will," I promised. "Have fun."

"We will."

I watched the loves of my life leave.

"She's darling," Sabine commented.

"She is, and very determined," I responded.

"I see that," Dean agreed.

A meaningful glance passed between husband and wife.

"You must be nervous about meeting your grandfather." Sabine reached her hand out to me.

I took it. "Very."

"He knows you're here," Dean informed me.

I squeezed Sabine's hand. "I should probably tell you I'm in therapy over all of this. My childhood left me with a lot of demons that I've been trying to put to rest. I know you know some of it because of the reports that private investigator sent every year, but that hardly scratches the surface of what my mother put me through."

Dean's face reddened and Sabine's eyes misted.

"I'm not saying this to garner sympathy. I just want to be honest with you."

"Oh, honey," Sabine cried, "you have more than our sympathy. We will help you in any way we can."

Dean placed his hand on top of Sabine's and mine. "I am so sorry. I've been sick thinking about how different your life should have been. How I should have protected you. How my father should have but didn't."

"It's not your fault. I know that. And I'm doing okay. I have a wonderful support system."

"Jonah." Sabine smiled.

"He's wonderful," I sighed.

"I can tell. He's a keeper, like your dad."

"How can you tell?" I knew that was a weird question, but I truly wanted to know how she knew my father was a "keeper." They seemed so happy together, so maybe she knew the secret to choosing a partner who would stand the test of time.

Sabine didn't act as if I asked anything out of the ordinary. Instead, she smiled at Dean like an infatuated schoolgirl. "When your father and I met twenty-six years ago, I was playing with the orchestra here as a guest pianist. He was attending one of their galas and when I saw him from across the room, I was instantly attracted to him. But when one of the waiters dropped an entire tray of appetizers and your father rushed to help them clean up the mess, I knew then he was someone I wanted to meet. He never lets people know how much his portfolio is worth, only how much they are worth to him."

I liked that. It sounded very much like Jonah.

Dean let out a heavy sigh. "I'm not always the best at that," he admitted. "I should have been more of a gentleman to your mom when we parted. I used to look back at that summer so fondly. A summer love affair with a pretty girl. I never even stopped to think of the potential ramifications. I figured she never called, so she must have felt the same. I should have called her. At the very least so she didn't feel as if I'd used her. I swear to you it wasn't like that. I did care for her, and it was all consensual."

I held my hand up, not wanting any details. "You don't need to explain. I knew my mother well enough to know she didn't have a lot of inhibitions."

Dean grimaced. "I don't want you to think ill of me. I want you to know I don't think of you as a mistake. I only regret not being part of your life before now."

"I don't think ill of you at all. Your father on the other hand . . ." I honestly admitted.

"As you should, love." Sabine put her napkin on the table.

"We should probably go upstairs," Dean suggested. "He's more lucid in the morning."

"You just be you and let it all out." Sabine pushed her chair back and stood. "No one is going to judge you. Dad knows he's in the wrong, so don't feel like you have to go easy on him. And when you're done, I'll have chocolate waiting for you."

I could already tell I was going to love this woman. "I always say chocolate makes everything better."

"You are my kind of woman."

"Are you ready?" Dean held his hand out to me.

I accepted his hand and a funny thing happened—I wasn't as frightened. "I think so."

chapter thirty

"I need to warn you before we go in." Dean stopped us at the door. I could already smell the antiseptic as if we were in a hospital, but a really fancy one. "He doesn't look anything like himself. He's extremely frail and he goes in and out of consciousness, so don't be alarmed."

"I watched my mother die in hospice, so I understand."

"Another thing I wish I could have helped you through."

"Me too. But I had Jonah."

"That was a long time ago. How come you and Jonah didn't stay together?"

"I promise to tell you after we talk to your dad."

"I would like that. Why don't we take a walk afterward, just the two of us?"

"In the cold and snow?"

"I always find it invigorating."

"Okay," I agreed. It would be nice to have some alone time with him.

With that, Dean opened the door and peeked in. "Can we come in, Lisa?" Dean asked the nurse watching over Roger.

Lisa greeted us at the door. "He's been expecting you. I'll give you some privacy. Push the button if you need me. I just administered his pain medication, so he won't be awake for much longer."

"Thank you, Lisa. I'll let you know when we're through." Dean ushered me into the low-lit room. A hospital bed sat squarely in the middle with monitors and machines surrounding it that were keeping Roger alive. They all seemed out of place in the handsome room filled with fine handcrafted furniture.

"Dad," Dean whispered, "I've brought someone to meet you." There was an edge to Dean's voice. I imagined he was just as upset with his father as I was.

My eyes adjusted and I got a good look at the man who had taken it upon himself to alter my life, to orchestrate it, in a way. His sunken cheeks and sallow skin spoke to his body being ravished by cancer. He hardly had the strength to turn his head our direction.

"Ariana, is that you?" he croaked out slowly and painfully.

Dean gave me a little encouragement by pressing his hand to the small of my back.

I bravely stepped forward. "I'm Ariana."

"Let me look at you," Roger begged.

I took a few steps closer. Enough to see how yellow his brown eyes were, and the few wisps of gray hair left to him.

"You look just like her," he cried and then coughed.

Dean rushed forward to help him sit up and take a sip of water through a straw. Once his coughing fit was over, he lay back down and closed his eyes for a moment.

"Why don't you sit down," Dean suggested. He pointed to the chair at Roger's bedside.

I took a seat and Dean stayed by my side with a comforting hand on my shoulder.

Roger opened his eyes after a few moments and looked directly at me. "You've come to haunt me," he said.

I shook my head.

"You've haunted me for a long time."

I wanted to say he deserved it, but his frail state wouldn't allow me to. Instead, all I could ask was, "Why didn't you help me?"

Tears filled his blurry eyes. "I tried." He still had some fight left in him.

"Your money?" I wasn't buying that excuse.

"She should have taken it."

"Maybe." But I had been thinking about the money. "You had to have known the chances of her using it wisely were slim to none. And that any of the men she was with would have taken advantage of it. It wouldn't have been much help to me. It would have only helped your guilt," I stated boldly, but without the heat I would have used had he been in better condition.

Dean squeezed my shoulder, letting me know my words were spot on and he was there for me.

Roger closed his eyes again. I wasn't sure if he was avoiding me or if the pain meds had overtaken him.

"I was protecting my son," Roger eked out. "She wasn't the first girl to try and trap him."

"Dad," Dean warned. "That's not fair. Joanie was telling the truth."

"I didn't know," Roger choked out, his eyes still shut tight as if he wished this was only a nightmare and when he opened his eyes it would all be better. "I thought someone else would help you. You had grandparents," he wheezed. "They should have done more. She should have taken the money." He was getting so worked up his heart rate increased more than it should have. His heart monitor started beeping loudly.

"Maybe I should go," I said to Dean. Despite what Roger had done to me, I wouldn't torment him in this state.

"Please don't go," Roger begged through labored breathing.

Dean adjusted his father's oxygen and helped calm him down. I watched as my father tenderly cared for his father. As sad as it was, there was something beautiful about it. It even made me think that someday I might get to care for Dean. It hit me full force that I had a parent. I never thought I would have one again. In some ways, I felt like I never had one. Tears filled my eyes.

Dean noticed the tears. "Are you okay, honey?"

"Yes."

"We probably shouldn't stay for too much longer."

That's when Roger reached out for me. His hand was bruised from what looked like old IV lines, and his skin was so translucent I could probably scratch him and he would bleed. "Please, you have to forgive me before I see her again."

I looked up at Dean. "See who?" I whispered.

Dean knelt next to the chair and brushed some of my hair back, like I had seen Jonah do many times to Whitney. "My mother. She would have loved you."

I wanted to ask my father if he could ever love me, but the words never came because I was afraid of the answer. Just like I had been afraid to love Jonah.

"Please take the money," Roger begged. He reached out farther. "I'm sorry I didn't help you. Please forgive me," he pled with all the breath he could muster.

I stared at his hand begging for me to take it. It was the hand I had wanted so desperately throughout my childhood to rescue me. And now here he was, needing me to rescue him from himself. In that moment, I found I didn't want to punish him, he had already done a good enough job of that himself. And withholding my forgiveness would only mean that I was giving him permission to continue to hurt me. I may have haunted him, but I wasn't going to let Roger Stanton haunt me any longer. And just because you forgave someone, it didn't mean that you had to love them. It didn't even mean that there wouldn't be times when I still hated him for what he had taken from me. But I wasn't going to let him take anything else from me. I knew the only way I could do that was to let this go.

I took Roger's cold hand. It felt nothing like Dean's. His was the hand I had truly wished for all my life. It was the hand mine belonged in. "I forgive you," I whispered.

Roger held onto my hand with all his might, tears trickling down his face.

Dean kissed my forehead. "Thank you, daughter."

And for the first time in my life, I felt like one.

I was glad I'd thought to bring all my winter gear while I walked with Dean on the Green Trail that ran behind his home. It was like a winter wonderland. Snow blanketed the ground and icicles formed in the trees, giving it an ethereal feel. There was even a frozen pond. A few teenagers were braving the cold and skating on it.

Dean and I walked in silence for a moment, partly because I was too afraid to breathe deeply for fear my lungs would freeze. But mostly because it had been an emotionally exhausting morning.

"Thank you for forgiving my father. I can, in some ways, relate to how hard that must have been for you. It's been difficult for me. He stole a lifetime from us, didn't he?"

Was it weird how happy it made me to hear that he felt that same pang? I tried not to tear up. I didn't need my eyes to freeze shut during such an important moment. "He did."

"You know, my father isn't a bad man. He's always been controlling, but he always wanted what was best for me. And I was the only person he had left after my mother died. He didn't want me to go away that summer and be a camp counselor. I had an internship with a colleague of my father's, but I wanted adventure. For one summer, I didn't want to be Dr. Stanton's son. I'd convinced him to let me go to Camp Alpine because the volunteer hours would look good on a resume. I had no idea how life changing that summer would be." He took my gloved hand.

"Will you tell me about my mother that summer?"

"Sure." He gave me a smile that said he had a feeling I would ask.

"You can leave out any gory details. I know how conception works, despite what you might think because of the whole bundling thing."

Dean barked out a laugh. "I didn't think you needed a talk about the birds and the bees, though I did make some great visuals for the boys when we had the talk many years ago. I think Sabine keeps them in the attic."

"I'd love to see them. I can always use a good laugh."

He chuckled and swung my hand. "So, your mom," he paused. "She was a breath of fresh air for me. She was different from any other girl I had dated."

"You dated?"

"Yes. I promise you, I wasn't the kind of young man only looking for one thing. We didn't sleep together until the end of the summer, after we had been on several dates. She was my first time. Which is probably more than you care to know."

"Actually, I think it's sweet, and it makes me feel better. My mom ended up with so many men who only cared about one thing. It was probably why she fell in love with you. I don't think she knew a lot of tenderness in her life in that regard."

"That is a shame. It makes me feel even worse that I never contacted her again. I did have tender feelings for her. I still do. She helped me see life in a whole new way."

I let out a high-pitched hiccup.

"Are you okay?"

"You just remind me of Jonah. He said the same thing to me a long time ago, when we were much younger."

"Why didn't you stay together?"

I looked out at the vast winterscape, which figuratively and literally took my breath away. "That is a long and complicated answer."

"Good thing we have plenty of time." He squeezed my hand.

I looked down at our clasped hands. I liked it. I liked it very much. "Well, for one, I promised my mother I would never marry, especially a *doctor*."

Dean chuckled. "We can be beasts."

"Jonah isn't, and I don't think you are either, but I always thought Roger Stanton was."

"I can understand that. But why didn't your mother want you to get married? She was married several times, if the reports are true."

"Oh, it's all true, and that's why. I didn't want to love Jonah only to lose him, like I saw happen over and over with my mom. But I can't solely put the blame on her. I had my own bad luck with men. Every man up to that point in my life had abandoned me. In some ways, even my own grandfather had—I guess both my grandfathers—though I know Grandpa Sam had no ill intent and it kills him that he didn't do more. But how can I trust Jonah if all the men in my life who should have loved me, left me?"

Dean tugged on my hand and we stopped. He breathed in deeply and let it out. A plume of warm breath formed between us. "You asked me a question before I left Colorado. You asked if I would have believed your mother had she told me about you. That thought has plagued me this past week. I would love to say with a hundred percent certainty that, yes, I would have. That I would have saved you from the cruel life you had. But this, dear Ariana, I can say and mean with all my heart. I always wanted a daughter. I always wanted you, and here you are. I promise I will never leave you." Tears formed in his eyes while he used his gloved hand to wipe the ones streaming down my cheeks.

It was like a dream come true for me to hear him say those words. Somehow, I felt them deep in my soul. I think I believed him. I threw my arms around him.

He embraced me like I had never been embraced before. "Ariana," he whispered, "to keep yourself from loving someone like Jonah, who clearly loves you, would be a greater tragedy than a man who never knew his daughter existed. To choose to throw away real love is the greatest travesty there is. You should be more afraid of that than anything."

Huh. I let that thought settle in my soul while I soaked in the warmth of my father. *My father.* It was there in his arms I knew what I had to do.

chapter thirty-one

While we all played a rousing game of Monopoly in our pajamas and stuffed our faces with the most delicious pizza I'd ever had as part of our New Year's Eve celebration, I looked around at everyone, both those old and new to me. This was my kind of family. They loved silly traditions as much as I did. Then it occurred to me that this was *my* family. I had a father, brothers, a stepmother who was quickly becoming a favorite of mine, and I had Jonah and Whitney.

What my father said to me on our walk kept playing in my head. I had been wanting to tell Jonah all about it and more importantly, how I felt about him, but we hadn't had a moment alone. I snuggled against Jonah after I'd collected my two hundred dollars for passing go. We were all on the floor surrounding the coffee table in their basement family room, which doubled as a theater room. I'd never seen such a large screen or so much tech.

"I think Ariana's cheating." Maxwell eyed my pile of cash.

Whitney perked up, offended on my behalf. "Ariana would never cheat. She just plays better than you."

I pulled Whitney onto my lap and kissed her cheek. "Thank you, honey."

Everyone around us laughed.

Sabine smacked Maxwell. "That's what you get for teasing your sister."

Whitney set her sights on Dean and Sabine. "How come your sons don't know a lot about dinosaurs? You should take them to the museum more. I had to tell them everything."

Dean tried to keep his smile under wraps. "I will rectify this situation immediately."

"I have notes you can use." Whitney just happened to have them with her. She had gone through them with me. She was well on her way to completing her doctoral thesis.

Dean took the notes Whitney handed over. "Thank you very much. Do you mind if I read them tomorrow?"

"That's fine, but it must happen before we leave because I have to share my findings with my friend Tabitha."

I honestly hated that we needed to leave tomorrow afternoon. I wanted to get to know my family better. I wanted to stay in this moment with Jonah and Whitney. At least they were coming home with me.

"I promise you will have them back before you leave." There was a hint of sadness in Dean's voice.

As we counted our way down to midnight, we laughed and tossed popcorn at each other when the other person made us pay for landing on their property. It was pretty much perfect. It was the family moments I'd always hoped for growing up.

When it was almost midnight, Sabine jumped up. "Ooo, I have champagne for those of us over twenty-one."

My brothers rolled their eyes as if to say she was crazy if she thought they hadn't had alcohol before, but they played along and took the sparkling cider offered to them. Whitney was long asleep with her head in my lap.

Jonah and I each took a glass of champagne and counted down until the clock struck midnight. We clinked glasses, and before we drank from them, Jonah pressed a kiss against my lips. "Happy New Year. May we celebrate many more together."

"Here, here." I took a sip of my champagne.

It didn't take long before we all retired to bed. It had been a long but good day, and I wanted to spend some alone time with Jonah. He had the same idea. As soon as I walked into our room from brushing my teeth, he swept me off my feet. "How about we spend the night on the couch? It's been a long time."

"What about our bundling sack?"

"I'll behave. Mostly." He nuzzled my ear.

I wrapped my arms around his neck. "You missed a spot."

He obliged and kissed my neck, driving me crazy. To the couch we went, where he gently set me down before joining me and taking me back in his arms. We lay in the dark, just holding one another.

"How are you feeling?" Jonah asked.

"Good. Actually, better than good. I feel light."

"I'm happy to hear that. I know today wasn't easy for you, but you stood up to your fears and Roger Stanton."

"I guess I did."

"Are you going to take the money?"

"I've been thinking about that. I want to give it to Dani for Children to Love. If I can help save one kid, this will all be worth it."

Jonah gazed down at me. "You are an incredible woman."

"I don't know about that."

"I do." He outlined my lips with his finger. "I love you, Ariana. Please let me love you."

I placed my hands on his cheeks, took a breath full of courage, and let it out. "Only if you let me love you back."

His wide eyes misted over. "Are you saying what I think you're saying?"

"I love you, Jonah. With all that I am, I love you."

epilogue

"Daddy," Whitney ran to Jonah when he arrived at the studio after work.

I loved to hear her call him that. I watched the scene that had played out almost every day this summer. Jonah knelt, kissed our girl, and asked her how her day was. She always had something to report. Today it was all about how she and Tabitha had discovered that they could make paint with milk. I was happy when I could impress her and teach her something new. Their designs were drying on one of the tables. Jonah admired them before he made his way to me at the workbench. He greeted me with a chaste kiss.

"How was your day?" I took one more kiss, because I could never get enough.

"Disgusting."

"How so?"

"Let's just say I saw a ninety-year-old man with a ball of ear wax that had been growing for at least half of a century, and we'll leave it at that."

"Say no more. I have better news. I got our wedding photos back today from the photographer."

"Perfect. I need something to wash the memory of today out of my brain."

"I'll get my laptop." I pushed the pieces of stained glass I was working on to the side before running to my office. I returned to find Jonah sitting at the bench admiring the piece I was working on for Sabine. My father had commissioned it. It was the silhouette of a woman sitting on piano keys.

"This is beautiful, as is my wife."

"Wait until you see the photos." I set my laptop in front of him and clicked on the folder that contained some of my favorite memories.

Jonah tapped on the side of his head. "I don't need photographic evidence. I relive the memories every day. Especially of our wedding night," he whispered with a wicked grin.

"I'd be happy to give you a live demonstration again tonight after Whitney goes to sleep."

He tugged me to him. "I do love you, Mrs. Adkinson. I hope you are well rested because it's going to be a long night," he groaned against my ear.

"Those are my favorite kind." I sat on Jonah's lap while we pulled up the photos.

The first one that popped up was a family photo of all of us after the beach ceremony in Oahu. I never thought I'd have a destination wedding, but Dean, I meant Dad, said that he wanted to throw me the wedding of my dreams. I told him as long as I could be barefoot in my white cotton sleeveless dress with Jonah waiting for me at the end of the aisle, I didn't care where I got married.

In the picture, we were all barefoot except Whitney, who'd thought it was inexcusable and had warned us all of the diseases we were potentially exposing ourselves to, and the glass and rocks we could cut our feet on.

She was in some cute white sandals. She looked so precious in her pink flower girl dress with her hair pulled up, flowers gracing her hair.

I touched the screen, reliving the best day of my life. My dad stood next to me, handsome and proud, Sabine, beautiful and happy. Grandma and Grandpa stood next to them, happy and adjusting. Grandpa and Dad had both walked me down the aisle. Dani and Kinsley were there and looking gorgeous as my bridesmaids in lace bohemian dresses. Brock and Brant looked stately and tan standing next to them. I could see the longing in Brock's eyes as he gazed down at Dani. My brothers were laying out in the front, being their goofy selves. They were laughing because they were probably thinking about all the condoms they had plastered on the honeymoon suite door.

On the opposite end of the spectrum, Jonah's parents stood to his side looking anything but amused. While they weren't outright rude to me anymore, they weren't warm and fuzzy either. Eliza had been invited as a courtesy but had declined to come. She was dating some CEO from Sweden and used that as an excuse. It didn't hurt my feelings.

That left me and my groom, who the photographer had caught kissing my forehead adoringly. It showed exactly how Jonah made me feel.

"We need to get this one framed," Jonah commented.

"I agree." I started to scroll through more of the photos.

"I've been thinking of something else we should do," he said casually.

"What's that?" I enlarged the next photo of us saying I do.

"I think we should have a baby."

"What?" I almost fell off his lap.

He steadied me. "You do want to have one with me, right?"

I readjusted myself so I could look at him. "Of course I do, but we've only been married for a month."

He leaned in and skimmed my lips. "I know, but you are the most wonderful mom in the world and more kids should get the privilege of having a mom like you."

"You're just trying to butter me up to say yes." I rubbed my nose against his.

"I mean every word. Please, say yes."

He had me at *we should have a baby*. "Yes."

sneak peek

IN NAME ONLY

A Pine Falls Novel: Book Two

I sat at my desk and stared at the photo of Brock and me at Ariana's wedding. I kept the photo in my top drawer and pulled it out to look at it more often than I should. I brushed my fingers over Brock. He looked amazing, his white linen shirt showed off how tan and muscular he was. And that look he was giving me. For the first time, I could tell he wanted me as much as I wanted him. At least I thought so.

That night, we had snuck away to take a long walk on the beach. The moon and stars were our only lights. While the waves crashed against the shore and washed over our bare feet, all I could think about was how thrilled I was that Brock had taken my hand, and how the way he held on felt like he never wanted to let go. Not a word was spoken. There seemed to be too much to say and neither of us knew where to begin.

But he didn't have to say anything. He tugged on my hand, making me stop and gaze up at him. He tucked some of my windswept hair behind my ear before brushing his fingers across my bare shoulder. Each touch sent shivers of pleasure down my spine. Then he leaned in, his lips teasing mine, so close but not quite touching.

He closed his eyes as if he had to think about what he was doing. It was a line we had never crossed but had tiptoed around for years. With a loud exhale, his lips crashed into mine. I slid my arms up his chest and around his neck. His lips stayed firm on mine as if he were soaking me in, but afraid to taste me. I wasn't sure how long we stayed like that, but he broke away from me too soon. Then he shoved his hands in his shorts pockets and we walked silently back to the hotel.

When we'd returned home last month it was business as usual for us. We'd never spoken of the kiss, though each time we were together, his eyes always seemed to drift toward my mouth. I wasn't sure if I could take much more of the cat and mouse game we'd played for years.

A knock and a head peeking in my door startled me, making me shove the picture under some paperwork on my desk.

"Hey," Brock's deep voice surprised me. "I hope I'm not interrupting."

I blinked a few times, wondering what he was doing here in the middle of the day. I thought he would be in surgery or at his office. "You're not." I rearranged some of the papers on my desk. "What are you doing here?"

He walked in and shut the door behind him. His tall, athletic body made my small office seem even smaller. Dr. Brock Holland had a presence to him that made him loom larger.

Brock approached my desk, clasping his hands.

I didn't think I had ever seen him nervous.

"Everything all right?" I asked.

He stared aimlessly at a paperclip on my desk. "I wanted to say goodbye before I left on my training mission." Brock was a major in the army reserve. As an anesthesiologist, he had treated soldiers and civilians all over the world on the battlefield and on humanitarian missions. This year he was headed to the Middle East for two weeks. It made me nervous.

"I thought we were all having dinner tonight?" Meaning our group of friends—Kinsley, Ariana, Jonah, and Brant.

He ran a hand over his dark hair that was cut military short now. "We are, but I wanted to talk to you alone."

I bit my lip. "Oh."

"Dani," he closed his deep blue eyes and paused before opening them and hitting me full force with them. "I think we should talk about *our* future when I get back."

"Ours?"

"Yes."

"What are you saying?" I could barely breathe out.

He flashed me his crooked grin. "That I'm going to miss you, and we'll talk when I get back in a few weeks." He always played it close to the vest.

"Maybe I'll be around," I teased.

He opened up his arms. I flew out of my chair, around my desk, and into them. He wrapped me up tight while I soaked in his peppermint and spice smell.

"Come back to me safe and whole," I whispered.

He kissed the top of my head. "I promise."

about the author

Jennifer Peel didn't grow up wanting to be an author—she was aiming for something more realistic, like being the first female president. When that didn't work out, she started writing just before her 40th birthday. Now, after publishing several award-winning and bestselling novels, she's addicted to typing and chocolate. When she's not glued to her laptop and a bag of Dove dark chocolates, she loves spending time with her family, making daily Target runs, reading, and pretending she can do Zumba.

To learn more about Jennifer and her books, visit her website at www.jenniferpeel.com.

If you enjoyed this book, please rate and review it on **Amazon & Goodreads**

You can also connect with Jennifer on social media: **Facebook & Twitter (@jpeel_author)**

Other books by Jennifer Peel:

Other Side of the Wall

The Girl in Seat 24B

Professional Boundaries

House Divided

Trouble in Loveland

More Trouble in Loveland

How to Get Over Your Ex in Ninety Days

Paige's Turn

Hit and Run Love

Sweet Regrets

Honeymoon for One in Christmas Falls

Second Chance in Paradise

The Women of Merryton Series:

Jessie Belle – Book One

Taylor Lynne – Book Two

Rachel Laine – Book Three

Cheyenne – Book Four

The Dating by Design Series:

His Personal Relationship Manager – Book One

Statistically Improbable – Book Two

Narcissistic Tendencies – Book Three

The Pianos and Promises Series:

Christopher and Jaime – Book One

Beck and Call – Book Two

Cole and Jillian – Book Three

The More Than a Wife Series:

The Sidelined Wife- Book One

The Secretive Wife- Book Two

The Dear Wife – Book Three . . . Coming Soon

My Not So Wicked Series:

My Not So Wicked Stepbrother

My Not So Wicked Ex-Fiancé

My Not So Wicked Boss

Pine Fall Novels:

Return to Sender

In Name Only… Coming Soon

Silent Partner … Coming Soon